Ménage

EMMA HOLLY

Black Lace novels are sexual fantasies.
In real life, make sure you practise safe sex.

First published in 1998 by
Black Lace
Thames Wharf Studios
Rainville Road, London W6 9HT

Copyright © Emma Holly 1998

Reprinted 2001 (twice), 2002

The right of Emma Holly to be identified as the Author
of this Work has been asserted by her in accordance
with the Copyright, Designs and Patents Act 1988.

Typeset by SetSystems Ltd, Saffron Walden, Essex
Printed and bound by Mackays of Chatham PLC

ISBN 0 352 33231 X

Ménage

I slipped my hands down Joe's back and under the waistband of his jeans, taking possession of his downy hindquarters. My nails curled into his buttocks.

'Kate – did you and Sean make love?' Joe asked.

'Not exactly. We did what you wouldn't let him do last night,' I replied, liquefying at the memory of Sean manoeuvring me into position; the way he'd shoved my knees apart with his boot; how thick he'd been when he'd breached me. Joe shivered in my arms and I realised he had his own memories.

'Next time, would you like to watch?' I asked.

'Next time I'd like to do,' he said.

Contents

To Viv – for going above
and beyond the call

Chapter One

The Former Mrs Robbyns

*O*n the night it began, I bounded up the stairs to my two-hundred-year-old colonial town house in the heart of Philadelphia. The shiny green shutters gleamed against the brick as if winking in welcome. Despite the tree-lined seclusion of Society Hill, the cacophony of rush hour sang in my ears. I loved this reminder of the city's vitality. My body hummed with its energy. My heart pounded, strong and free. My skin tingled in the brisk autumn air and under it all, like a fruit ripening for harvest, my cunt warmed at the thought of the half-read erotic novel waiting by my bed.

Masturbation first, I thought, then dinner, then TV, then to bed with my smutty book.

Back then nothing made me happier, or hornier, than a productive day at work – preferably a long one. Not only did it prove that, at thirty-three, I still had plenty of go in me, it proved I was as good a breadwinner as Tom – better, in fact, because I didn't have to be a lawyer to do it.

'First thing we do, let's get rid of all the lawyers.' Kicking off my Adidas, I tossed my keys on to the Queen Anne side table in the hall. My hair clip followed.

With a sigh of relief, I dug my fingers through my sheep-thick curls and massaged my scalp. Heaven. I

1

flicked on the lights. Apart from its usual creaks and groans, the old house was quiet. My lodgers must be out cruising the bars on South Street.

A thrill ran through me as I imagined the picture they'd make: one dark, one fair, both gorgeous and young, both fairly reeking with erotic possibilities. The connection between Sean and Joe was palpable. I could almost smell the sex on them, like animals in heat. Could some of that heat be for me, I wondered, or would they keep it all to themselves?

Pondering that very question, I smoothed my black riding jacket over the swell of my breasts. I loved the way the black velvet hugged my generous curves before nipping in at my waist. Paired with a snug pair of Levis, I knew the jacket bordered on obvious, but I wasn't one to hide my figure – not when I worked so hard to stay in fighting trim.

In any case, having two scrumptious young studs in the house tended to make me clothes-conscious. And body-conscious, I thought, peering up the narrow spindle-banister stairs to make certain I was alone.

No shadows moved on the landing. No Robert Cray Band growled seductively through the hall. I'd never heard Robert Cray before Sean and Joe moved in, but once I had I was hooked. That man really knew how to sing about love. I could have eaten him up just listening.

My sex melted like butter at the thought. I loved giving head, which probably kept my marriage together longer than anything else. Seventeen year olds simply don't do that sort of thing well.

Smirking to myself, I took the stairs two at a time.

Maybe I'd slip into Joe's room and borrow the CD. He wouldn't mind. Despite Sean's attempts to make me – and Joe, for that matter – believe he was one hundred per cent boy's boy-toy, I knew Joe was sweet on me. Sean had an early accountancy class, so every morning Joe and I ate breakfast alone. Lately I'd been coming down in my embroidered silk kimono. How he blushed if I bumped his leg under the table or bent to drag the frying pan out of the cabinet.

Of course, my derrière is one of my best features. Power walking will do that.

Anyway, most days Joe finished breakfast with a boner too big to let him stand. There he'd sit, a napkin draping his humped-up dick, a prisoner of my erotic torment – and his own shyness. Sometimes I'd press a goodbye kiss to his clean-shaven cheek for the sheer pleasure of watching that napkin jump.

Joe made me enjoy being a woman again.

Reaching the landing, I saw he'd left his door open. I caught a whiff of soap and Aramis, the purest aphrodisiac I knew. My palms tingled with excitement. I didn't intend to snoop, merely grab the music and go. Even so, my heart skipped at the prospect of having his private space all to myself. Who knew what I might stumble across?

As though it divined my thoughts, Joe's *Phantom of the Opera* poster glowered as I sauntered to the CD player. Robert Cray's *Strong Persuader* lay on top of the stack. Joe knew I liked the album, and knew I might wander in if he played it. I suspected he played it as often as he dared. I tossed the plastic case into the air, caught it neatly, then stopped in my tracks.

Joe's jockstrap hung from his bedpost. The white pouch sagged with the memory of its burden. I knew from our breakfast sessions that he was well-hung. Oh, yes, Joe was a six-foot, hard-as-a-board, twenty-three-year-old stud.

I fingered the sweat-dampened cotton. The mouth of my sex gave a little gasp and a trickle of warmth ran out.

This was too kinky. What the hell, though. Men liked women's lingerie. Why shouldn't I be aroused by a jockstrap? I brought the cotton to my nose and sniffed the combination of good clean sweat and young man's musk. Immediately, I felt an urge to keep the thing, to sleep with it under my pillow or press it between my thighs while I stroked myself to climax.

I told myself the urge was juvenile, not to mention thievish, but I shoved the underwear in my pocket and ignored my twinge of guilt. Worse, I continued my survey of his room. I touched the military crease at the bottom of his mattress, evidence of Joe's self-disciplined nature. It was a young man's bed, narrow, the sort a man could carry from his parents' house because he couldn't afford to buy something bigger. That bed made me think of raging, unrequited hormones, of jacking off with his big brother's *Playboy*, or waking up to sticky sheets.

God, I was crazy to even consider messing around with someone that young.

Annoyed with myself for more reasons than I could name, I turned to gaze at my reflection in the small, square mirror on the back of his door. At five foot five, I could see myself from the neck up.

Trying to be both fair and honest, I faced a smooth-skinned woman with wide blue eyes and a mop of unruly auburn curls. My fitness walking, in addition to keeping my curves where they belonged, lent me a flattering outdoor blush. My lips were generous, softly pink, and my cheekbones owed a debt to some forgotten Scandinavian ancestor. All in all, my face appeared a good deal more open than I really was. People would never guess at my reserve from looking at me. Only when I smiled would the twinkle in my eyes lead anyone to suspect I harboured secrets.

My lips curved upward. In my opinion, that grin and the mischief in it were my best features. I shouldn't have let my sense of fun become a stranger to me. I'd been burnt by my divorce, it was true, but that was no excuse for failing to take advantage of the opportunity Fate had so kindly set in my path. Joe was twenty-three, an adult. If I had any nerve at all, I'd let him know – in no uncertain terms – that I was more than ready to play.

Unfortunately, that was easier said than done. Losing

4

my smile, I sighed and shut Joe's door behind me. The third floor called: my bedroom, my big grown-up bed, my two hundred pages of masturbation aid.

A sound halted me at the door to my room: a rhythmic rattle, like a blind flapping against the window – except the sound was too fast for that, too fast and getting faster.

'Slow down,' hissed a voice: Joe's voice. 'I think I heard someone.'

Another voice groaned something coaxing. The rattling slowed but did not stop.

My hand flattened over my pounding heart. Joe and Sean were fucking in my room. A wave of heat swept me from scalp to ankle – instant, intense arousal. I didn't even have time to take offence. Awash in cream, my clit beat a frantic tattoo against the seam of my jeans.

My knees gave way. My hand brushed the door. The latch clicked. The door swung open an inch. Wincing, I grabbed the frame for support.

I could see them through the gap in the door. Oh, could I see them. Both men were stark naked. Joe was bent forward at the waist, his arms propped straight on my footboard. His legs were straddled wide; every muscle in his thighs and calves stood out with tension. There was no mistaking what that tension was, either – Sean was sodomising him. The force of his thrusts made the bed rattle. His tight pink buttocks clenched as he forged in and out.

What a cute rump Sean had. I'd been so distracted by Joe's crush on me, I'd never noticed. Now I longed to kiss it, to bite it. My knuckles whitened on the door. With an effort, I forced myself to remain still.

Sean was shorter than Joe, but he looked at home on top. He caressed Joe's hair-shadowed torso with a handful of yellow silk. Its trailing edge brushed Joe's upthrust cock, which bobbed like a spring at the contact. Sean chuckled and repeated the tease.

Apparently, he enjoyed tormenting Joe as much as I did.

But what of it? Sean wasn't my concern. Joe was. I turned my attention to my favourite tormentee.

Sweat spiked Joe's straight dark hair. His face red, he grimaced – but not, I thought, with pain. As I watched, he arched his back and tipped his buttocks higher.

Accepting the offer of access, Sean gripped his shoulders and levered deeper. 'Gotta have it, don't you? Can't hardly go a day without it. Hell, if I did you every hour, you'd still want more.'

'Fuck you,' Joe responded, even as he pushed whole-heartedly into the next thrust.

Sean laughed. He nipped the apple of Joe's shoulder and rubbed his cheek across the smooth olive skin. The gesture made my insides turn over. I hadn't thought Sean capable of tenderness – or that his relationship with Joe was more than a power trip.

'Would she do this for you?' he asked. 'Would she lay you over the end of my bed and bugger you till you begged?'

She? I wondered. She as in me?

Joe choked out a laugh. 'That would take some doing, considering her equipment.'

Sean laughed, too, and then I really felt like an intruder.

But it was my room! Taking a quick breath for courage, I shoved the door open. The lovers froze, mid-stroke.

'Shit,' said Sean.

'Oh, my God,' said Joe.

Young Joe's face was a canvas for his emotions. I read contrition in the compression of his lips, embarrassment in his flaming cheeks. 'Kate. We didn't expect you back so early.'

'I guess not,' I said.

At the dryness of my tone, he tried to disengage. Sean wouldn't have it. His muscular arms formed a vice around Joe's waist. With a short grunt, he slung himself deeper. Joe couldn't stifle a groan of pleasure.

That groan was all the impetus I needed to step inside.

Joe's head came up. His cognac-coloured eyes dark-

6

ened. That's when I knew my lodgers were here, in my room, because the chance I might walk in lent a thrill to the proceedings. But I could live with that – considering the thrill they'd given me.

Hiding a smile, I shrugged out of my jacket and hung it over a chair. One pocket bulged with Joe's stolen jockstrap. What a bad girl I was, and getting badder by the minute. Beneath my apple-red turtleneck the tips of my breasts felt cold, as if they'd been capped in steel.

Sean was the first to notice. His thrusting stuttered to a halt.

'Well, well, well. Looks like our landlady isn't miffed, after all.' He circled one finger around Joe's nipple, a tiny mirror of my own. 'Why don't you ask her if she wants to join us?' Clearly, Sean expected me to run from this challenge.

'Yes, why don't you?' I said, my voice as sultry as I could make it.

Joe's gasp sounded loud in the hush of my attic bedroom. His prick bobbed up another inch – and stayed there. Had I ever seen anyone swing so high? I stepped closer. The tip of his penis was shiny and full, plum-red, plum-shaped. I licked my lips. Joe moaned.

Behind him, Sean eyed me like a snake eyes a mongoose. He didn't pull free, though. Maybe he didn't realise I wanted him right where he was.

I circled the locked pair, savouring the sheen of sweat and the ripple of lean male muscle. They made a pretty picture, what with Sean so fair and Joe so dark. Sean's buttocks tightened as though he could feel my eyes on them. Then I reached the other side.

No one could miss how my perusal had energised Joe. His erection grazed the skin beneath his navel. I suspected it was painful. It looked good enough to eat.

He looked at me and bit his smooth lower lip. 'Do you – do you want to join us?'

'That depends on your partner,' I said. 'Were you serious about the invitation, Sean? Or testing whether I'd bite?'

'Try it and I'll bite back.' He bared his teeth. 'And I do like women – in case that's what you really want to know.'

Smug, sexy bastard. I'd deal with him later. In fact, I was looking forward to it. For now, though, Joe and his beautiful boner were my primary concern.

I gestured towards my shirt, capturing his eyes. The soft cotton clung to my tautened nipples. He stared at the little nubs. 'Would you like me to take this off?' I asked.

'W-would I?' He shook his head to clear it. 'Of course I would.'

Sean snorted. I ignored him. Grasping the hem in both hands, I pulled the shirt over my head, then shook out my auburn curls. Now I wore nothing but jeans and a lacy black push-up bra. Both men's eyes widened, visibly impressed.

See, I mentally told my ex. Some men appreciate what I've got to offer. Some men wouldn't trade me for a raft of flat-chested teenagers.

Emboldened, I ran my hands up my sides and cupped my breasts. I lifted their weight the way a man might; my nipples crested the edge of the lace. A low cry broke in Joe's throat.

'Amen,' Sean seconded. His gaze roved my chest as he used the bundled silk to draw a slow figure-of-eight on Joe's belly. I had the oddest feeling he imagined he was touching me.

Curious, I tugged the yellow cloth from his hand. When I shook it out, it turned out to be a skimpy silk teddy. It did not belong to me, but someone had sprayed my Chanel No. 19 all over it. I did not know what to make of this, or of Joe's cringe of horror.

'Whose is this?' I asked.

Joe's eyes flew open. 'I thought it was yours.'

Sean cleared his throat. He looked embarrassed. 'Um, that's what I told him. I thought he'd – well, I didn't want him to mess up your nice underwear. I have sisters. I know how women get about that stuff.'

I pressed my lips together against a laugh. 'Very considerate, Sean.'

Joe frowned – not a reaction I wanted to encourage, so I tossed the lingerie aside and shimmied out of my jeans. That got his attention, especially when I dropped to my knees and scooted under his arms between him and the footboard. I considered his rigid penis. It was long as well as thick. This was going to be a challenge, but a nice one. Knowing he watched, I circled my tongue suggestively round my lips.

'Oh, God,' Joe moaned.

Sean's hands were all that held him back, all that held himself firmly lodged. Both men were panting now, caught on the hook of my suspense. A sense of incredible power sang through my veins. I let my breath wash Joe's groin. His hips bucked forward.

'Please, Kate, I can't stand it. Please touch me.'

I touched him. I rubbed my face like a cat along the 'V' of his inner thighs. I kneaded his calves until the knots softened under my palms. I kissed the smooth thrust of his hip-bone. I speared my fingers through his lush pubic hair and then, when his breath was coming in sobs and Sean's hands had clenched into white-knuckled fists, I opened wide and took one drawn-up testicle into my mouth.

'Kate.' Joe stroked my curls with a trembling hand. 'Kate.'

I knew then that, no matter how good Sean made him feel, no one existed for Joe but me. I mouthed my way around both sides of his sac, testing his weight and fullness, smoothing the dark wire-silk hair with my tongue.

'Ready?' I asked, treating the root to one tiny, teasing lick.

Too breathless to answer, he yanked his other hand off the footboard and buried it in my hair. I'd almost licked my way to the head when his fingers tightened and jerked me back.

'Wait,' he said in a high, thin voice. 'I need a condom.'

Sean cursed. Obviously, he'd had enough delay. 'Don't be such a prude. Just pull out before you come.'

'But I'm dripping.'

He was indeed. Tiny droplets of preorgasmic fluid seeped from the eye of his prick.

'I'll take care of it,' I said, and did the honours with the stash I kept in my bedside table.

When I took Joe's cock in my mouth again, he sighed, long and liquid. I felt as if I were the kindest woman alive. This time I swallowed all I could reach, bearing down and up in a steady rhythm that had nothing to do with teasing and everything to do with relief. Sean began to thrust in time to my sucking, bumping Joe forward. Ever the gentleman, Joe braced his legs to prevent being pushed too far down my throat. He couldn't know I loved the added pressure; loved the sensation of witnessing and doing at the same time.

Too turned on to resist, I moved Sean's hands on to Joe's balls. Sean gave them a squeeze.

'Oh, yeah,' he said. 'Buddy, you are primed.'

That taken care of, I was free to see to my own pleasure. I slid my hand into my lacy panties.

Joe's cock abruptly changed angles in my mouth. He was craning around to see. Had he watched a woman masturbate before? The thought that he might not have tightened the coil of heat in my belly. Maybe he'd enjoy seeing more.

I brought my hand back to the lacy waistband. 'Would you like me to take this off?'

'Yes.' He was so breathless I could barely hear him. 'Please.'

I released him long enough to twist out of my panties, then slid two fingers between the slippery petals of my sex. Joe's tongue curled out to wet his upper lip. He swallowed. I promised myself I'd let him taste what he was hankering for before the night was out.

Then Sean broke the heated moment. 'Think we could hurry this up? I can't hold out much longer.'

'So come,' Joe said.

'I want to come with you.'

'So grit your teeth. Ah, yes.' Joe hummed with delight as I bore down towards his root. The sound drove me wild. I frigged myself faster and spread my knees as far as I could so Joe could see. He could hear, too. My fingers made a rapid, squelching sound in all that juice. Joe's shaft thrummed its approval against my palate. Under his velvety skin, he was hard enough to hammer nails. I tongued the sweet spot beneath the head. His knees threatened to buckle.

'Do that again,' he said. 'Oh, yeah. You're going to have to hold on, Sean, because I intend to make this last.' His hands stilled on my head. 'Unless you're tired?'

I laughed and sucked harder. Years of practice had given me jaws of steel. I'd last as long as he could, which – from the feel of things – wouldn't be much longer. No one could get that stiff and not be close to blasting off.

'Oh, man,' Sean complained.

'Oh, yes,' Joe praised.

Their reactions were too much for me. I had to come. With one hand gripping Joe's knee for support, I rubbed my rosy bud faster, chasing the pleasure.

Caught up in his own chase, Sean lost the last shreds of his control. 'Come on.' His belly slapped Joe's back as he went into overdrive. 'Do it, do it, I can't – I'm coming, damn you.'

My fingers slid through my excitement. I thrust the longest into my wet, summery heat, felt the muscles flutter and clutch, felt the achy sweetness spread.

But Joe beat us both. His cock jerked an instant before Sean moaned like a foghorn, an instant before my body spasmed in ecstasy. Lost to everything then, the orgasm shook me like a rag doll, jerking me from the inside out until my legs collapsed and my head thunked against the bed.

Joe immediately slipped from Sean's hold to kneel beside me.

'Kate. Sweetheart.' He gathered me against his body. 'Did you hurt your head?'

'I'm all right.' I rubbed the sore spot, more dazed by his concern than by the thump I'd taken.

'Poor thing,' he murmured, rocking me.

Left without his partner, Sean stepped towards the window and turned away. The setting sun gilded the curve of his spine. He raked his short blonde hair back. His shoulders sagged. A little worry tightened my throat. What if he really cared for Joe? Then a truly horrible thought brought my hand flying to my mouth. 'Oh, God, Joe, I didn't bite you, did I?'

He kissed the tip of my nose. 'No, sweetheart, you let go just in time.'

With a flattering lack of effort, he scooped me off the floor and set me on my king-sized bed. Sleepy and warm, I let him remove my bra – which was the only clothing I had left. His hands passed over my breasts in gentle exploration, a strangely comforting gesture. Then he pulled the chenille coverlet up to my neck.

To my surprise, considering Sean's possessive streak, both men settled on either side of me. Sean snuggled against my back and sighed with exhaustion. I patted the arm he draped around my waist. In all my fantasies, I'd never dreamed of seducing him.

Of course, I hadn't really seduced him tonight. He'd just gone along. Well, more than gone along – he'd enjoyed himself. So why did I feel as if I'd stolen something from him? Why did I feel protective? Most of all, why did I wish we could do it again – not just Joe and I, but the three of us together?

Divorce rebound, I thought. You figure if one man will prop up your self-esteem, two should send it through the roof. I didn't believe that, though. I'd caught a glimpse of the real Sean tonight, and it had struck a chord.

We had more than our lust for Joe in common.

The question was, what did I intend to do about it? Keep it light, I thought. Treat it like a game and no one will get hurt.

The object of our affections lifted the erotic novel I'd

left by my bed a lifetime ago. 'Hm,' he said. One finger stroked the naked clinch on the cover. 'I'm sure you sleepyheads don't need it, but I think I'll read you a bedtime story.'

The sound of furious whispers woke me, that and the circling caress of a hand on my hip: Joe's hand. Already I recognised the long fingers, the gentleness all out of proportion to his years. Or perhaps his gentleness depended on youth. Perhaps life would roughen his soft edges.

The thought disturbed me. In fact, being disturbed disturbed me.

I feigned sleep, which was not an easy task. Sean's naked front spooned my naked back and his erection nuzzled the crease of my buttocks. Lust told me to squirm closer. Curiosity told me to be quiet and listen. Curiosity won.

'What is your problem?' Sean hissed.

'She's asleep.'

'Don't worry. She'll like it.' Sean's chest was damp with excitement, his nipples pebbled and hot. Whatever 'it' was, I suspected he'd like it, too.

'But I've never done it before.'

Sean reached over me to ruffle Joe's hair. 'It's not hard. Hell of a lot easier than going down on a man.'

'What if I can't find it – and how do you know?'

'I had a life before I met you, you know. Just because I like men better doesn't mean I can't appreciate a good-looking woman.'

'But I thought – You never said –'

This was getting too private for me. 'I'm awake,' I said and laid my hand on Joe's belly. His stomach muscles jumped.

'Oh,' he said, and, 'Oh, man,' when my fingers ventured lower.

Grasping the root of his erection, I pulled slowly until the flare of his glans crossed my palm. He caught my hand before I could stroke him again.

13

'Behave yourself,' he said. He threw the covers off the three of us and stared at me in the moonlight. His hand trailed down the curve of my side. 'You are so beautiful.'

My skin heated under the compliment. Had anyone said those words so convincingly before?

The mattress creaked as he scooted lower on the bed. I heard the coverlet fall to the faded Turkish carpet; heard the rush of Joe's breath. Did those hastened exhalations signify anxiety or arousal? I prayed he wasn't doing something he didn't want to do. He kissed the tender skin beneath my navel, then rubbed his face across my fleece. Aside from the endearing gesture, which he repeated, he didn't seem to know where to start. My concern intensified.

'Here,' said Sean. He lifted my upper thigh and arranged it over Joe's shoulder. The scent of male sweat and female musk perfumed the air.

Joe kissed one plump lip.

When he went no further, Sean said, 'Watch.' His hand, callused from the construction work he did every summer, slid down my belly. He combed through my curls to part my labia.

He did indeed know what he was doing. His first and second finger slid into the slick valley either side of my clitoris. Up and down he rubbed, the smooth pressure tugging skin and nerves and spreading my gathering moisture until my whole sex felt oiled. Finally he squeezed the tenderest morsel between two fingers. The tip bulged towards Joe's waiting mouth.

'See,' Sean said with a hint of triumph. 'No trouble finding that.'

'No trouble at all,' Joe agreed, and his tongue curled out to lap the delicate offering.

His touch spurred a delicious throb of sensation. I fought not to squirm. Joe licked me again through Sean's tight fingers, more firmly this time. Oh, he had a good mouth, a natural-born, pussy-loving mouth – soft, but not too soft, curious and flexible. Every nerve jangling contact called a sound from my throat. Helpless to stop myself, I clasped his silky head and pulled him closer.

'Let go,' Joe rasped.

I stiffened but, to my relief, he meant Sean. Pushing his friend's hand aside, Joe surrounded the apex of my sex with his mouth. His lips tugged my clit while his tongue massaged it. I began to struggle, my orgasm just out of reach. He stroked the inside of my wrist with his thumb. 'Hush,' he said.

But I couldn't hush. It felt so good. I wanted to come so badly. My hips rocked into each suckling pull. Sean pushed forward, helping me, branding my backside with his cock.

Then Joe let go. 'Switch on the light,' he said.

Surprisingly obedient, Sean yanked the chain on the Tiffany lamp. Red-amber light bathed our tangled bodies. Like neon, the glow highlighted muscled arms and thighs, wide chests and soft breasts – three healthy animals rubbing against the boundaries of love.

Joe backed away to view his handiwork. His thumbs spread me wide. The sight of my glistening sex seemed to mesmerise him.

'Don't stop now,' I said, caught between laughter and frustration.

'Just a sec,' he assured me.

His head came up at something Sean was doing behind my back. 'No, man. You're too big. You'll hurt her.'

Well. That made me turn.

Sean was twisting the top off a tube of lubricant.

'I wasn't going to,' he said, all innocence. 'Besides, she's not that much smaller than you.'

He looked to me for permission, hope kindling in his face. Rather than give in at once, I measured his cock with my eyes. What he lacked in length, he more than made up for in girth. Sean cringed. If he could have made it smaller, I think he would have.

'He's too thick,' Joe said.

'But not too long,' Sean wheedled, then sighed. 'I suppose you're an arse virgin.'

'I'm afraid so,' I admitted. 'Nothing bigger than a finger.'

He looked so crestfallen, I assured him I wasn't saying never. Sean had made sacrifices tonight, and had been a sport about it. He deserved to be able to play his favourite game – and who could say I wouldn't enjoy it? Joe obviously did.

'That's settled then.' Joe planted his hands on his hips. 'Fingers only.'

'One or two?' Sean teased.

Joe shook his head at him, but the corners of his mouth twitched. He settled back between my legs, not so nervous this time. 'Now.' He parted me again and licked me once to say hello. 'Where were we?'

Sean waited until I was squirming against Joe's mouth to begin his probing entrance. Despite my resolve, I couldn't help tensing. My ex had done little more than rub me there, and that only when he thought I was taking too long to come.

'Relax.' Sean pressed the edge of his teeth into my nape. 'Easy now, easy.'

Joe hummed the echo of this croon while Sean pushed two lubricated fingers past the furled rosebud of my anus. Goose bumps prickled along my arms. In his fingers slid, to the first knuckle, then the second. When they hilted, he massaged me from the inside in slow, firm strokes.

The surprising burst of pleasure made me groan. He scissored his fingers apart, widening me, no doubt preparing me for the day when he would storm that fortress with his cock. I groaned again. His unfamiliar intrusion woke a hidden set of nerves. They lit up like sparklers under his expert touch. Suddenly Joe's suckling seemed not too gentle, but almost too intense to bear.

'Good girl,' Sean praised, his voice shaky with arousal.

His hips rocked mine forward, the demands of his sex too urgent to ignore.

He shifted behind me and rearranged himself. His shaft moved, practically scalding the crease of my inner thigh. With his free hand, he pressed it up against my pussy. The shape of him, the smoothness of his skin, the frantic pulsing of his veins, called down a gush of cream.

'Oh, yeah,' he said, anointing himself with the thoroughness of a connoisseur. 'Baby, you are hot.'

Joe nuzzled lower, taking a taste for himself. From the way Sean whimpered, I knew he'd received a lick, too.

'I'll get to you,' Joe promised him.

But first they got to me.

'Faster?' Sean said, increasing the stretch of his fingers.

I could only gasp.

Joe took that as a 'yes' and increased his efforts. In seconds, the first climax hit me. My neck arched, my legs stiffened. Joe reached up to squeeze my nipples between his fingers and a second drum-roll shuddered through my sex.

Feeling it, he laughed and flicked my clit with his tongue in a lightning-quick rhythm I thought Sean must have taught him. Crying out loudly enough to wake the neighbours, I ground my pussy into his face and came again.

'Cool,' said Joe, when I finally floated back to earth.

'Come here,' I said with the ragged remains of my breath.

He slid up my body and we kissed, our first kiss – hungry on his part, languorous on mine. He tasted of me and himself, a combination of sharp and sweet. To my surprise and pleasure, he kissed without coyness or hesitation. His tongue delved into my mouth as if he couldn't get enough of me, as if he wanted to pass his fever for me through the kiss. It was catching, all right. In minutes, I was ready to take him.

Too overwhelmed to speak, I took his sex in my hand and guided him towards my gate.

He stopped me with a tiny shake of his head.

17

For one awful moment, I feared I'd mistaken the extent of his interest. If he didn't want vaginal sex, maybe he wasn't as bi as I'd thought.

'No,' he breathed a millimetre from my ear. 'When we're alone.'

Our eyes locked, just for a second, but long enough to shock me with the intensity of emotion that passed between us. I couldn't define the feeling. Longing was part of it, and fear, and hope. Hope was the scariest, I think.

Sean stirred behind me, breaking the spell. He reached for Joe, took his cock from my grasp and smeared it with lubricant until it glistened in the lamp light, cherry-wet, cherry-red. I felt Joe's body tremble. His eyes lifted and searched mine. Focused on his own goals, Sean tugged until their shafts nestled side-by-side between my thighs.

'Press tightly,' he said, and pushed my leg down with his hand.

The pressure jammed their pricks together. Joe's slipped on my skin, on Sean's skin. Joe hesitated. His lips moved with words I never heard – an apology, I believe. Then they embraced each other around my body, kissed each other wetly beside my ear, and buffeted me with the fervour of their grease-slicked thrusts. Sean gripped Joe's buttocks so hard the indentations turned white. Joe flattened my breasts with his chest. Their grunts and gasps aroused me all over again. I could have listened all night, but neither man was in a mood to dawdle. Watching me take my pleasure had cranked them up. Now they wanted theirs, right away, and no monkey business.

They came simultaneously and so quietly I felt embarrassed for crying out.

Sean rolled away from me first, then Joe. Snuggling up to my favourite pillow, Joe promptly fell asleep.

'Thanks,' Sean mumbled from the other side of the bed. 'That was fun.' Then he was out, too.

Some things never change, I thought. Still, there was a

spring in my step as I padded into the shower to wash off the night's adventure.

The water streamed over me, soothing my tired muscles. My soapy hand drifted between my legs. I'd have one last firework before sleep. As my fingers pursued the little explosion, a single refrain beat through my head: *When we're alone. When we're alone.*

Chapter Two
All Work and No Play

*I*left them sleeping the next morning. I tried to wake them, but a few grumpy mumbles were all I got for my trouble. Even as I dressed, Sean squirmed over to Joe's side of the bed and wrapped his hand around his cock.

If that didn't wake Joe, nothing would.

For the first time, I noticed Sean wasn't circumcised. Still buttoning my sheer silk blouse, I walked around the bed to get a closer look. His relative slightness might have exaggerated the effect but – goodness – his equipment was large. The foreskin hugged his heart-shaped glans like a smooth pink turtleneck. I put one knee on the mattress and kissed the little dimple at the base of his spine. He stirred. He smacked his lips. Encouraged, I tongued the honey-gold down that shadowed his tailbone.

'Mm-bm,' was all he said.

I peeked over his hip. His penis had begun to wriggle against the white sheet, filling from the bottom up. The head poked out a smidgen more. I sighed. I remembered how men got in the morning. He and Joe were sure to have a quickie when they finally woke. I wished I had time to stay and watch – and help, of course!

Later, I promised, but it was hard to drag myself away, even if I was late for work.

My resentment faded as soon as I hit the great out-doors. The day was beautiful: bright blue sky, flaming autumn leaves. The walk from Society Hill to South Street led through the city's best-kept eighteenth-century buildings. If that weren't satisfaction enough for one morning, three male joggers turned to check the poste-rior fit of my yellow Capri pants. I congratulated myself for pairing them with the matching crop jacket, and rewarded my best-looking admirer with a wink. He promptly tripped over his shoelaces.

During the ensuing 'are-you-all-right?' exchange, he passed me his card. I appreciated the gesture, but wondered how compulsive you had to be to carry business cards out jogging. Plus, he wasn't built as nicely as Sean or Joe.

Good grief, I thought. One night of Rocky Road and I was spoilt for plain vanilla.

I glanced at the card as I crossed Fifth Street. 'L. Kingston Waters,' it said. 'Estate Agent.' He might as well have been a used car salesman. He did have nice blue eyes, though – bedroom eyes, with curly black lashes starring the lids.

The door to my bookshop jingled as I pushed it open. My heart warmed at the sight of so many customers browsing the stacks. Everyone told me you can't sell romance in the city. You've got to locate in the suburbs to catch the bored housewives. Luckily, I didn't listen. One year later, Mostly Romance out-grossed the local chain and the popular new age bookshop two doors down. Our atmosphere accounted considerably for our success. We boasted oak panelling, moulded ceilings and comfy chairs. A jungle of greenery enhanced the scent of leather and printer's ink. We also served the best coffee in town. Women came in giggling carloads from as far as Virginia. Men shopped for their wives or tried to pick up dates. People couldn't find what we had anywhere else, and once you took our back room into account, we were well-nigh irresistible.

The back room was my special baby. It housed a

collection of erotica from all over the world, a real treasure house of delights. Customers wrote thanking me for creating a safe space to buy and explore. I was happy to do it; I knew how they felt.

I pondered, as I'd begun to do lately, whether it was time to open a second shop.

Flushed with my own success, I waved to Keith, the morning sales assistant, declined his offer of coffee, and headed for the office I shared with my partner Marianne. Marianne was my sister-in-law – actually, my ex-sister-in-law, since my big brother had done a moonlight flit. For years she'd been my closest friend, the only friend who stuck by me after my own divorce. Living with Tom had brought out my bitchy side. He was the charmer, not me. Consequently, our mutual friends had no trouble believing his version of the facts. To them I was the harpy wife, and he the long-suffering soul of patience.

Sometimes I thought the only reason Marianne knew better was because Tom had run off with her daughter.

At my tardy entrance, she looked up from the computer inventory. She arched one thin brow. 'Late night?'

I hummed evasively. Marianne liked sharing her exploits, but I preferred to keep mine private – especially since I'd discouraged her from making a play for my lodgers by swearing they were absolutely, positively, one hundred per cent gay.

Now she spread her silver-tipped fingers across the surface of her desk. Marianne had gone Gothic lately: white face, ink-black hair, skin-tight leather. She carried it off with *élan*, one of the few women who could without looking like death warmed up.

At my continued silence, she pursed her lips – her bee-stung, scarlet lips. 'I suppose you don't want to hear about my encounter with Keith, then.'

In spite of myself, I was interested. 'Our Keith, from out front? Marianne, he's barely eighteen.'

'Nineteen,' she corrected with a Cheshire cat grin, 'and very hormonal.'

My glance flashed around the room looking for signs of coitus – semen smears, lipstick on the wall.

'Not here, silly.' Her eyes sparkled. 'I bumped into him in Rittenhouse Square last night. He was cycling; I was strolling. We stopped to chat. It turns out, he's the one who's been "borrowing" my nice Italian shoes.'

Grabbing my chair, I rolled it to the front of her desk and sat. 'He's a transvestite?'

'No, no.' She waved her silver claws. 'Just a foot fetishist. He says I've got the best arches he's ever seen. I never knew how inspiring that kind of admiration could be.' Her sooty lashes dipped with pleasure. 'You know the wall behind the big wading fountain in the park?'

I nodded.

'After I let him know his confession didn't disgust me, he parked his bike there and set me on the seat. He swung his leg over the bar, facing me, and pulled off my shoes. First he massaged my feet, ver-ry slowly. Oh, it was nice, especially since I could see how much he enjoyed it. His hands were shaking. He could hardly sit still. He was wearing those stretchy biker's shorts.' She smiled creamily at me. 'No jockstrap and hard as a rock in about six seconds. I could see everything – every vein, every ridge. He has the biggest balls I've ever seen: each one a handful, you know?'

I didn't, but I could imagine. I pressed down hard on the cushion of my chair. Why did I let Marianne do this to me? 'And then what?'

'Then he licked me. Not just the toes, but everything – heel, ankle, the long bones on the top. I never knew my feet had so many lovely nerves, and every one connected to my pussy. I tell you, I was ready to screw the bike seat.'

'Did he want to screw?'

'Do ducks quack? Fortunately, I was wearing my favourite black mini-skirt, the one with the studs up the side. He pushed it up a bit and whipped out his Swiss Army knife.' She laughed and tossed her straight black

23

hair. 'I love a man who carries his own tools. Anyway, he sliced the crotch of my underwear and pushed real close so no one could see what we were doing – except kissing, of course. He was a nice kisser, too, lots of tongue action. I pushed those lycra shorts down until he sprang out and then I slid straight down on him. It was nice, Kate, hot and strong.' She fanned herself. 'Young men do get so desperate.'

'Especially when they're acting out their fantasies,' I said, thinking of Sean and his tube of lubricant.

'Exactly. He didn't take but a second to come. I was disappointed, until I realised he was just warming up. "Please don't go," he said, when I was about to climb off. "When someone gets me this hot, once is never enough." As you might imagine, I was happy to oblige. The second time did last forever. We had to be careful, with all those people walking by. We couldn't thrust really hard – just little shakes and rolls with that bike seat digging into me the whole time. Deliciously frustrating. He had to grind his thumb over me before I could come, but when I did, I thought the top of my head would fly off. Then we adjourned to my car.'

'To your car?' Marianne owned a classic Volkswagen Beetle.

'He wasn't going to make it all the way to my house. I'm telling you, Kate, the boy was pneumatic. The back seat was cramped, but – hey – I'm flexible. He took me twice before I drove him back to campus. He's a student at the University of Pennsylvania.' She tapped her nose with one finger. 'I wonder if he knows your lodgers.'

I sensed visions of orgies dancing through her head. Alarm bells rang in mine. Despite my fondness for Marianne, I had no desire to share my sex life with her, or my new playmates.

'Sean and Joe are postgraduate students,' I said. 'Keith is only in his second year.'

Marianne shrugged. 'Just a thought. No need to get miffed.'

Her indifference was feigned, of course. If I gave her

the least encouragement, she'd have us all in bed within the hour – though my presence was probably optional. I didn't know what she'd do if she discovered I'd lived out her fantasy already. Marianne had a competitive streak as wide as the Ben Franklin Bridge.

I pulled my chair back to my walnut roll-top desk and started slitting correspondence – bills, authors' fliers, a postcard from my favourite publisher's rep. Sorting them like a robot, I thought: Better make sure she doesn't find out. Otherwise, I'll never hear the end of it.

Sean wandered in at noon, carrying a bouquet of yellow chrysanthemums. I thanked God Marianne was out to lunch.

'For you,' he said, then turned full circle to view the shop.

I watched him from behind the counter. Joe had dropped by many times, but never Sean. Two college girls pinkened as his gaze passed over them. He didn't seem to notice, which worried me. Was his attraction to me a big exception for him? If it was, our trio could break up awfully quickly. I wasn't sure how Joe would react to that. Joe was very loyal. He might give me up, too, if he thought his friend wasn't happy.

'This is nice,' Sean said, his scrutiny complete. 'If I were a woman, I'd shop here.'

'If you were a man looking to pick up girls, you might shop here, too,' I said, then blushed for what I might have implied. 'Um, what are the flowers for?'

He grinned. 'What do you think? They're a thank you from both of us – and an apology. We meant to wake up early and, you know, fit one more in, but I'm afraid neither of us is a morning person.'

This must mean my standing breakfast date with Joe was more of a tribute than I'd known. Annoyed with my pleasure at the discovery – for hadn't I promised to keep things light? – I reached under the counter for a vase. 'They're beautiful. Are you on your way to class or can you stay awhile?'

25

My invitation brought him up short. For a second, he looked like a wallflower who couldn't believe he'd been asked to dance. I felt good for asking, if a little worried for feeling good.

'I can stay,' he said.

'Good. I'll show you around.'

I gave him the grand tour: new books, used books, the coffee lounge on the balcony. We finished in the back room. He headed straight for the old-fashioned rolling ladder and climbed to the top. The kid in me took over.

'Hold on,' I said, and shoved him the full length of the wall.

He whooped in delight. 'I love these things. My mother was a librarian. She never let me play with them.'

'She probably wasn't allowed to.'

He nodded, his face shadowed with conflicting emotions. How complicated people are once you start to know them. He rubbed the bridge of his nose. 'Does that door lock?' he asked.

'Yes, but –'

Without waiting for me to finish, he clambered down and latched it.

'A customer might want to get in,' I said, but the determination in his face weakened my resistance, and my knees.

He plastered his back to the door. 'Come here.'

I closed the distance between us and waited. His wavy gold hair swooped over one eye. Long in front and short in back, the style suited his sullen, bad-boy looks. Accountancy student or not, Sean had the face of a handsome day labourer. With his rugged features, his full, sensual lips and heavy-lidded eyes, he looked like a man who'd drink too much on weekends, keep his wife popping out babies, and shout obscenities during sporting events.

Apart from a fondness for obscenities, none of it was true.

'I haven't kissed you yet,' he said. 'He has, but I haven't.'

I stroked the side of his face. He wasn't more than an inch taller than me. 'Don't kiss me because Joe has. Kiss me because you want to, if you want to.'

'If I want to –' He captured my hand and dragged it down his black T-shirt. His body felt warm – too warm. My fingers snagged on his waistband, then settled over the impressive swell behind his buttoned flies. He covered my hand and pressed hard. His erection barely gave. My pulse shifted into high gear. Maybe Joe wasn't the only one who wanted to get me alone.

'Now, does that feel like I don't want to kiss you?'

'If you're trying to prove something –'

He cut me off with an impatient *tut*. 'I don't have to prove anything. I sleep with people I like, people who impress me. I admit they're usually men but, hell, sometimes lightning strikes in funny places.' He squeezed my hand over his cock again. 'I'm not arguing with ol' Willy here. He knows what he likes and he never lies.'

'That's very flattering but –'

'Be quiet,' he said, and yanked my head to his for a kiss.

His tongue pressed directly home, subduing mine with force and expertise. His hand clamped the back of my neck, steel-hard and work-rough. Something flowered in me at this treatment, something secret and dark. I struggled against the kiss for the sheer pleasure of inspiring more displays of mastery. His arm tightened on my waist. He lifted me, turned, and shoved me back against the door. The weight of his body trapped me in place, and the strength of his legs. He ground his hardness into my softness. Wanting more, I slung one leg high on his hip, clamped both hands on his adorable butt, and rocked back.

'Like that, bitch?' His teeth nipped my earlobe. Though the name shook me, I laughed at him. His hazel eyes narrowed. 'I'll make you beg,' he said.

'Yeah?' I blew a stream of air through his fringe. 'You've got fifteen minutes to prove it. Marianne will be back in twenty and I'm not in the mood to share.'

He flashed his teeth at that, half grin, half alpha wolf display. Before I could wonder what he'd do next, he attacked my side zip and yanked my snug yellow trousers to my ankles.

'Hands and knees,' he said. When I stubbornly shook my head, he dragged me to the rolling ladder and manhandled me into the position he wanted. He was so powerful he didn't even have to hurt me to do it. He simply moved me as he pleased and I wasn't strong enough to stop him.

Panting with excitement, I grabbed the second rung. Joe couldn't protect me now. Sean would take me any way he wanted, as hard as he wanted, as fast as he wanted. He pushed my knees wider with the tip of his construction boot. My bottom felt chilled, exposed. A drop of sexual moisture ran down my inner thigh. I knew he must be staring at it.

'I'll give you one thing,' he said. 'That is one prize-winning, wet-and-ready arse. Too bad I haven't got time to spank it.'

'You and whose army?'

This time he laughed at me. I heard buttons popping, foil tearing. I turned my head. He'd shoved the flaps of his jeans down past his bare hips – he wore no under-wear – and was slathering lubricant up and down his thinly sheathed prick. His motions were quick, but not so quick he couldn't enjoy them.

'Eyes front!' The heel of his boot reinforced the whispered order, pressing my buttocks hard enough to shock.

'Fifteen minutes,' I reminded him, defiant to the last.

'Eleven. And don't think you aren't mine already.'

He dropped to his knees behind me, surrounding me in warmth like cocoa on a cold day. He didn't remove my short jacket or my blouse: merely shoved my silky shirt-tails to my waist. Considering I was bared like a surgery patient, I couldn't believe how comfortable I felt.

Customers trod the aisles mere feet away. I heard the floorboards creaking under their shoes. A man I scarcely knew was about to initiate me into a potentially painful sex act and I'd never felt safer in my life.

'I must be losing my mind,' I said.

'No, babe, you're about to find it.' Sean laced our fingers together around the ladder rung. He cupped my pussy from the front and rotated my sex against my pubic bone. If anything, the rough handling made me wetter. His fingers slid through my juices.

'Take a deep breath,' he said. 'Remember how good this felt last night.'

I willed myself to relax. His hand left my sex to pull one cheek from his target. An unaccustomed draught cooled my flesh before his cock-head probed me, slick and hot. I arched my back and it pressed inside. His sudden exhalation burned my neck, but he didn't speak, just grasped my hip and pushed again.

'Halfway there,' he said and I thought, my God, half is plenty. The pressure was incredible – not painful exactly, but alarming. Was he really going to fit?

He heaved once more, grunting this time, and this time my body engulfed his root. I felt his balls press up against my cheeks, felt the prickle of his thatch. Inside, my body twitched and flamed. I thought my bottom had grown a second heart, the pounding there was so intense. A moan rose in my throat. If he moved, I'd come.

'Good?' He chuckled as if he knew exactly what was happening to me. 'Feel like begging yet?'

I almost said 'no' but I remembered how few minutes remained. Should I beg? I suspected he could hold out longer than I could. If I begged now, he might get me off a few times. I knew my day would be miserable if he didn't.

'Please beg, Kate.' His hips shimmied with urgency, bringing me closer to the edge.

I bit my lip and tasted blood. 'How should I say it?'

'"Please" is good enough. Just make it quick. I'm dying back here.'

29

'Please, then, Sean. Please fuck me in the arse.'

The hand that held mine tightened. The other found my pussy again. He kneaded the soft, wet flesh as he slowly dragged back out of me. Halfway out, he pushed, using his grip on my mound to anchor his return. My untried state prevented him from going far. His chest rumbled. I sensed his impatience with my tightness, but also that he loved it. He throbbed inside me, pulses of fire that vibrated through the barrier between my anus and sheath. If Sean and Joe both filled me, would they feel the passage of each other's shaft? I came at the thought, a long ripple that oscillated like liquid gold between back and front.

'That's it. Give it up,' Sean said as the climax eased me. He began short-stroking in quick, eager drives. 'Ah, you're smooth as silk. I wish I had all day for this.'

I shuddered again, this orgasm a brief stab of pleasure, there and then gone. His thrusts lengthened. He groaned and said: 'God, this is good.' Another climax broke at his praise, his deeper strokes touching it off further inside me, making it hotter. As soon as that one faded, the hunger built again. My pussy clenched, desperate for something to hold. I fumbled for his hand and urged two fingers inside my dripping sheath.

'Oh, man.' His fingers stroked me inside, their movements agitated. 'Oh, man, I'm a goner. Spread your legs wider. I gotta get – I'm gonna shoot. Oh, yeah, babe, that's it. That's it.'

His groin slammed my cheeks as if someone had kicked him from behind. His prick stiffened even more. I knew I had seconds to finish – milliseconds. I mashed the heel of his palm over my bud and gyrated hard. My climax burst in a shower of hot, red darts. My body tightened, round his fingers, round his prick . . .

'Oh, sh–' he hissed as his hips began to jerk. He shook for a good while, a marathon orgasm.

Afterwards, he held me longer than he had to, longer than I understood. I rubbed the side of my head against his face, trying to give him whatever it was he needed. His cock softened, slipping from me.

'Kate,' he whispered. 'Pretty Kate.'

He bit my neck before he let go. Leaving his mark, I suppose. Limbs shaking, I pulled up my trousers and sagged back against the bookshelf. Sean dropped down beside me. He took one look at me and stripped off his T-shirt.

'Here, wipe your face. There's got to be a dry spot somewhere.'

'Good thing I don't wear make-up.'

'You don't need it,' he said.

The unexpected compliment inspired a silence. I wiped my face and returned his sweaty shirt, which he dazedly pulled back on. If I looked anything like he did, we could have passed for train wreck victims – not only for our dishevelment, but for the expression on our faces. We'd surprised the hell out of each other.

'I didn't expect this to happen,' I said.

He scrubbed his hair back from his face, making his biceps pop in unison. 'Me neither.' He looked at his watch and grimaced at the time. 'I'd better leave. Your employees will wonder what's going on.'

'Sean.' I paused to measure my words. 'We should go somewhere and talk. We . . . we kind of jumped into this – last night, too. I want to make sure no one gets hurt.'

He rubbed his palms down the front of his jeans. 'I know. I didn't expect it to be so –'

'Intense?'

He nodded, then looked away. 'There are some things you need to know about me and Joe, things you might not understand.'

I had no doubt of that. By mutual accord, we struggled to our feet and shook out our wrinkles.

Marianne walked in the street door just as we walked out. Her cool grey eyes took in our rosy cheeks and rumpled clothes, and branded me a liar. I'd pay later, I knew, but at the moment I didn't care.

'Two,' I said and held up a victory sign, our private code for a long lunch.

'Looks like you had two already,' she called after us from the door. That's how I knew she was angry.

We walked to a shabby, basement-level restaurant in Little Italy. White fairy lights festooned the age-browned murals. Plastic flowers graced the tables. Early or not, the place was suspiciously empty. I didn't understand why Sean had chosen it until the waiter came to take our order.

'We'll have two double scoops of *gelato*, one lemon and –' Sean squinted at me as though reading my aura '– one raspberry.'

For a young man, he was mighty dictatorial. Unfortunately, raspberry was my favourite, so I couldn't countermand him.

The rich, fruity treat made a perfect post-coital snack. We traded bites from each other's dishes like an old married couple. The analogy summoned a shiver of foreboding. I knew I shouldn't be getting so comfortable.

'I don't know where to start,' he said.

'Why don't you tell me how you and Joe met?'

His smile said the memory was sweet. 'We had a class together last year – Film Appreciation. Joe didn't know me from Adam but I noticed him straight away: that blue-black hair, those eyes, that skin. I wanted to lap him up the minute I saw him, but he was off in his own little world. I couldn't tell with him, either. Was he gay, straight, or somewhere in between? All I knew was he was sexy, as if God turned up the voltage when he made Joe.'

I tucked another sugar-tart spoonful into my mouth and let it melt. Sean rubbed his jaw. His faint stubble was a shimmer of gold beneath his skin. 'That day, the professor was screening *Blue Velvet*. You know, the one with Kyle MacLachlan and Isabella Rosellini?'

'I've seen it.'

'Then you know it's pretty hot. We had a break

32

between reels, so I went to the men's to take a leak. Everyone else stayed to suck up to the prof – or so I thought. I went in. I saw an empty cubicle. I had a half-hard now, 'cause of the film, and was thinking: do I want to jack off or would I rather wait? 'Cause if I do it now, I'll have to hurry and waiting can be good unless you lose the edge altogether.

'Then I heard it, a little noise in the next cubicle. I know this noise, of course. I'm a master of the silent public wank myself. I don't know if you've heard it, but a fist makes a tiny shishing noise as it pumps a cock, especially if you've got a little sweat and juice to slick up the skin. Fucking your hand has a rhythm, too, like sex, only it's one person's rhythm instead of two. You can slow down or speed up whenever you like. It's sexy as hell to listen to. Plus, you can learn a lot about a guy from the way he does himself.'

Sean reached across the table and took my hand as though he knew the precise instant my sex overflowed. His thumb circled the sensitive cup of my palm.

'This guy has done this before, I thought. His strokes were real sure, real steady. He knew what he liked. He wasn't in a hurry, but he wasn't dilly-dallying, either. And he was breathing through his mouth so he wouldn't make much noise.

'By then, my half-hard was whole hard and then some. I started to take it out, thinking I'd give this guy some silent accompaniment and then I thought: Sean, babe, why not introduce yourself? Maybe you'll meet someone you like. At the very least, you'll get a good laugh. So, as quietly as I could, I climbed on the seat and peeked over the wall. Imagine my surprise when I saw it was him, sexy old whisky eyes. He looked up, turned beet-red, then burst out laughing.

'"Hello there," I said, as suave as you can get when you're standing on a toilet. "Like some help with that?" He thought about it a minute – the longest minute of my life – then says, "Sure. Come on over." Well, I didn't need more encouragement than that. I nipped inside and knelt up facing him on the throne. He still had his dick in his hand. He was still hard. In fact, he was harder than he was a minute ago. "What now?" he asked. My heart just about stopped. "You've never done it with a guy?" He said he'd thought about it lots of times. What about girls? I needed to know. "Once," he said and he made this face, as if it wasn't worth mentioning.

'I could read his whole sexual history in that one word. Good kid, good girlfriend. Probably met at church. His hormones raged. Hers didn't. She gave it a try – 'cause she loves him – but neither of them knew more than Peg A fits Slot B. Naturally, the whole messy business ended in disaster. Nobody had fun. Afterwards, they couldn't look each other in the eye. They broke up. Good kid started wondering if something was wrong with him. He'd been daydreaming about guys lately. Maybe he was gay.'

Sighing, Sean lifted my hand and kissed it. He didn't seem to notice my palm was sweating. 'Finding Joe was like a sugar addict getting his own sweet shop. Horniest guy I'd ever met and a virtual cherry. Never had a decent orgasm he hadn't given himself. I felt like whatsit, the real My Fair Lady guy.'

'Pygmalion?'

'That's the one.' He shook his head and clasped my hand to his chest. 'I decided to go down on him. I knew he'd never had anyone do that and I knew he'd love it. I think I sucked him for ten seconds before he flashed.'

'"Flashed?"' I asked, my voice husky. Despite the fact that homosexuals are one of my kinks, the terminology was new to me.

The corners of Sean's mouth twitched. He resumed his sensuous circling of my palm. 'Take your shoe off and slide your foot over here. Then I might tell you.'

I did as he asked. He trapped my instep against his bulge by pressing his thighs together. He was big already, but he grew bigger when I curled my toes.

'Bad girl,' he said, but he didn't tell me to stop.

Instead, he continued his story. '"Flash" means to give yourself away as liking men too much. Joe flashed because he came almost as soon as I touched him – too fast for me. I wanted to drag things out. Luckily, the whole thing excited him so much he didn't even go soft before he stiffened up again. "More?" I asked. I think he said something like, "Gee, would you?" – as if I wasn't delighted to do it. After that round, he remembered me. Some guys don't, you know. Some guys think as long as they don't do anything back, they can't be gay, as though being inconsiderate makes you straight. Not Joe, though.

'Would I like him to return the favour? he asked. Would I ever – only I wasn't about to trust ol' Willy to a neophyte. "Why don't you see if you like the rear door?" I say. Lord, he was so afraid he'd hurt me, I was laughing by the time he finally got it in. Then he put his hand on my cock, in that gentle way he has, like my dick was something precious. I melted then and there. I vowed I'd keep him, by hook or by crook.' He screwed up his face at this admission.

'He really likes you,' I said, reading his embarrassment. 'He wouldn't stay with you if he didn't want to.'

'Maybe not.' Sean released my hand and clinked his spoon through the melted yellow soup in his *gelato* dish. 'Thing is, the first time I saw him ogle a girl, I knew I was keeping him from half his nature. He wanted to try again. I could see it in his face.'

'I'm sure he wanted to try again because you restored his confidence.'

'But I let him know, in a hundred ways, that I'd be upset if he did try.'

'What of it? Who wants their lover to sleep around? You would have been upset. Joe chose not to upset you because he cares about you. None of that seems wrong to me. What I want to know is what changed your mind? Why did you make an exception for me?'

'Honestly?'

'Of course, honestly.'

'At first, it was just because I knew I couldn't stop it.

35

He had it bad for you from the start. I mean, his appetite was always big, but since we moved in with you I'd take him three, four times a day and still hear him beating off before he went to bed. Every time you stopped to chat, to listen to that damn album or whatever, he'd be a maniac afterwards. He tried to hide what was making him so horny, but I knew. He started mumbling your name in his sleep. Once he even called out "Kate" when we were having sex.'

'I'm sorry, Sean. That must have hurt.'

He waved my concern away. 'Not so much. By then I was starting to get off on it. He wanted you so bad, and thought he'd never have you. I loved watching him sweat.' He stuck his spoon in his mouth and pulled it out upside down. 'Just like you do. Anyway, I knew you had the hots for him, even if he didn't. I started to think: what if I set it up for him? What if I make myself part of it? I've been with girls before and with some of them, it was good. And you remind me of him. You've got that glow like something's simmering inside. It isn't obvious, but someone with my radar can pick up on it. You like sex as much as Joe does.'

I raised my eyebrows at that. 'I've never had it four or five times a day.'

'Haven't you?' He leant forward, his forearms flush with the Formica tabletop. 'Not even doing it for yourself?'

That brought the colour to my face. I had, of course – not every day, but plenty of days. My ex, a two-fer at the most, had never wrung it all out of me.

'If you haven't, you could,' he said in his know-everything way. 'Between Joe and me, you could certainly give it a try.'

My heart played Fred Astaire for a couple of beats. Sean was offering me my fantasy on a platter – except he wasn't a fantasy. He was a real person with real feelings. I might promise to keep things light, but one of us was bound to end up hurt. Maybe all of us would. Life had taught me that lesson to the full.

I shifted on the seat, conscious of the heat between my legs. This was a once-in-a-lifetime chance. Would I kick myself worse if I grabbed it, or if I let it go? Coward that I was, I threw the decision back to Sean. 'Is that what you really want? To start up a threesome?'

'You bet,' he said, without a moment's hesitation. 'I can't hold on to Joe forever. Might as well go out with a bang.'

Chapter Three
Out of the Frying Pan

I returned to Mostly Romance at a pace too ambling to qualify as exercise. Sean's story had plumped the folds of my sex. The sensitive tissues chafed with my steps, but I ignored the discomfort.

My thoughts required my full attention.

Sean seemed to assume he'd lose Joe, that Joe would choose me over him. Did he expect me to make Joe choose? I thrust my hands in my pockets and worried my lower lip.

'On your left,' someone warned me from behind. I looked back. An inexperienced rollerblader was headed straight for me. I sidestepped towards a shop window to avoid getting bumped.

The next fellow wasn't so lucky.

'Watch where you goin', man,' said that dreadlocked individual.

The scolding rattled the skater so badly he wobbled into the path of some Japanese tourists. Skirting them by inches, he veered towards the kerb. A balding Italian man grabbed his waist, neatly rescuing him from careering into traffic – for which feat a young punkette with a nose-ring yelled, 'Good save!'

Yes, indeed, this place had all kinds. Philadelphia might not always act like the City of Brotherly Love, but the diversity of her inhabitants gave her plenty of chances to practise.

I admired Philly's ability to encompass so much variety. I admired it in myself. So why should I make Joe choose? Why shouldn't all three of us be happy? My gloomier half said, 'Because that sort of thing never works.'

As if on cue, Marianne stuck her head out the shop's entrance and grabbed my lemon-yellow lapel. She tugged me behind her to our office. As usual, she'd closed the mini-blinds; said too much sunshine gave her a headache. I opened the blinds halfway, pinched a brown frond off the asparagus fern and turned to face her. I expected a dressing-down, but instead she bubbled over with news of a good-looking man in an Italian suit who'd dropped by to ask me out.

I said I couldn't imagine who it might be.

'You couldn't forget him. He's scrumptious. Sexy eyes. Gold Rolex. He said his name was Larry.'

I hung my jacket over the back of my old-fashioned swivel chair and sat. 'I don't know anyone named Larry.'

'Of course you do.' With the persistence of a bloodhound, Marianne parked her leather-clad bottom on the corner of my desk. Her miniskirt rode up her sheer black stockings. She wagged her pointy four-inch heel. 'You met him this morning. He gave you his card.'

'Oh, that guy.' I opened my centre drawer and pawed through the clutter for a piece of chewing gum. 'I don't know what you're so excited about. He wasn't anything special.'

'Are you kidding? He's totally beddable.'

'Maybe the suit hid his love handles.'

'The Italian suit,' she clarified. 'The expensive Italian suit.'

I popped the last stick of spearmint into my mouth. 'Tom wore nice Italian suits.'

My partner snorted. 'Tom, may he rot in hell, is history. It's time you got back in circulation.'

'I am in circulation. Besides, I don't think I want to

start up with anyone else right now. My life is complicated enough.'

This admission was a mistake. Marianne stood, clenched both hands in her satiny black hair and pulled. 'I knew it. You're having a rebound thing with those limp-wristed lodgers. Kate, Kate, Kate, can't you see there's no future in that?'

Determined to play it cool, I swung my feet on to the blotter and crossed my ankles. 'Aren't you the one who's always saying "live for the moment"?'

'If only you would!' Marianne plopped back on her own desk and tugged her gold-braided bolero jacket over her tiny waist. 'At least give the man a call.'

'If you like him so much, you give him a call.'

'You're impossible.'

'And you're so jealous you could spit.'

She glared at this, but her anger faded to a pout a moment later. 'Maybe I am, but that doesn't mean sleeping with them isn't a stupid idea.'

'It wasn't stupid when you wanted to do it.'

Since she couldn't think of a comeback for that, she sniffed haughtily and swept out of the room muttering that I'd better not come crying to her when my heart got trampled.

Her warning hit home. I had a tendency to get serious about the men in my life. This fling with Sean and Joe was the closest I'd come to breaking my habit of serial monogamy. Already, I liked Sean far more than was convenient, and Joe –

I squirmed lower in my chair. Joe was so yummy it was dangerous.

Joe was cooking when I returned home that evening. I have a nice kitchen with exposed brick walls, herbs hanging in bunches from the beams, and lots of fancy pots. I don't cook much, but I like the cosy way it looks.

I liked the way Joe looked in it, too. I stood in the doorway watching him slice vegetables at the big butcher's-block island. He wore stone-washed jeans and

40

was bare-chested. A freshly ironed blue shirt draped the back of a kitchen stool, which was where it belonged, in my opinion. Muscles flowed beneath his bare skin as he chopped. Joe had an awe-inspiring set of shoulders, very broad and very firm. He didn't work out much, though. Twice a week, maybe, he joined Sean at the gym or rode his bike along the river to Boathouse Row. He was just one of those lucky people who are born lean.

He was born tuneful, too, I thought, listening to him hum. He had a nice tenor, with the slightest hint of huskiness. Unless I was mistaken, the tune was Nat King Cole's 'Rambling Rose'. He'd been into my CDs again.

'Hey there, Mr Capriccio.'

He spun around as if I'd caught him jacking off. Appropriately enough, the top button of his jeans was undone, revealing a silky line of hair that dived from his navel to his crotch.

'You're early,' he said, doing up the button and grabbing his shirt off the stool.

Before he could get more than a hand in the sleeve, I ran my palms from the sinewed balls of his shoulders to his elbows. 'I'm not early. I simply left on time today – and don't dress on my account. I like ogling your hairy chest.'

His blush enchanted me.

'I didn't want to ruin the shirt while I was cooking. I've just pressed it.'

My hands reversed direction, skimming up his arms and down the centre of his chest. I spread my fingers across his board-flat abdomen. His warm, satiny skin twitched like a horse with a fly on it. The temperature of his groin jumped and, to my delight, his goods began to swell. 'You pressed that shirt for me?'

'Uh huh.' His diaphragm jerked with a quick breath.

My hands wandered higher, over his ribs, on to his pecs. His nipples were small, no bigger than pennies. The nub of erectile tissue in their centres stood out sharply and a tinge of blood-pink excitement painted their tips. Joe lowered his head, watching my hands,

41

watching his body react. My own nipples ached at the sight. Feeling naughty, I took the tiny beads between thumb and forefinger and pinched.

'Kate,' he gasped, and backed me into the island. Drawer handles jabbed my thighs – not that I cared. His heavy erection dug into my front, hard and getting harder. His hips swivelled until the pressure nearly lifted me off my feet. 'Lord, you make me crazy. I've been thinking about you all day. I could hardly sit through class. I kept getting hard, remembering the things we did yesterday, and the things I want to do tonight.'

'Such as?'

'Oh, man.' He grabbed my hips and kneaded. 'Don't get me started. I want everything to be perfect, the food, the wine, the dessert. Sean is staying with friends tonight. We have the place to ourselves.'

'I see. And does everything have to happen in order – food first, sex last?'

Confusion creased his brow. 'I don't want you to think I'm just some horny kid. I'm making salmon with orange sauce, steamed artichoke hearts and –' he consulted the open cookbook '– Indonesian rice salad.'

I slipped my hands down his back and under the waistband of his jeans. He wore them looser than Sean did. I had room enough to take possession of his downy hindquarters. He went up on his toes as I stroked them. What a sensitive boy he was. 'That sounds delicious, Joe. Is anything in the oven yet?'

'No, but –'

I silenced him with a deep, open-mouthed kiss. He tasted of ginger and oranges. He moaned, then filled my mouth with his tongue, slow, forceful spearings that probed my palate, then my cheeks. My nails curled into his buttocks at his sudden switch to aggressor. He didn't even flinch, he was so focused on his explorations.

I fumbled for his zip. 'I think I need an hors d'oeuvre.'

The sound of the tag ripping downward brought him to full alert. His long, strong fingers folded over my

42

wrist. 'No, no, no. I waited all day for this. I can wait a few hours longer.'

'Can you?' His prick sprang through the vent of his briefs. How could I have forgotten how impressive he was? Veins stood out along the stalk and a drop of clear fluid seeped from the slit that pierced his glans. I swiped it off with the pad of my middle finger. At my touch, the passage gaped like a tiny mouth. A second drop squeezed through the contraction, this one large enough to roll sinuously down the head. I licked my lips. Hors d'oeuvre and then some. 'You look ready to go right now.'

'I can wait,' he insisted, though he was dancing on the spot.

I collected another drop and carried it to my lips. Salty. 'Maybe I can't wait.'

'Please,' he said, eyes glued to my sucking mouth. 'I want to keep my edge.'

I settled my cheek on the perspiring curve of his shoulder. 'From what Sean says, your edge doesn't take long to recover.'

He grasped my arms and pushed back. 'When did you and Sean have a chance to discuss my "edge"?'

'When he brought the flowers.' An idiotic rush of embarrassment heated my cheeks. Obviously, Joe didn't know about our tête-a-tête.

He touched the telltale colour with the back of his hand. 'You're blushing. Did you and he – Kate, did you and Sean make love?'

My embarrassment deepened. 'Not exactly. We, um, we did what you wouldn't let him do last night.'

Joe slammed his fist into the cutting board. 'Shit. I wanted to cop your cherry myself.'

I had to laugh at that. 'And here I thought you were concerned for my well-being.'

'I was! I mean, that was part of it. He's hung like a damn horse. Oh, hell.' He pushed his hair back with both hands. 'I'm sorry. Of course you and Sean have the right to do whatever you like. It wouldn't be fair for me to keep all the good stuff for myself.'

'Well.' I shimmied closer. 'I hope you don't think that's all the good stuff there is. In any case, I didn't think you wanted to cut Sean out.'

'I don't.' His arms circled me and he rested his cheek on my hair. 'I just want to have some time that's only for us, like tonight.'

'That's fair.'

'I guess I didn't think Sean would want to have you to himself.'

I chuckled. 'I don't think Sean expected that, either.'

'He didn't hurt you?'

'No-o.' I liquefied at the memory of him manoeuvring me into position, the way he'd shoved my knees apart with his boot, how thick he'd been when he breached me. 'It was . . . interesting. He's very commanding.'

Joe shivered in my arms and I realised he had his own memories.

'Yes,' he said. 'Very.'

I assessed his distant expression. 'Next time would you like to watch?'

He shivered again. 'Next time I'd like to do. Then maybe I'll want to watch.'

'Fair enough.'

But first we had to get through dinner.

Oddly enough, one hunger sharpened the other. Joe cooked well. The salmon melted in my mouth, the artichoke slid tenderly off the spine, and the rice was nice and spicy – not unlike me! I spent a good portion of the meal moaning over how delicious everything was. Joe relished that, in more ways than one.

When he stood to help me clear the dinner table, he had a hard time straightening. His erection, thick as Philly bratwurst, extended into the left leg of his jeans. Grimacing, he tried to tug the denim off the bulbous head.

I hid a smile as I preceded him into the kitchen. 'You've got a choice.' I set the first few plates into the sink. 'I can help you load the dishwasher, or I can get a head start on my shower.'

Joe latched on to me from behind and rubbed his erection down the outside of my thigh. Unbelievably, it stretched at the treatment.

'Boo-hoo,' he pretended to cry. 'My balls are bluer than Frank Sinatra's eyes. Why do you have to take a shower?'

Now was probably not the time to mention I might be a little fragrant from my morning encounter with Sean. 'Because women are funny that way?'

'All right,' he said with flattering reluctance, 'but save some good spots for me to wash. I'll be up soon.'

I started stripping on my way out, divesting myself of blouse, shoes and trousers before I hit the threshold. Once there, I turned and posed for him. Beneath my clothes I wore the yellow teddy Sean had tried to pass off as mine. Braless today, my nipples flirted with the peek-a-boo lace, hard as gumdrops – and twice as tempting, to go by Joe's expression.

He shook his head at me. His hand cupped his crotch as if to hold back imminent explosion. 'I'll be up very soon. In fact, if you don't hurry, I'll beat you there.'

Giggling as I hadn't in years, I scampered upstairs, so elated my feet barely touched the treads.

True to his word, Joe didn't keep me waiting long. The bathroom door slammed open minutes later. For a moment, he stood watching me through the shower's rippled glass. I could hear his heavy breathing over the spray. He must have run upstairs. When he'd gazed his fill at my blurred image, he shoved the door along its track. Pushing my wet hair from my eyes, I saw that he'd stripped, too.

I lost my breath. There was something about having him here, standing outside my shower, stark-naked and ready to rut. My eyes raked him up and down, taking in the well-shaped hairy legs, the narrow hips, the perfect development of his torso. His pecs were high and flat like a young girl's. He hadn't been kidding about having

45

blue balls, either. Tinged with teal, his testicles had drawn up so high they kissed the base of his cock. While I stared, they jerked in their sac as if with a life of their own.

'Well?' he said, unable to read my awe.

'I think I'm going to faint.' I was only half joking. Waves of heat pulsed through my body and my head swam as if I'd stood up too fast.

'Please don't,' he said, with a hint of a smile. He tossed a handful of condoms on to the sink. They weren't my brand. What a sweetie he was. Most guys would have exhausted my supply before they'd even consider buying their own. Joe's mother must have raised him right. I watched him don one with a deep, proprietary pride.

'Now I'm ready for anything,' he said, and swung his long bronzed legs into the tub.

I opened my arms and he stepped into them.

'Oh, Joe.' I hugged him tightly, too tightly maybe, but he felt so good, as if we'd been made to fit together. 'I can't believe you're really here. I spent so many nights fantasising about you.'

He swayed me from side to side, his cock a thick, hot prong between our bellies. 'Good. I shouldn't be the only one losing sleep.'

'You're not.' I sleeked his hair back from his forehead.

His eyes closed at my touch. His hands drifted to my front and squeezed my breasts. I groaned at the moulding caress.

'Sweet,' he said, circling the heavy globes. 'You've got the prettiest breasts I've ever seen. They're nice and full, but they hang just right.' He nuzzled the tiny curl in front of my ear. 'I love your hair, too. It's like caramel with the sun shining through it.'

'Anything else?' I asked, basking in the compliments.

'Oh, yeah.' Sheeting water, his hands cruised down my sides and around to the small of my back. 'Your butt is to die for.' He gave the hard, high cheeks a squeeze. 'No wonder Sean couldn't resist you. And no man alive could look at your legs without wanting them wrapped around his waist.'

'No man alive, huh?' I hid my smile against his left pectoral.

'Not if he were eighty and bedridden. And then there are these little beauties.'

Leaning forward, he dragged his chest across my puckered nipples. The contact sent a twang directly to my sex. 'Perfect. Like raspberry cream, sweet and sharp and smooth as velvet.'

Inspired by his own words, he bent to suckle me. At the first worshipful tug, the difference between my lovers was clear. Sean zeroed in on what he wanted, but Joe's appetite for touching knew no bounds. Every part of me enthralled him: the back of my knees, the inside of my arms, the hollow at the base of my throat. My navel had to be laved and pinched to full erogenous life; my thigh had to be nibbled; my fingers sucked. Joe found his pleasure in pleasing. He imposed nothing. He offered everything.

Now he knelt before me, his thumbs lightly stroking the petals of my sex. He pulled me gently apart. I tensed. I was so aroused I could scarcely stand still. He bent closer and bathed me with his warm, gusting breath. He licked me once with the flat of his tongue.

I couldn't contain a cry. His head jerked up in alarm. 'What's the matter?' he asked.

Too hungry to accept more foreplay, I held out my arms. 'I don't want to come until you're inside me and I will if you kiss me there. Please, Joe, take me now.'

'Here?' His eyes cut towards the bedroom.

I tugged his sinewy shoulders. 'Now. Please.'

His gaze heated at my plea and he shot to his feet. As he backed me against the tiles, water fountained off his shoulders, casting a halo of steam around his head. His big hands gripped my buttocks. He lifted, arms bulging, jaw set. I swung my legs around his hips and locked my ankles in the small of his back. Secure now, I reached between us, caught him beneath the head and played him between my lips. His cock juddered in my hand. He slipped against me, around me. I pressed him tight to my swollen bud.

'K-Kate. God, I can feel you. You're hard for me.'

I squeezed the neck of his cock.

He cursed, a good curse, so I did it again. His face turned as red as his erection. I heard his teeth grind with his effort to control himself. One hand released my buttock and fumbled between our bodies. Looking down, I saw him take a good hard grip on his balls and tug.

Then I capped him.

'No,' he moaned, but his hips undermined the protest by surging forward. He filled me in a single stroke. His hand flew back to my bottom, pulling me close as his cock flexed inside me.

'Oh, yes,' I sighed. I wound my arms behind his neck, my entire spine stretching with pleasure.

He cried out at the subtle writhing motion. 'Don't move. Do not move.' His legs shook with strain. He was panting.

'Am I too heavy?'

He laughed, then groaned when my vagina fluttered on his shaft. 'Honey, oh, honey, you're just right. You're like heaven inside, so warm and wet. I can't believe how good this feels. Just be still. I can't – I don't want to lose it. Just give me a minute.'

Stretching my neck to reach, I nipped his earlobe. 'Are you going to flash?'

He started at that, then chuckled. 'You and Sean must have had some talk. I'm afraid I might flash, all right. I might come with the first thrust and give away how much I like you.'

'How awful.'

He smiled into my eyes, his lashes starred with shower spray, his hair plastered against his handsome young face. His affection shone through the perfection of his features. His cheeks were pink with it, his mouth tremulous. His dark amber eyes crinkled at the corners, teary-bright.

'I don't care what happens,' I said, misting up myself. 'We'll have plenty of chances to make love.'

'That's why I want the first time to be right. Because you're so damn sweet. Now hold still.'

Pressing a quick kiss on my forehead, he shifted his grip so he could curl his thumbs down the crease of my thighs. He slid them forward until they met at the top of my labia. Gently, he caught my clitoris, hood and all, between the pads. My breath hitched at the direct stimulation. Gaining confidence, he pressed harder, then rotated the love-slicked folds against the tender shaft. 'If I rub you like this, can you come just from that?'

'Three guesses,' I said, already gulping for air. I tried not to churn my hips, but it was hard to restrain myself. The ache went all the way to my womb and the jutting rod that split my sex was exactly what I needed to cure it. 'Oh, please, Joe, can I move a little?'

'Let me do it,' he said. Muttering a prayer for fortitude, he rocked me in quick little surges. The red came back to his face as soon as he began.

'Geez,' he gasped. 'I think my balls are trying to crawl inside my body.'

He couldn't tug them back this time. His hands were busy with me. I lowered one arm to reach around his body.

'Careful.' His feet slapped the wet porcelain as he spread his legs and braced himself.

Too naughty to resist, I curled my fingers into his crack and followed it down. He jumped when I tickled his perineum. 'Kate,' he warned.

I bit his shoulder. 'Almost there.' His scrotum swung against my hand. 'How hard should I pull?'

'Hard,' he said through gritted teeth, but I was afraid of injuring him.

My experimental tug made him groan miserably and hitch me closer. I tried again.

This time, he groaned even louder. 'Are you trying to make me come faster?'

Abashed, I let go.

'Just finish yourself, honey,' he said. 'Just take what you need. I'll try to hold on.'

Taking him at his word, I ground my pubis to his root, tightening myself around him to gather in the sensations. I added an inch to his abbreviated thrusts, then two. I knew this was straining his limits, but, lord, it felt good to massage that killing itch. His thumbs circled faster, trying to keep me with him. Sounds broke in his throat, choked and harsh. I looked down at his cock on my next withdrawal. The taut skin glistened with my juices, russet red. I knew he couldn't last much longer.

'Soon.' The wave rose inside me. 'Just a little – oh, God.'

My head snapped back as it broke. Joe cried out, rocketing through my spasms with a flurry of long hard thrusts. He marked the end of each stroke with my name. Each repetition shot another spear of pleasure through my loins – Kate, Kate, Kate – withdrawing to the brink and hammering back like he meant to drive his cock to my heart.

Then he came. His penis convulsed inside me as though milked by an invisible hand, strong, dramatic contractions – five, six, seven – each shaking his body from scalp to toe. Finally, after the tenth hard spasm, he sighed, a sigh of the most intense relief I'd ever heard.

'Kate,' he murmured again, sagging against me until the tiles supported both our weight. He held me like that for a minute, then let me down and unclamped his fingers from my cheeks. He'd gripped me so tightly my nerves tingled from lack of circulation. 'Wow.' He shook the stiffness from his hands. 'That was good.'

'Good enough to count as a flash?'

He wagged his finger at me. 'I'm all flashed out, Miss Kate. So you can worry about your own darn self.'

But how could I worry about betraying my passions

when he treated me, and them, with such tender loving care?

He carried me to my bed wrapped in a big yellow towel.

'You'll spoil me,' I purred as he rubbed me dry.

He feathered the glossy triangle between my legs. 'Believe me, it's a luxury. Sean never lets –'

He stopped speaking, either because he didn't want to bring Sean's name into 'our' time, or because he didn't want to betray a confidence. Rather than pry, I rolled to my side and stroked his thigh as far as the edge of the towel he'd tucked around his hips. He shifted his knees apart. Accepting the wordless invitation, I slid my palm up the near-hairless skin of his inner thigh. My knuckles joggled his weighty shaft, causing his breath to hiss through his teeth. He unwrapped the towel.

'Suck me until I'm hard again,' he said. 'That is, if you wouldn't mind.'

I smiled. 'Of course I wouldn't mind. I love going down on you.'

To prove it, I bowed over his lap, lifted the head on the cupped flat of my tongue and tipped it into my mouth. Heavy as he was, I had to trap him in my lips to hold him steady. Then I licked him, large circles and small, pausing now and then to flick the tiny blind eye or the sensitive array of folds on the underside of the head.

My efforts were not in vain. In less than a minute he'd reached full tumescence. He put one hand on his shaft and urged himself an inch farther into my mouth.

'A little more,' he said. 'Please.'

What red-blooded male only wanted a little more head? But he'd learn to ask for everything he wanted, once he discovered how happy I was to give it. I swallowed more of him, tonguing first beneath the flange, then to the edge of his gripping fist. Bit by bit, I coaxed his hand away until I was bobbing slowly up and down his length. My throat relaxed as I found my groove. My hands kneaded his thighs like a pampered cat. I thought – as I had many times – that I'd been born to do this, born to feel this smooth, tropical flesh slipping between cheek and tongue and palate.

Joe breathed deep and slow, obviously enjoying this, obviously trying to stay loose. 'Oh, man, look at you.' He slid his hands down my back and kneaded the muscles of my bottom, pulling my cheeks apart with each circling squeeze. 'Oh, man, you are so gorgeous. I love watching you suck me, the way your whole body moves with it, the way your mouth hollows when you pull, the way you make me wet from tonguing me so well. It is so fucking sexy.'

His praise made me want to please him all the more. I sank forward till my nose brushed his crisp, black thatch.

'Oh, honey. Oh, yeah. Turn for me, sweetheart. That's right. I want to do it for you, too.'

Careful not to lose his mooring, he rearranged us on the bed until we both lay on our sides. He kissed my cunt so tenderly it made my neck go limp. He kissed me the way most men only kiss women's mouths, as though the flesh there were beautiful and delicious – infinitely desirable, endlessly lovable.

I hummed my enjoyment into his erection, running my hand in long, grateful strokes down his legs. He hummed back and burrowed deeper. His chin settled over my clit, rocking it hard. The remnant of his beard, faint from his recent shave, burned pleasantly over the hood. I might be sore later but now the friction was just what I needed. He probed my sheath as deeply as he could with his tongue, spearing in and out like a small, flexible penis.

It felt so good, I wanted to thank him somehow.

I thought of Sean. With a shudder of anticipation, I dipped two fingers into my juicy well. Joe started in surprise, but quickly resumed what he'd been doing – until I pushed the lubricated digits between his buttocks. He grunted as they slid past the ring of muscle guarding his gate, stiffened when they reached the first knuckle, and moaned when the webbing struck home. The smoothness of his passage surprised me, and the tightness. No wonder men liked this. I wiggled experimentally.

His cock leapt in my mouth and his anus clenched my fingers. His reaction excited me so much a gush of cream welled from my sex.

'Mm.' I pulled up my favourite lollipop until it slipped free with a smack. 'Say, Joe, where would I find your prostate?'

His laugh sounded more like a cough but he did answer. 'Towards the front, right about where your fingertips are. But, Kate, wait a second before you go exploring. You might get more than you bargained for.'

To my surprise, he reached down and repositioned his cock between the meeting of my breasts.

'Hey,' I protested.

'Forget it, Kate. Try concentrating on one thing at a time.'

He had a point there.

'Will I feel anything?' I asked, probing the soft, silky walls.

'You might.' He squirmed under my manipulations. 'You might feel a firm swelling, about the size of a walnut.'

'Oh! There it is. I feel it.'

Joe felt it, too. He moaned loudly, his body undulating against the sheet, his cock stiffening between my breasts. 'Rub it, Kate. Yes, right there. A little harder. Long strokes. That's it. Just like that.'

Massaging the hidden gland was like doubling the voltage through a wire. Within seconds, he was panting and shaking. His movements ragged, he took me in his mouth again. With one taut hand, he cupped the side of my breast, pressing it against his rigid shaft to make a cosy tunnel. He must have wanted to thrust but he kept himself on a brutally short rein, making do with tight jerks of his hips. Everything followed the rhythm with which I rubbed his hot spot – his abbreviated thrusts, his sucking, his repeated gasps for air.

With that kind of inspiration, I came long before he did, in a shower of sparks that burst from the heart of my sex and spread out in delicious rippling tingles, making my back bow and my toes curl.

'Again,' he pleaded, bucking harder between my breasts. 'Come again, Kate.' But I was determined not to miss his fireworks.

They were worth waiting for, too. A warning flush darkened his body a second before he came and his anus clamped my fingers like a vice. It took all my strength to continue the massage, but it was worth it to hear his rapturous groan, to feel his seed shooting hot and strong along my belly. He settled slowly, still twitching as I petted him down.

'Man, you wrung me out,' he said in a tone of amazement.

I wriggled around until we lay face-to-face. His eyes were closed but he pulled me into a sweaty embrace.

'I need a nap,' he mumbled. 'Wake me in an hour.'

An hour? I thought. Try eight.

In actuality, it was more like thirty minutes – and he woke me. The next time was slow and sweet. Sensing my exhaustion, he rocked me like a baby in a cradle, keeping me on the brink for ages. When I was ready to weep with longing, he pushed us both over the edge in a deep, muscle-wrenching climax. I stayed awake long enough to sample the brandy-soaked pears he'd finally remembered making, after which I sank into a billow of pleasant dreams.

At 3 a.m., a metallic rattle disrupted my slumber. Heart pounding, I bolted up in bed. Someone was trying to force the lock on the front door.

I flashed back to the months following my divorce when I was a woman alone in a big city living in a creaky old house that, for all I knew, was haunted by the ghost of my dear-departed lesbian aunt. Mind you, Aunt Sally loved me enough to bequeath me the house, but she was also the sort to drop in uninvited, just to say 'hi'. Frankly, I didn't welcome a visit from the Other Side any more than I welcomed a visit from a burglar.

A snore from Joe returned me to the present. Thank God. 'Joe, wake up.' I shook his shoulder. 'Wake up!'

'Wha–?' He lifted his head and rubbed his eyes.

'I think someone's trying to break into the house.'

His head flopped back down. 'Prob'ly Sean.'

'Sean has a key.'

'Prob'ly drunk,' he said, and closed his eyes again. 'Knew he wouldn't stay away all night.'

To a panicked woman, who was only half-awake, this conclusion represented too big a leap to reassure. I grabbed the fireplace poker I kept for just such an emergency.

Joe struggled up on his elbow. 'Don't bash him. He's the best friend I've got.'

I should have bought a dog, I thought, clumping down two flights of stairs with the poker held before me like a sword. A big, scary dog with sharp teeth and a loud bark. Something crashed in the vicinity of the kitchen. I froze. Then I heard a curse that was, indeed, familiar.

It was Sean.

I flicked on the light and found him trying to pick the pieces of a broken glass off the linoleum. He blinked owlishly in the sudden glare. I noticed that my yellow trousers, and Joe's jeans, lay in a tangle by the refrigerator. Sean must have tripped over them.

'Kate,' he said, his eyes bloodshot, his sensual mouth slack. 'You're up.'

This is what I got for starting an affair with a twenty-three-year-old. No, with two twenty-three-year-olds. Sean swayed on his haunches.

'Couldn't stay,' he said. 'Too many illegal substances. I don't party like that any more.'

This declaration would have gone down better if he weren't totally sloshed.

'Come away from that glass.' I pulled him up by the arm. One of his palms was bleeding, a long thin cut, like boys used to swear by in the old days. He stumbled against me as I guided him to the sink. I opened the tap and held his hand under it.

'Ow,' he said, but I didn't see any glass. 'Can't drink like I used to. Only had three beers – okay, maybe four. And look at me. I'm a mess.'

'That you are.'

'Hate a sloppy drunk.' Unable to keep his footing, his elbow thunked on to the counter. 'He won't love me any more.'

Trying not to laugh at his theatricals, I wrapped a paper towel around his palm and applied pressure. 'I'm sure Joe has seen you drunk before.'

'No, not because of that. Because I stole your cherry – your arse cherry,' he enunciated, in case it wasn't clear. 'I knew he wanted it, but I stole it anyway. In fact, I stole it because he wanted it.' His face settled into mournful lines like the tragedy mask at a drama club. 'Kate, sometimes I'm so bad I don't know what to do with myself.'

When I smiled at him, tears stung my eyes. I remembered being his age, and remembered a few of the lousy, selfish things I'd done since then. 'Everyone is bad sometimes, Sean. That doesn't make it right, but it doesn't make you a monster either.'

Nodding, he sniffed hard and wiped his eyes on his sleeve. His muscles bulged with the motion. Some tough guy – and that black T-shirt had seen better days.

'Whew.' I waved my hand in front of my nose. 'You smell like a brewery.'

'Some stupid first-year shook up a beer can and sprayed me with it.' He pushed carefully off the counter and tested his balance. 'Better take a shower.'

'Better let me help you,' I said, easing his arm around my shoulders.

In fits and starts, we shuffled up the stairs to the second floor, to the bathroom he and Joe shared. The air smelled of shaving cream and cologne – Joe's Aramis, Sean's trendy Calvin Klein. I propped him on the toilet and turned on the spray. Once it was going, I knelt down to remove his shoes.

'You gonna wash my back, too?'

I didn't answer, but that didn't seem to matter to him. The three, or maybe four, beers had loosened his tongue. 'Nobody ever washed my back, not even my mom.'

That tugged my heartstrings, too. What a softie I was. 'You could have asked Joe.'

He shook his head, that hound-dog look on his face again. 'Joe gave me so much. I couldn't ask him to baby me, too.'

I peeled off his socks. 'Sure you could. But you would have had to give up your nice, dominant position.'

His glare told me I'd hit a bull's-eye. His mouth opened on a stutter. Then he closed it and started again. 'You've got a sharp tongue, Mrs Robbyns.'

'Ms Winthrop,' I corrected, levelling him with the gimlet eye I used to save for Tom. Unlike my ex, Sean met it like a man.

'You think I wouldn't let Joe baby me 'cause I wanted to stay in charge?'

'You tell me.'

He rubbed his face with both hands. When he let go, the mournful lines were gone. A sly smile had taken their place, one I found altogether too charming. 'I'm letting you baby me.'

I braced my hands on my knees and stood. 'That doesn't count. You're not in love with me.'

His grin faded. He couldn't deny my words, or that he was in love with Joe. With a weary sigh, he stripped off his stinky T-shirt and tossed it into the hall.

'Thanks, Kate,' he said. He appeared almost sober. 'I think I can take it from here.'

Joe was sitting on the stairs when I emerged, his head in his hands, his back bowed over his knees. He'd pulled on a pair of briefs and nothing else. I sat next to him on the faded cabbage-rose carpet runner. He gathered my hand on to his knee. My guess was Sean had never said he loved him.

'You heard?' I said.

'Yeah.'

'You know, we can stop this any time you want – before anyone gets hurt.'

'Do you want to stop?' His eyes were brilliant in the low light from the hall.

I shook my head.

'I don't think Sean wants to stop, either, Kate.'

'But –'

He silenced my protest with a petal-soft kiss. 'You have to be brave to have an adventure.'

I snorted. 'Yeah, and you can't make an omelette without breaking eggs, but I don't want you or Sean to end up cracked.'

He bussed the tip of my nose. 'I'm not a coward and neither is Sean – or you.'

I leant my head on his shoulder and thought that over. Cowards don't divorce their philandering husbands, or start their own businesses, or form *ménages à trois*. Maybe I could handle this. Maybe.

'We'll wait until he comes out,' I said. 'He can spend the night with us.'

Joe squeezed my shoulder in approval. 'That's a girl. We'll make an adventuress out of you yet.'

Chapter Four

Intimate Notions

The next day was Saturday. Mostly Romance didn't open till noon. A quickie to start the day would have suited me, but Sean was too grumpy and Joe was too hungry. The rumbling in his stomach distracted me from my goal.

As a result, we all rolled out of bed together.

'Bagels, coffee, fruit,' Sean said in his curt morning rasp. 'Be at the table in half an hour.'

Fortunately, this meant he was preparing the meal. I'd just finished setting the kitchen table when the telephone rang. More at home now that he'd tupped the lady of the house, Joe grabbed the cordless receiver. He frowned at the voice on the other end.

'It's Larry,' he said, and thrust the phone in my direction.

For a moment, I drew a blank. Then I remembered. L. Kingston Something-or-other.

'Oh, damn. Marianne must have given him my number.'

'Indeed, she did,' said L. Kingston as I lifted the phone to my ear. 'She also gave me to understand you were available.'

I noticed Larry had my ex's knack for turning any statement into an accusation. Switching hands, I tried to unhunch my shoulders. Both Sean and Joe had crossed their arms across their chests. I didn't know who made me angrier, this obnoxious estate agent or the two Stone Age men who'd suddenly appeared in my kitchen.

'As it happens, Mr, um –'

'Larry.'

'Larry. As it happens, Marianne mistook the situation. I'm not currently available. Marianne, on the other hand, is – and finds you quite attractive, I might add.'

'I'm not interested in Marianne.' He rolled her name off his tongue as if it were something nasty. 'Look, you're not married, are you?'

How dare he? He should be so lucky to find an uninhibited woman like Marianne. 'Look, Larry,' I said, giving his name the same disparaging intonation. 'My marital status has nothing to do with it.'

I guess he realised he wouldn't endear himself to me by insulting my friend, because at once he was full of apologies.

Thirty seconds into his backpedalling, Sean grabbed the phone. 'Hey, dick-head, the lady's not interested.' And he slammed it down with a flourish.

I stared at him, astonished by his gall.

Amusement tugged the corners of his mouth. 'Breakfast was getting cold. Come on. Sit, you two.'

Against my better judgment, I sat. I accepted the toasted bagel half Sean handed me, but I wasn't forgetting what he'd done. 'You had no right to do that, Sean.'

Completely unperturbed, he poured a glass of juice and pushed it to my elbow. 'Why not? You wanted to get rid of him, didn't you?'

'But you were rude.'

'So were you.' He passed the honey-walnut cream cheese. 'I just got rid of him cleaner.'

I couldn't deny that, though I wanted to. Feeling vaguely in the wrong, I knifed a smear of cream cheese across my bagel. 'Well, next time, let me handle it.'

'So long as you do.'

'You do not dictate who I see, Sean Halloran.'

Joe inhaled sharply at that statement, but Sean didn't bat an eyelid. 'Baloney. We all know this cosy arrangement goes to hell the minute one of us decides to two-time the others.'

'I agree,' Joe piped in. He reddened when I cocked one brow at him but he didn't back down. In fact, he seemed disappointed in me. 'You have to agree it's safer this way.'

Chastened, I dropped my gaze to my plate. 'I didn't actually intend to sleep around.'

'Then it's settled.' Sean flaunted his victory with a flash of teeth. 'All for one and one for all.'

I said nothing. A knot of stubbornness tightened in my chest, the same perverse love of resistance for resistance sake that had made me struggle against him in the back room. I wanted, no, *hungered* to humble him. He knew it, too. His grin widened. 'You and whose army?' he mouthed, throwing my words back at me.

'What?' Joe asked, sensing the hidden currents.

I suspected Sean preferred them hidden, so I answered. 'I'm going to take him on, Joe. I'm going to see him on his knees to me.'

'Who?'

'Me,' Sean answered, still grinning.

Joe laughed – until the steely set of my face stopped him. 'No, really, Kate.'

'Yes, really.'

'But why?'

'Because he needs it,' I said, and exulted in the flinch Sean couldn't quite hide.

'In your dreams,' he said. He ate in silence after that, chewing angrily and casting the occasional dark look from under his golden lashes – sometimes at me, sometimes at Joe – no doubt trying to predict how sides would form up for the coming battle. That battle was inevitable. I'd upped the stakes with my challenge and, worse, my claim that he secretly wanted to submit. He'd have to devise a truly devious response. The prospect quivered like mercury through the folds of my sex, icy-hot and dangerous. Getting the best of him wouldn't be easy.

I smiled to myself even as Joe tried to cover the tension with idle chatter. He needn't have bothered. I knew I'd revel in Sean's revenge as much as I'd revel in my own eventual victory.

The woman appeared near closing time. I was working in the coffee bar on the balcony so I had a perfect view of her show-stopping entrance. Everywhere I looked, patrons – male and female – gaped at this living goddess.

She had to be six feet tall. A mouth-watering ivory suit draped her hour-glass figure. Its thin velvet lapels swooped over the ski slope of her breast, and its mid-thigh-length skirt bared a pair of lean, seemingly endless pins. Her hair swung towards her chin in a 1920s bob, mahogany-brown and patent-leather shiny. Behind its teasing sway, I caught a glimpse of full red lips and huge, long-lashed eyes.

She glided to a halt beside the Hot New Authors table and paused to survey her temporary kingdom. Intuition told me Sean had sent her, so I was not surprised when her gaze climbed the second storey and locked on mine. My heart rolled over with a funny hiccup. I didn't usually react to women this way, but she was so beautiful it was like meeting a famous fashion model outside the dry-cleaner's. The shock sent my normal barriers crumbling.

Along with everyone else, I watched her spectacular legs mount the spiral stairs.

'Hello, there,' she said when she finally reached me. She leant across the coffee bar. Her silk blouse released a whiff of Chanel No. 19 – my scent. Somehow, I didn't think the choice coincidental.

'I'd like a tall mochaccino, double whip,' she said, her eyes never leaving mine. She had a slight Southern accent. Her voice was rich and sweet, not unlike the coffee she'd ordered.

'Not worried about insomnia?' I teased, my hands admirably steady on the machine.

The woman shrugged with an insouciance that requires either years of practice or being born French. 'Whether I sleep or not, I'm always entertained. Aren't you?'

'Things have been looking up lately.'

Her painted lips curled at my admission. She tapped her perfect red nails against the black marble counter, then nodded at me. 'Those are lovely, dear. By far the prettiest I've seen.'

Out of reflex, I looked down at myself. I wore a grey cashmere V-neck and jeans, and no jewellery. I couldn't imagine what she might be complimenting, but she soon enlightened me. 'Your breasts, darlin'. They're nice and full, but they hang perfectly.'

Her words unnerved me. Besides the fact that they were uttered by a woman, they seemed so familiar.

Now she tilted her head to one side. Her shiny hair brushed her shoulder. 'Now don't get agitated, dear. I'm not here to pick you up – though, believe me, nothin' would please me more. No, I'm just here to deliver an invitation from a friend.'

'A friend named Sean?' I slid her foam-topped coffee across the marble.

Her laugh tinkled like the proverbial silvery bells. The bearded gentleman at the corner table closed his eyes. 'Precisely,' she said and, with a coyness worthy of a Hollywood screen legend, withdrew a note from her cleavage.

She pressed the folded slip of paper, now warm and fragrant, into my palm. That's when I noticed the back of her hands were shaved. My eyes flew to hers and she laughed again, a throaty chuckle this time. 'That's right, darlin'. She's a he.'

Her mission complete, she/he tossed what I now recognised to be a very expensive wig. He wiggled his elegant manicure as he backed away. 'Don't you be late – and have some fun for me, you hear?'

Boy, I thought, when Sean planned a scene, he really pulled out all the stops. Curious, I unfolded the invitation. I found a Pine Street address, a fifteen-minute walk from my shop.

'Nine o' clock sharp,' ordered his imperious scrawl. 'Be there or be square. P.S. Tonight's safe-word is "Uncle".'

Apparently, whatever the little devil had planned required safe-words. Trust Sean to choose the one I'd choke before saying. When I was a kid, crying 'Uncle' during a game was the ultimate expression of surrender. But we'd see who'd surrender tonight. I slipped the note into my back pocket and took a fortifying sip of the mocha cappuccino his gender-bending friend had failed to collect.

Insomnia, be damned. I had a feeling I'd need all the fortification I could get.

The address occupied the basement level of an attractive brownstone house. *Intimate Notions* said its discreet, hand-lettered sign.

The windows were dark and a CLOSED sign hung in the door. Nonetheless, I was sure of my welcome. I descended the four concrete steps and peered through the glass. A small blue light burnt in the back, revealing nothing but shadows. I felt both foolish and excited, which was probably what Sean intended.

Determined not to quail before I'd crossed the starting line, I jammed my thumb over the buzzer. Before the grating echo faded, an invisible someone opened the door.

'Come in,' said the shadow, a diminutive female shadow. She closed the door behind me and pulled a filmy curtain over the glass. 'One moment,' she said. I heard high-heeled footsteps moving quickly across a carpet, and then a teardrop chandelier filled the room with a soft, sparkling glow.

Red struck my eyes: lush, venereal red. It lacquered the walls of the octagonal salon. It upholstered the plump, satiny chairs. It swirled across the savage Chinese carpet, and swayed among the rails of multi-coloured silk confections that obviously formed the shop's mainstay. Camisoles and teddies hung from ribbon-padded hangers, along with morning gowns and corsets and brassieres of every imaginable style.

At the centre of the room a headless mannequin stood. She wore a matching bra and panty set with the nipples and crotch cut out. I choked back a laugh. I'd always found that sort of get-up ridiculous, a dirty old man joke; not something a woman would choose for herself.

Or so I thought.

'Dear me,' clucked the woman who'd admitted me. 'I can see I've got my work cut out for me.'

For the first time I turned to her. My jaw dropped. She was a little doll, a spun-sugar, sweet-as-cherry doll, round where a woman ought to be round, and slim where she ought to be slim. Her bright blonde hair framed her innocent face in thick, marcelled waves. Her rosebud mouth barely looked large enough to hold a spoon. Celestial blue eyes widened at my lengthening stare, but I couldn't restrain myself.

Again, I sensed deliberation in Sean's choice of accomplice. What evil genius had led him to pick the two women in all of Philadelphia who would tickle my erotic fancy? Or was I kidding myself about the set-in-stone nature of my preference? Was that the humbling message Sean meant to convey?

To my relief, the delectable cream-puff wore ordinary business clothes – a black angora turtleneck over tapered beige trousers.

'Come,' she said. 'I need to fit you.'

At once, I pictured her fitting me, her soft white thigh pressed between my own, her pink cheeks hollowed to suckle my nipples to aching points.

Shuddering off the image, I followed her through the opulent, overheated salon. Gold accents glittered about the room. They danced on a floor-length mirror framed in rococo gilt, on the chain from which the chandelier hung, on the –

My hand flew to my throat as I noticed a gold-plated phallus twirling from a wire above the entrance to the changing room. Feathery wings, also gold, extended from the gleaming prick's sides – the shop's guardian angel, I supposed. My body responded to the flying dildo with a rash-like prickle of heat.

Sean's accomplice turned her kittenish chin towards her shoulder and winked at me. 'My name is Amy,' she said. She blew the phallus a kiss as she passed beneath it.

Resisting an urge to do the same, I entered the changing room. The curving space was divided into separate cubicles, all doorless and all mirrored. Here, blue struck the dominant note, colouring the carpet, the walls and the scroll-backed café chairs. The ceiling was lacquered a rich indigo and stars were spangled over it. To my right loomed a Chinese-style ebony and brass cabinet. Amy turned to it and opened its folding doors, exposing a multitude of tiny compartments.

'You can strip off now,' she said, occupied with the contents of a drawer.

Well, really, I thought. But I did as she asked.

'The centre cubicle,' she specified, when I would have chosen another.

I could think of only one reason to choose this cubicle over the others. I studied the mirror. Though the lighting was artful, a hint of smoky indistinctness revealed its two-way nature. Tiny hairs stood in an icy wave along my arms. Aside from that, however, I don't think I betrayed my knowledge that others would watch me disrobe.

I undressed without any special grace, the same as if I were alone. I didn't bother to ask if I should remove my underwear because I knew I should. Once naked, I gazed at my reflection, outwardly dispassionate, inwardly seething – and not with anger. I saw my body as a stranger might: the mixture of lean and soft; the pleasing

66

arrangement of my bones; the arrow of hair that pointed to my secrets, a darker auburn than my head but just as curly. I saw that I was beautiful and that others would desire me for no better reason than that. The knowledge did not displease me. I would take them, or not, as the spirit moved me. I was the master of my flesh.

But not tonight. Tonight I delegated responsibility for my pleasure to more imaginative hands, the hands of the man who had to be behind the mirror: Sean Patrick Halloran. I felt no fear, merely anticipation and a certain curiosity – not only for what was to come, but for how it would make me respond.

Amy handed me a corset-like contraption of burgundy silk and lace. 'Let's see how this fits,' she said. She stood behind me and slightly to the side. Her eyes were quiet on my naked body but something inside her fizzed. Her nipples distended her fuzzy sweater, and when she steadied my elbow so I could step through the leg holes, her palm was damp.

Taking me by the shoulders, she turned me to face the outer salon and began to tighten the laces. I closed my eyes at the unfamiliar sensation. As she pulled, the bodice gripped my torso like an elastic bandage. I could not begin to explain why this impersonal embrace aroused me, but it did. Maybe the lack of breathing room was making me light-headed.

'Suck in,' she ordered, and gave the ties a final heave. 'Now be still. Do not move.'

She circled around to my front and resettled my breasts to sit more comfortably in the lacy cups. Her hands were hot but not wet. I knew she must have dried them on her trousers. Once again, she turned me to face the mirror as if I were a child. 'Open your eyes.'

As soon as I did, I burst out laughing. This contraption looked even sillier on me than it had on the mannequin. My nipples, and a good bit of my breasts, bulged out from the cut-out cups like old-fashioned bomber noses. The laces cinched my waist to cartoon-like waspishness, and my pubic hair showed through the crotch like a squirrel peeping through a stage curtain.

'No, no, no,' Amy scolded, her pretty face flushed. 'It is not funny. You look beautiful.'

Exotic dress-up was obviously her kink, and I had as good as mocked it. Ashamed, I wiped tears of laughter from my eyes and apologised. I could not, however, contain a few last snorts.

'I should beat you,' she said, giving my arm a little slap. That quieted me, because I wondered whether she would – and if I would like it. 'Besides,' she added. 'I'm not finished.'

I hoped whatever remained wouldn't be so humorous.

All too soon I remembered the old saying: be careful what you wish for. Amy removed a small pot of body paint and a finger-wide brush from one of the cabinet's mysterious drawers. Sticking the end of the brush between her teeth, she squinted at my reflection.

'Tits first, I think.'

My nipples sprang to attention. Amy smirked as though to say: now, that's better. She opened her paint pot. Its contents matched the burgundy silk I wore. Her fingers were slim and dexterous as she dipped the brush in, then scraped the excess against the rim.

I braced for the first touch of the sable wedge. When it came, I had to bite my lip to keep from crying out. The tight fit of the corset cups had trapped the blood within the peaks of my breasts, sensitising the nerves. The merest brush stimulated as strongly as a pinch. Amy bent closer. Her hot, shallow breath dampened my skin. Bit by bit, she dabbed me with the cold, wet paint. As it dried, the cosmetic warmed and tightened, making me feel she touched me even when she didn't.

She saved my nipples for last and those she brushed back and forth until uncontrollable whimpers broke in my throat. I wondered if Sean could hear as well as see through the mirror. Was he touching himself? Was Joe with him? Would they reach out and fondle each other's hard, straining pricks, the way they must have done a thousand times before?

I wished I could see them and yet the fact that I couldn't, and could only imagine, had its own erotic power.

'There,' said Amy. She stepped aside so I could admire her work. 'Two perfect raspberries.'

A wisp of déjà vu tickled my subconscious, just as it had when Sean's transvestite friend complimented my breasts. But Amy was waiting for a response.

'I see what you're aiming for,' I said, my voice so thick I had to clear my throat. 'Unless you looked carefully you'd think I was fully covered.'

She beamed at me. 'Exactly. Now, turn around and bend over. Yes, grab that chair and lean your hands on it. I need to do your back.'

My 'back' required considerably more coverage, since nothing but a snug-fitting thong covered my muscular bottom. I melted under the endless strokes. Having my hair washed at the salon made me horny, no matter if some fat hairy guy was doing it. This was a hundred times worse – or better, I suppose.

'Mm,' I sighed, and wriggled my bottom in Amy's direction. Sean must be getting an eyeful. In this position, all that concealed my sex was a thin strip of silk: a thin, sodden strip of silk.

'Oh, Kate,' said Amy, surprising me by using my name. 'Your butt is to die for.'

A muffled protest penetrated the barrier of the mirror, followed by a hollow slap, as if a hand had been clapped over someone's mouth. I added it up then. The source of the compliments I'd been receiving today was Joe. Sean must have tricked him into talking about me. I could easily imagine the conversation. 'Kate's got nice tits,' Sean would say, oh-so-casually. 'Oh, yeah,' Joe would agree, happy to discuss his current object of obsession. 'They're nice and full, but they hang just right and the nipples, mm, they're like sweet, creamy raspberries.' On it would go until Sean had an entire battery of compliments, one of which Joe was bound to have used in what should have been a private moment.

How upset Joe must be, thinking I'd think he'd betrayed an intimate secret!

And what a nasty girl I was, because the thought of his entirely unnecessary anguish made my sex grow moist and warm.

Amy distracted me from the delicious throb of guilt by sliding the thong to the side and beginning to paint my cleft. I flinched at the cold touch on this more sensitive skin. 'Shh,' she murmured. She ran the brush from stem to stern in long, hypnotising strokes. 'Just relax.'

Without warning, she reversed the brush and inserted the first slim inch past my sphincter. Shocked, I went up on my toes, then sank back to take it. She turned the inch of polished wood in a knee-melting circle, soothing an itch I hadn't known I'd had.

'Oh,' I said, feeling my bowels flutter wildly.

'That's a beautiful little rosebud,' she said, and I wondered if these, too, were Joe's words. 'It's so tight and puckered. It looks as if it wants a kiss.' She sighed. 'Too bad I've painted it so nicely. I wouldn't want to ruin it.'

Go ahead, ruin it, I almost said, but I wasn't ready to go that far. Removing the paint brush, she leant closer to blow me dry. The warm puffs stirred my pubic hair, heated my lips, and made my stiff little button feel as if it had been set on the grill.

'Bend over a bit more,' she said. She stepped away from me and pulled open another drawer in the magic cabinet. 'Now don't look up, Kate. We mustn't spoil the surprise.'

I heard a cap twist open; heard liquid glugging and then a cap – no, two caps – being replaced. She moved behind me again. I felt something new probe the pucker of my anus, something thick and firm that dripped oil down my quivering furrow. Whatever the something was – a dildo, I suspected – it flexed as she pushed, then slid inside in one lubricious rush.

My passage embraced the intrusion, squirming with rapture. I marvelled at how quickly one could develop a taste for these things. Sean, of course, would not neglect such a detail. Every part of me must be tightened round the screw of desire, but especially the part whose virginity he had claimed.

'There.' Amy patted the plugging end. 'Now you're dressed for success.'

I laughed, but this time she didn't take offence, just stood me up and turned me around to face the mirror. I seemed a different woman, my eyes starred with lust, my cheeks flushed and my limbs liquid and loose, despite my constraining garments.

Amy grinned at me, reading the change as clearly as I did. She pulled two dressmaker's pins from her pocket, which she used to secure the crotch flaps out of her way. With an efficiency she hadn't shown before, she camouflaged my curls with the burgundy paint.

'Tut, tut,' she clucked as the brush approached my swollen labia. 'This area is much too wet to paint. Guess I'll have to clean it up.'

Before I could move, she wriggled her tongue up and down my folds, exploring the wet, quivering flesh as if she'd been waiting all evening to do it. A hopeless squeak caught in my throat. As my hips pressed helplessly closer, the dildo rocked inside me. I realised then that it was filled with oil, oil that sloshed back and forth with the effect of a miniature water bed. The combination felt incredible – the hardness in my bottom, the softness lapping my sex. I couldn't imagine Amy's activity was drying me, but I was wound up so tightly I welcomed any prospect of relief.

'There,' I moaned, as she teased the slippery hood with the very tip of her tongue. 'Oh, please, a little harder.'

For one heavenly moment, she obeyed. Then, with a

small sigh of regret, she pulled back. 'Sorry, Kate, but orders are orders.'

If the mirror hadn't stood between me and Sean, I think I would have strangled him. 'Sure,' I said, my body shaking with frustration. 'I understand.'

'There's just one more thing you need.'

'An orgasm?' I suggested.

She pouted and shook her finger at me. The 'one more thing' turned out to be a blindfold.

'Oh, no,' I said. 'I don't like having my eyes covered.'

'Too bad.' She dangled the red velvet eye cover from her forefinger. 'Anyway, you know the safe-word. If you're ready to give in, just say it.'

I glared at her pink-cheeked innocence. 'Well?' she prodded.

'Fine,' I said, without one iota of good sportsmanship. 'Do it and get it over with.'

'Now remember –' she stood up on tiptoe to tie it on '– taking this off without permission is as good as saying "Uncle".'

To my dismay, the blindfold was very thick and very snug. As soon as she secured it, the world went black. I gritted my teeth against a wave of discomfort. When I was eight, my big brother socked me in the eye with a baseball, and not – as he swore to our parents – accidentally. For weeks I wore a big cotton eye-patch and ever since I'd loathed any impairment of my sight. To me, being blindfolded was a reminder of vulnerability, not to mention injustice.

But cry 'Uncle' over a bad childhood memory? Not Kate Winthrop.

I tried not to stumble as Amy guided me to the outer room. I felt much more naked with my eyes covered. The air seemed colder, the room larger. A draught chilled the painted skin of my mound so I knew we approached the street door. I stopped in my tracks, panicked at the thought of going outside.

'Be brave,' said Amy. 'This part is difficult. There's a cab waiting directly opposite. I want you to open the door, walk up the four steps and straight ahead. When you bump into the cab, open the door and get inside.'

I'd been shaking my head as she spoke but now I dug in my heels. 'No, I can't.'

Amy stroked my arm, her hand warm and comforting. 'Remember, you can stop any time you want, Kate. In fact, if you're really scared, you should stop. I don't think you're a coward, though, do you?'

'I'll be arrested,' I said through the nervous chattering of my teeth.

'Nonsense. It's pitch-dark out, the cab driver was specially hired, and if anyone should see you, they'll think you're a pro on her way to work. No one will know how bare you really are.'

I must be crazy, I thought, but I took a deep, steadying breath and reached for the door. I hit the knob on the second try. I turned it and pulled. The cold air hit me like the slap of wet cotton.

I trust Sean, I told myself. But if that cab wasn't there, he'd think Lucrezia Borgia was a saint compared to me. I hobbled forward, stubbed my bare toe on the first step and lifted my foot. The handrail bumped my side and I used it to ascend the last three steps. A car rolled by on Pine Street. It honked. A hysterical giggle rose in my throat. I must have looked a sight in my blindfold and tart's get-up. Please, God, let no cops drive by, I thought.

Hands waving through the air in front of me, I took one shuffle forward on the pavement, then two, then three. At six I bonked my knees on the side of the cab and spent fifteen endless seconds searching for a door handle. Finally, I found it, yanked the door open and threw myself inside. My body shook so hard it looked as though I had nerve damage. The oil-filled dildo felt like a vibrator.

Well, okay, that part was nice.

'Hello,' said the cabbie, as though he did this every day. He had a young voice. Nigerian, I thought – another of Sean's cronies, no doubt. 'You will please wait for our other passengers.'

I hoped there would be other passengers. I'd just remembered my handbag was sitting back in that midnight-blue changing room.

Minutes passed. The cabbie slid a cassette into his tape deck. Guitars twanged and wailed and Robert Cray began a gravelly croon. That cheered me. I was nodding my head to 'Nothin' But A Woman' when the doors opened on either side of me. Two people entered – Sean and Joe by the smell of them. Then the front door opened and someone else got in.

What the –? Was Amy invited to the second act as well?

Damn Sean anyway. I knew guys fantasised about women together, but were we supposed to perform in front of them? What if I couldn't? Imagine how rotten that would make Amy feel. For the first time that evening, anger rose. I'd get him for this. I didn't know how, but I would.

Without a word from anyone, the cab swung into motion. Sean took my hand and pressed it to the inside of his thigh. Fine, I thought, let's see if you're ready to rock and roll. For good measure, I squeezed Joe's thigh, too, and slid my hands up to cup their groins. Joe was bulging, but Sean was a rock. Sweat dampened the cloth that strained across his prick. His breath whistled when I scratched my thumbnail down the arch. A seam creaked in the breathy silence, lending new meaning to the phrase 'too cocky by half'.

Good, I thought. The bigger he is, the harder he'll fall.

Chapter Five
The Joys of Submission

My hand fumbled over a wrought-iron railing, over chilly rosettes and swirls. The design was familiar. The cabbie must have driven us home.

By this time, Joe's jacket draped my shoulders. If Sean had let him, I think he'd have carried me over the threshold, as well, but at least I wasn't in danger of shocking the neighbours. In my part of town, women rarely ventured outside in red silk corsets – with or without nipple coverage.

'Who's got a key?' I asked, my tension abating at the prospect of reentering my safe, cosy nest.

No one answered. To my amazement, the door creaked open. So much for safety.

'Well, hello,' drawled a creamy Southern voice. It belonged to the she-male from the bookshop. 'I'm glad to see you survived your ordeal. My name's Lulu, by the way, but my friends call me Lou.'

Bemused, I allowed her – him – to usher me into the hall. This adventure was getting crowded. I supposed I should be grateful the cabbie hadn't stayed.

Lulu, or Lou, pulled me into the sitting-room. I heard the crackle of a fire. A pair of hands, I don't know whose, took Joe's jacket from me.

Lulu whistled. 'You look scrumptious, darlin'. What I

wouldn't give for a pair of tits like that – as long as I could take 'em off at the end of the day.'

I laughed at the image this inspired. A hand slapped my painted buttock hard enough to sting. 'Ow.' I rubbed the sore spot. The hand slapped me again. This time I identified Sean's callused palm.

'Take it like a man,' he ordered.

I simpered as well as one could behind a blindfold. 'Why don't you show me how a man takes it?'

Amy giggled at that, a hint of insubordination I filed away for further reference.

Sean was not amused. 'I see you want to do this the hard way.'

'The harder the better, big boy.'

He snorted as though he doubted my capacity to take what he could dish out. The air between us thickened. I was breathing harder and I could hear everyone else breathing harder, too. The challenge I offered turned everyone on. How long would Sean take to master me?

Forever, I swore, but even then I knew he wouldn't. He was too good a mind-fucker to fail. The crazy thing was, I was looking forward to breaking. To pit my will against his, no holds barred, and to know that in the end I'd give him what we both wanted, made my hot little snatch quiver like a rabbit.

'Hook her up,' he said.

Two pairs of hands grabbed me under the arms. Neither was Sean's, and neither gripped me with authority, so I twisted until I broke free. If Sean wanted to 'hook me up', he'd have to do it himself.

The third time I escaped Sean grabbed me around the waist and wrestled me to the carpet. Then I really let loose, growling and kicking like a madwoman. The oil-filled anal plug flexed and sloshed inside me as we rolled, goading me to twist even more. I knew how strong he was, and how quick. I could do what I wanted without much chance of hurting him. It felt good to act out my aggressions, especially when I hooked one foot behind his ankle and tripped him. Once I had him down,

I ground my sex over his groin so fast I stunned him. He actually pushed his cock at me, until he noticed he wasn't in charge any more. Then he flipped me off and trapped my wrists in the small of my back – with one hand. He lifted me, still squirming, off my feet. When I tried to knee his balls, he yanked my arms back hard.

I must have winced because Joe begged him not to hurt me.

Sean blistered the air with his curse. 'I ought to beat you for even thinking it.'

The threat inflamed me. My blood zinged from our wrestling match and the feel of his cock jabbing me through his clothes was far from calming. I wanted to spread my legs and take him, just tug down his zip and impale myself through that ridiculous crotchless corset. He must have read my mind because he grunted, hitched me higher and headed towards the fire. Setting me down, he forced me to my knees on a padded platform. Blindfolded or not, I knew it wasn't part of my original decor.

My nostrils flared. Above the tang of communal arousal, I smelled leather and beeswax. I could well imagine what uses the leather might be put to.

'Give me a hand,' Sean said to the others.

They leapt to do his bidding. This might have been my house, but tonight Sean ruled.

His cohorts wrapped my wrists, waist, and lower thighs in fur-lined manacles. Clinking chains held the bindings taut and held me spread-eagled on my knees. The waist-belt hugged me from rib to hip. The thigh manacles were almost as big, but the wrist-cuffs matched the width of a woman's hand. As much embrace as restraint, the get-up inspired the same pleasure the corset had. I could struggle as hard as I wished with no fear of getting free. I moaned when someone patted my bottom. At that point, I didn't care how loud I was or how many people heard me.

I hoped enjoyment wouldn't be mistaken for submission, because I couldn't hide what this did to me. I threw my weight against the chains, testing their comfort and strength. The fur was soft, the leather hard. The metal clanked like Charles Dickens' Christmas ghost. It was good.

'Babe,' Sean said, 'you were born for bondage.'

The air moved as he bent closer. To my surprise, he kissed me – a hungry, open-mouthed kiss, really eating at my mouth as if he couldn't bear to leave one morsel unsucked. As though that were a signal, the watchers closed in on me. Soft lips captured the peak of my breast. Amy's, I thought, until I felt the slightest scrape of beard. A zip rasped. A long, hard cock caressed the back of my thigh. Hands teased the hair that curled from my mound, fluffing and tugging, but never touching skin. Someone licked the crook of my elbow. I shivered. That had to be Amy. The unfamiliar cock slid higher until its swollen knot pressed the curve where my buttock met my thigh. Its owner moaned and clenched my hip. A drop of pre-come wet my skin. My pussy heated and swelled. My clit peeped out between my lips, catching the brush of a small, light finger. I twitched at the glancing contact and kissed Sean harder, vowing I wouldn't plead – not me – but, boy, was I tempted.

All at once, my tormenters fell away. Someone did up his trousers. I steadied my breathing as well as I could.

Sean's rough hand swept a curl from my forehead. 'Now say thank you, babe.'

'Thank you, babe,' I parroted.

This time my cheek received the open-handed slap. 'Say "Thank you, sir" or I won't remove that blindfold.'

I hesitated, then decided getting the damn thing off would be worth it. 'Thank you, sir.'

He laughed. For a moment, I thought he'd leave the blindfold on just to tease me, but to my relief he removed it.

I blinked to clear my vision and again to clear my head. My cosy living room had been transformed into a bondage chapel. Flowing black velvet masked the windows, my antique furniture was shoved to the walls, and white candles flickered on every surface that would hold them. If I'd known, I'd never have dared wrestle Sean to the floor. Lou had thrown something into the fireplace to make the wood burn blue. The eerie light glinted off the stainless steel apparatus that held me prisoner.

Have bondage frame, will travel, I thought. I concluded the contraption must belong to Lulu or Amy. It certainly wasn't mine. I'd never tried anything this kinky – though I might have fantasised once or twice about tying down my ex.

A man I'd never seen before stepped into my field of vision. He had big brown eyes and an ash-brown crew cut – a regular GI Joe in his khaki T-shirt and camouflage trousers. Shoeless, his bare feet paddled in the carpet, long and thin. Even by firelight, I perceived a body so honed he could have done fitness ads. He had big shoulders, a narrow waist, and precious little body hair. His equipment filled his trousers like an extra pair of socks. Did that bulge contain the towering love tool I'd felt rubbing up my thigh? Whether it did or not, I must admit my jaw dropped in admiration.

'Like my toy?' he drawled, gesturing to the rack. His voice gave his identity away.

'Lulu,' I exclaimed. 'I mean, Lou.'

'In the flesh.' He preened and I saw a shadow of the striking woman who'd delivered Sean's invitation.

'Enough chatter,' Sean said. 'Pull the rack to the centre of the room.'

Both Amy and Lou jumped into action. They unlocked the wheels and turned me around until the fire warmed my front. Then they locked it down again.

'Lean forward and stick your butt out,' Sean ordered. 'Further! Joe, you and Amy steady her shoulders. Lou, you're on clean-up duty.'

Clean-up duty involved removing Amy's paint job with a chamois cloth soaked in oil. Lou had nice hands, really nice. Strong but slow, they kept me at a fine pitch of arousal, lingering long enough to let me know he didn't mind feeling up every bit of a woman there was.

Sean certainly had a flexible bunch of friends, up for anything. I squirmed as Lou's chamois-draped thumb made a thigh-quaking journey around the inner folds of my labia.

'Sweet as honey,' he murmured for my ears only. His hip spooned mine. 'You tell me the minute Sean removes the PRIVATE PROPERTY sign, 'cause I sure would I like to dip my stick in that pot.'

Suiting deed to word, he sneaked one finger out from under the cloth and curled it into my dripping sheath, a quick, deep probe – in and then gone.

Sean didn't notice the pass, but Joe did. His hand tightened on my shoulder. His lips thinned. Was he jealous? Anxious? Or just hot? All three, I hoped, too aroused for scruples. Arching my back, I thrust my buttocks higher.

Joe made a sound, both pained and hungry, and Amy reached over to cup his crotch.

At once I wanted to tear her hand off at the wrist. I hated her touching him, but couldn't look away. She palmed his arch, then squeezed. Joe shifted on his haunches. His buttocks tightened, lifting him into her hand. I ground my molars together. How could he? Then his dark-amber eyes met mine. His lips moved. *I love you*, I thought he said. Hot confusion burst in my chest. Had he said it? Did he mean it? Did I want him to mean it?

I barely heard Sean order Amy to remove the paint that covered my nipples.

Her first touch brought my attention back, however, as I'm sure Sean wanted. I had no experience with female lovers and her performance of the intimate task unnerved me. I didn't want her touch to excite me but it did. She didn't give me a chance to hide it, either. Long after the paint was gone, she played with my nipples, pulling and twisting them. After a while I was heaving in the chains, trying to get more. She knew exactly how hard to tweak me so the pain increased the pleasure. She knew when to stop, too. Between her ministrations and Lou's, I soon verged on coming. She gasped to Sean that they'd better call a halt. My nails bit my palms, but I did not cry out.

'Right,' said Sean. 'Now, we'll warm you up properly.'

As if I weren't warm enough already!

The first spank came without warning, a loud smack across the meat of my right buttock.

'Ow,' I complained, in spite of myself. Joe squeezed my shoulder in commiseration, but this time he knew not to protest.

'"Ow"?' Sean repeated. 'That earns you twenty more.'

Ten came in a flurry, covering my buttocks with a delicate glow of pain. Left, right, up and down they smacked and then – whack – caught my cheeks from beneath. After that he slowed, letting me appreciate each blow individually: the initial sting, the sharp sound, the jiggle of the dildo as my flesh shook under the spanking.

I'm not sure when I began to enjoy it – maybe from the start. After the first rain of smacks, the skin from my thighs to my waist radiated heat and tingled with sensitivity. My sex felt thick, juicy, and my arousal endless. I could go on like this forever, just slowly spiral upward getting hotter and hotter until my hunger grew as sharp as coming. I know I stopped counting after ten and could have spat with annoyance when Joe gasped that I'd had enough.

'She's pink,' he panted, as though he'd been beaten, too. 'Give her a rest.'

I moaned and wriggled my bottom in the air, pleading without actually opening my mouth to say the words.

Sean knew better than to let me get away with that.

'What do you think, Katie?' He settled one hand over my burning flesh. 'Do you want me to stop?'

I whimpered, hardly believing that sound was coming from my throat.

'Do you?' he whispered.

'No,' I whispered back.

'No!' He roared with laughter. 'Then we definitely should stop.'

If I'd been free he wouldn't have wrestled out from under me then. As it was, I yanked at my bonds, writhing in anger.

'You know the word,' he mocked. 'Say "Uncle" and I'll let you go.'

'Damn you,' I said. 'If you think you can master me with a two-minute spanking, you're crazy.'

'Wants more, does she? Well, I'll give you more. On one condition.'

I bit my lip, not daring to ask.

'What condition?' Amy whispered, almost melting into the floor at the signs of my suffering.

Sean walked around the frame and kissed her. That infuriated me, too, though I couldn't keep my eyes off their working cheeks and tongues. Wasn't I supposed to be the centre of attention? And why did she have to be so pretty, with her shiny blonde waves and her pert little breasts heaving on her rib cage like a pair of tinned peaches? Sean covered one with his palm, squeezing it through her kitten-soft sweater. Joe watched the byplay as avidly as I did, his breathing quick and shallow. While one hand clutched my shoulder, the other rubbed his cock and balls. Too horny to resist, I guessed.

I despised them all; yet I wanted to screw them all.

'What condition?' I demanded, making Sean's head snap around.

He wiped Amy's lipstick off with the back of his hand. 'On the condition that Joe takes the whip.'

Joe ceased rubbing his goods. He wagged his head from side to side. 'No way, man. Not me. You know I can't stand to hurt anyone.'

Sean laughed, and not very nicely. 'Does she look like she's hurting? Or does she look like she'll cream the floor with a little more discipline?'

My heart sank at Joe's tortured expression. He wasn't going to do it and, damn it, I wanted him to.

'I can't,' he said, his eyes pleading me to forgive him.

82

His skin glowed like old ivory in the candlelight. I stared at his graceful, restless hands, at his rising and falling chest, at the pulse beating hard and quick in his throat. He wanted to beat me so badly that he could taste it.

'I can hardly bear to watch,' he said, but his body denied the lie. I think he knew it, too, because his expression grew even more miserable.

I looked away.

'C'mon, you do it, Sean,' Lou coaxed. He gave Joe a sympathetic wink. 'You know you want to.'

Sean glared, but I could see him waver.

I wanted to shake him. A true master would have used this chance to break Joe. And why should Lou have a say? Wasn't he a slave here, too? Even as my body tightened with frustration, my brain toyed with a plan. Sean's indecision opened a window of opportunity. All I had to do was figure out how to crawl through.

'Fine,' said Sean, oblivious to the whir of my mental gears. 'I'll do it.'

He extended his hand to Lou, obviously the keeper of the toys. Grinning, Lou pranced over to the holdall he'd stowed on my camel-back sofa. Without wig, make-up, or heels, Lulu appeared, as he tossed paraphernalia from the bag – a jockstrap, a padded bra, an assortment of black velvet ties and, finally, a mahogany-handled, velvet-tongued whip.

He slapped it neatly into Sean's waiting hand. 'Whip away, my master.'

Despite my amusement, a trickle of cream ran down my thigh.

'Oh, man,' said Joe. Still kneeling in front of me, he caught the trickle on his finger and carried it to his mouth.

Sean made us all jump by cracking the whip through the air.

The first lash stung like hell, as did the second. I knew at once I didn't like this as well as the spanking. The whip wasn't as intimate, and the glow it raised was less sensual. By the fourth lash, I was debating whether to cry 'Uncle'. It didn't hurt too badly, but it wasn't much fun.

To my surprise, Joe stood before the whip could fall again.

'Sean.' He held out his hand. 'Your aim sucks. Hand it over.'

'What?' Sean and I said at the same time. What happened to my protector, the man so soft-hearted he couldn't bear to watch? Sean wound the tail of the whip around his palm. 'What makes you think you can do any better?'

'I used to play flick the can with my Dad's bull whip.'

'Your Dad's bull whip?'

Joe shrugged. 'We weren't allowed to use the deer rifles. I always beat my brother, and he was two years older than me.'

Joe had a brother? How could I not know that? Why hadn't he mentioned it?

The first crack of the whip startled the questions from my head. This time, I knew an expert held it. The velvet licked my hip and tickled my belly. Again it descended, and again, never settling in the same place twice. It fell without hesitation, but in a pattern too subtle to predict. My body danced to its stinging syncopation. I swayed in my bonds and dreamt of a smoky jazz club – me on the stage in a long, slinky gown, tugging off a glove, easing a satin strap down one shoulder. They watched me, all of them. Their lust beat at me through the dark.

Dimly, I heard Joe sobbing for air, but the whip seemed separate from his distress, as if it whipped me by itself.

My sense of yielding increased, of being able to sink deeper and deeper into arousal. Through slitted lids, I saw Lou stagger back into an armchair. He unzipped his khaki trousers and drew out a long erection. He punched one fist down it, then the other. I cried out under the whip – for him and for the love of that long, rigid stalk.

My cry pushed Amy over the edge. She yanked the black angora turtleneck over her head, baring breasts

84

every bit as soft and delicate as I'd imagined. Her upper body glowed in the glimmering light, and she pulled and twisted her nipples just as she'd pulled and twisted mine. Lost in a private dream, her hips churned on nothing. Her expression was so concentrated she might have been solving the mysteries of the universe. In my current state, nothing seemed more natural than a crowd masturbating to the music of a whip whistling towards my back – watching me and being watched. The lash curled between my legs and hugged my pubis for one brief instant. I shuddered with pleasure. Joe was so good at this. He had no idea.

Overwhelmed with sensation, I sagged in my chains.

Immediately, Joe dropped the whip and ran around the frame. 'Are you all right, Kate? Did I hurt you?'

His concern pulsed through me like living fire, but I couldn't answer. I could only moan with longing. A Trappist monk wouldn't have mistaken the sound for distress, but Joe crawled on to the platform and hugged me.

'I'm sorry, Kate. I'm sorry. Please, please don't hate me.'

'Kiss me,' I said, slurring like a drunkard.

With a cry, he captured my mouth. We kissed desperately, as if the world were ending, as if we'd never make love again. My body ached for him to fill it. I wanted to ram myself over him as brutally as I could, and at the same time, I wanted to soothe every salty tear – to be kind, to be sweet, to wrench his heart with the pain of falling in love.

To devastate us both.

'Enough,' Sean said, a cold, cutting order.

Joe ignored him. If anything, he clung tighter. The whip sang down, striking Joe's back. Everything stopped at once – our kiss, Lou and Amy's masturbation. Even the fire seemed to hush. Joe stared at his friend as though he'd lost his mind, but Sean stood firm.

'Back,' he said, pointing with the doubled whip. 'Now.'

Joe moved back, slowly, but he moved.

Sean replaced him before me, his belt at eye level. He unfastened the buckle, then pulled it from the loops so fast the leather hissed. For a heart-stopping moment, he swung the belt from side to side, then tossed it to Lou. The whip followed. Such arrogance, I thought. But it was merited. He didn't need those tools to master me, only the one between his ears.

Knowing it would tease me, he dragged his hands up the bulge of his balls and dick. A wet spot at the midpoint of his zip proved how ready he was. I licked my lips.

At my telling gesture, Sean whipped open his trousers and released his swollen cock. It sprang out hard and full, bouncing once before rebounding towards his belly. His foreskin clung to the base of his glans, as though the head was too swollen to allow full retreat. My sex contracted, wanting to test just how swollen he was.

'Eat me.' He pushed his rod in my face. 'Nice and slow.'

At that moment, getting someone else off was not my first priority, but a woman like me is always game to take a taste, especially when the cock *du jour* is such a fine, vigorous specimen.

My hair fell forward as I circled his glans with my tongue. Sean's knees locked.

'Easy,' he said. I hadn't licked him hard but he was primed to blow.

I licked again, even more softly, directly across the eye of his cock. His thighs flexed and released. The prospect of a good long suck had weakened his guard. If I played my cards right, that guard might fall altogether. 'Make it last?' I asked.

'Oh, yeah,' he growled. 'Make it last.'

I leant closer to get at him. The chains rattled. Sean shuddered once at the sound, and again as I licked my way slowly up his under-ridge. I knew he'd lose it if I sucked him, so that's all I did: licked him up and down and all around. I kept my tongue soft and wet – a comfort lick.

Sean liked it so much he clasped his hands on either side of my head. His guidance was firm but gentle. Perhaps he feared a tighter grip would lead me to intensify my efforts, which would bring him off sooner than he wished.

Perhaps, too, he did feel some affection towards me.

As I lapped him with all the delicacy I could muster, his thumbs traced the arc of my brows, smoothing them along the bone. Soon his fingers explored me as well, curving over my cheekbones and nose and jaw, as though he loved the structure of my face.

Could I really plot revenge against a man who touched me so tenderly?

That's when it hit me. Tenderness and domination were not inimical. They fed off each other and strengthened each other. If Sean had succumbed to doubt, the way Joe had, he would have robbed me of a rare pleasure. His carefully restrained violence opened a side of my nature I'd never suspected.

If I cared for Sean, could I do any less?

No, I thought. No.

Confidence fountained up through my sex and belly. My brain hummed with clarifying energy. I could do this. I was chained but he was putty in my hands. His hips rolled forward. I gave him the increase in pressure he craved, but slowed until he sighed with every lick and his ribs swelled with all the air he could draw. The skin of his prick tautened, strained to its limit. He was fast reaching the point where he'd think he'd die if he didn't come, where he had to, fucking had to have it.

I ventured on to the crown again, teasing the rim of his crinkled foreskin, giving it the tiniest nibble with the edge of my teeth. His pelvis jerked; he groaned. I backed off and closed my mouth. He took himself in hand and pushed the head towards my suddenly inhospitable lips.

'Suck it,' he said in a voice like sandpaper. 'Open your mouth and suck it.'

I opened my mouth all right – just wide enough to say 'Uncle'.

Sean gripped my jaw. 'Don't fucking "Uncle" me now. Suck it!'

Teeth clenched tight, I shook my head.

Lou burst out laughing. 'Oh, darlin', she's got you now. She doesn't have to do nothin' once she cries "Uncle".'

'Shit, Kate, don't do this to me.' It was much more plea than order.

I cocked my head and contemplated his poor bobbing willy. 'I might suck you off, on one condition.'

Sean crossed his arms. He knew he wouldn't like it.

But Joe thought he would. 'What condition?'

'On the condition that Sean lets me tie him up.'

'Forget it.' Sean's hands slashed the air. 'I don't care how blue my balls are. The slave does not bind the master.'

But he didn't reckon on his fractious cohorts.

'Cluck, cluck,' Lou mocked. 'What's the matter, Sean, not man enough to take it?'

'Yeah, Sean,' Amy said, giving her breasts an impudent shimmy. 'Afraid to take what a woman dishes out?'

Then all three of Sean's handmaidens joined the fowl chorus. His curse was too blue to repeat, but as sure as chickens lay eggs, it held surrender. Yo-ho-ho, I thought, my arousal surging back in full measure. My turn.

Chapter Six
Cruel to be Kind

*T*he rack held no terror for Sean, so I couldn't tie him to that.

I tapped my lips in thought. He stood rigid before the fire, his erection jutting through his gaping flies. Joe and Lou held his arms. He could have broken free, but that would have meant bruises all around, which was not the point of this game – at least, not the way Sean played it.

'Amy,' I said, 'why don't you undress him?'

I suspected he'd find her attentions as uncomfortable as I did. Amy's sexuality was so visual her scrutiny could make the comatose squirm.

Sean did bristle as she pushed his T-shirt up his ribs. Still topless, her back was a vision, ivory-pale and curved like a violin.

'Does that tickle?' she asked in her sweet doll's voice.

Sean gritted his teeth. Lou and Joe lifted his arms so that Amy could remove the shirt.

'Oh, come see.' She waved me closer. 'His chest hair looks like gold in the firelight.'

I went to see. His hair was fine and fair, and the steely hummocks of his chest spoke of long hours at the gym. My hands joined Amy's in exploring his torso. I skirted round one pec with my fingertips, then meandered down

89

the valley of his breastbone. Sean's tiny nipples beaded in excitement.

Amy and I exchanged glances.

'One for each?' she suggested, and we twined our arms around his waist.

Sean moaned as we captured his nipples. He pushed his chest towards our mouths and tried to wrest free of Joe and Lou. Neither allowed escape, but Lou pressed behind me and ironed his cock into the small of my back. Joe did the same to Amy. Bodies surrounded me – Sean's hard silk to my front, Amy's soft silk to my side, and the friction of cock-filled cotton to my back.

'Hold on,' I said, my voice ragged. 'Let's get his trousers off.'

Amy took charge of that. She bared one hip at a time, then dragged jeans and briefs to his ankles, effectively hobbling him. Crouched at his feet, she sighed at the picture he made.

'Shoes, too?' she asked reluctantly.

Amy did not like simple nudity, but I did. I nodded.

When she'd stripped him off, we stepped back to admire him. The men held his arms out from his sides. I'd seen weight-lifters without Sean's definition, but he wasn't bulky. The curves of his muscles flowed smoothly along his limbs. Of course, the best curve of all was the upswung hook of his erection.

'You have a gorgeous body,' I said. 'You make me want to pull you into my arms and samba.'

To my amazement, Sean dropped his eyes. Had no one gushed over him before? That would have to change.

It would wait, though, for now. Rather than speak, I circled him. My eyes traced the high, taut swell of his buttocks, the vulnerable hunch of his shoulder blades. Lured closer, I dragged one finger down his vertebrae to his cleft. Gooseflesh broke out across his skin. A spring entered my step. My limbs, so recently released from bondage, swung strong and light. Now was the time to plan, before my head grew fuddled with lust.

What fear did Sean most need to overcome?

'Tell me something, Joe,' I said.

Joe blinked as if awakened from a dream.

'When you and Sean make love, who's on top?'

Joe laughed. 'Oh, Sean's definitely a top.'

A top. The way he said it suggested a code – not only the person on top, but the person in control. Hm. A pulse of interest flickered in my womb. I remembered him saying Sean never let him be tender.

I didn't want to ask my next question in front of our victim, so I beckoned Joe to the sitting-room entrance. We put our heads together beneath the wide arch.

'When Sean climaxes, are you ever face-to-face?'

Joe tugged his earlobe. 'To tell the truth, I couldn't tell you what he looks like when he comes. What he sounds like, yes, but . . .' His voice slowed. 'I think he feels too naked at the, uh, crucial moment. He doesn't want anyone getting too close.'

'That's what I thought.' I steepled my hands before my mouth.

Joe watched me for a moment before a beatific smile lit his eyes.

'I get it,' he said. 'You intend to kill him with kindness.'

I smiled back. 'Something like that. But I need your help. He's too proud to say "Uncle". I want you to watch him. If you think I've gone too far, you call a halt for him.'

'I hope that's not all you want me to do.'

I turned my head towards the sitting-room. Sean's golden brows shadowed his eyes, creased by his stormy emotions. 'No,' I said. 'I want you to do the things you've dreamt of doing, the kindnesses he'd never accept. But I think Lou and Amy will have to keep back. I don't want anything to ruin the sense of intimacy I'm trying to create.'

'I'll tell them.' Joe rubbed his freshly shaved jaw. 'They won't mind watching.' He said this as if he knew their preferences well. How many games had he played with them? He smiled at my suspicious expression. 'I'm guessing,' he said. 'Don't you know what people enjoy almost as soon as you meet them?'

I didn't, as a matter of fact. But if Joe did, no wonder Sean had kept him under wraps. I walked back to the others. 'We're going upstairs,' I announced, 'to my bedroom.'

Sean flinched at that. Moving the game to my territory gave me the upper hand. Plus, it might seem irrational, but sex in a bed felt more serious than sex on a sofa. Fortunately, Sean couldn't protest against a simple change of venue when I'd accepted a whipping.

Amy scooped Lou's holdall off the couch. 'I'll bring the toys,' she chirped.

'I'll blow out the candles,' said Lou.

Sean displayed no such cheer. He trudged to my room like a prisoner being led to his death. His little death, I gloated as my new recruits manoeuvred him on to my bed and stretched him out.

'Restraints?' Amy suggested. She snapped a black velvet strip in front of her blossom-pink bosom.

'Be my guest,' I said.

Naturally, she made a show of it, bending over and wriggling her bum as she bound each wrist and ankle. My bed sat in a heavy mahogany frame with a tall headboard and a low footboard. Pineapple-shaped crests topped the four posts. Amy looped the long black ties over their spiky crowns, criss-crossing the cloth like a ballerina's laces. When Sean was laid out in a handsome 'X', she and Lou retired to the dormer window seat. She dropped her trousers before sitting, leaving nothing but a tiny triangle of emerald satin to shield her from the world.

'Nice,' said Lou, and pulled off his khaki T-shirt.

Amy's pout stopped him from removing his baggy army trousers, though she did allow him to unzip them and pull his cock through the vent of his tight black briefs. She wrapped her hand around the shaft, holding but not stroking. The sight of her delicate fingers on that long pole sent a shiver up my sex. Shivering a little himself, Lou hugged her waist and cupped her mound through the green G-string. They sat like a pair over-sexed teenagers at a film, cheek-to-cheek and hand-to-sex, waiting for the show to begin.

I hoped the show wouldn't disappoint them.

Joe and I consulted by the foot of the bed. Sean stared daggers at us, but his cock stood as eager as ever, a thick red stake angling back towards his belly. 'What first?' I asked.

Joe's fingers drifted over the swell of my nipples. 'Nothing too direct. We don't want him to come straight off. Maybe a massage?'

Sean growled at that idea, but Amy popped up like a jack-in-the-box and dug a bottle of oil from Lou's bag. Joe caught it one-handed. He flipped the top up with his thumb and sniffed the subtle almond fragrance. He tipped the bottle towards me. 'Do you want the honours?'

'Oh, no, I think this is a four-handed job.'

'Cripes.' Sean squirmed against the covers. 'Some dominatrix you make.'

I smiled to myself. Sean wasn't used to a top as devious as me. 'I didn't give you permission to speak. Perhaps we should gag that pretty mouth.'

'Fuck,' said Sean, so I had to gag him.

He struggled as I tied it; he couldn't seem to help himself. I guess the gag threatened his control as strongly as the blindfold had threatened mine. Once he was gagged, there would be no more wisecracks to obscure his reactions. His body would speak for itself, loud and clear.

'I think we should strip off,' Joe said.

I hesitated, conscious of our audience, but he was right. To create the atmosphere I wanted, we had to be as vulnerable to Sean as he was to us. We removed our clothes as though no one but Sean was watching. The corset laces had left red marks on my belly. Joe set the oil on the mattress between Sean's legs so he could massage them, clucking and kissing away the angry

93

weals. A gasp from Amy told me she liked the look of that. Joe heard it, too. His lips curled against my navel. Straightening, he tucked the oil between his thighs to warm it, which reminded me my hands needed warming.

I ran my palms up his sides to the tufts beneath his arms, burrowing through the musky tangle in search of skin. He jumped when I found it, then bent his neck to kiss me. His tongue teased the silky inner surface of my upper lip, then the lower, then slid sinuously along my tongue. A quick pull of his cheeks closed us both within the liquid cave, licking, sucking, penetrating deeply before withdrawing. I rose up on tiptoe and mewled for more. He gave it to me, covering my breasts and compressing them in a slow, circling caress. My nipples budded between his fingers.

Our show proved too much for Sean. Pained noises issued from behind his gag. I imagined how he must be feeling and moisture welled inside me. Joe's hands contracted, squeezing my rosy nipples out where his friend could see them. Sean thrashed against the sheets. Excited by his reaction, Joe's cock bobbed between our bellies, swaying like a metronome. I shuffled close enough to still it with my belly. Joe kissed me harder.

'Warm enough?' he breathed against my lips.

I nodded, probably as starry-eyed as he.

We turned to Sean. His legs scrabbled on the mattress as if he could run from what was coming, but Amy's elegant knots prevented more than an inch of play.

'Shh.' I grabbed his nearest foot and kneaded it. Sean's back arched off the bed.

'His feet are very sensitive,' Joe confided. He grinned at Sean's muffled protest and poured a little slick of oil into my palm.

I knew why Sean wanted to keep his secret as soon as I rubbed the oil into his instep. Each stroke made him twist in his bonds until tendons stood out along his joints. Looking down at him, I felt a surge of maternal affection. He was so adorable in his resistance. To me, at least, his tough-guy facade was entirely transparent. Inside was a stubborn-jawed toddler insisting he always be in charge of himself. *Me do it, Mommy. Me.*

Giving in to an impish impulse, I took hold of his big toe and wiggled it back and forth. 'This little piggy went to market,' I crooned.

Sean's expression of outrage was priceless. He was fighting so hard not to enjoy this. Too bad ol' Willy gave him away by throbbing in time to the nursery rhyme, virtually begging for more.

Happily, 'more' was my middle name. I bent over the last little piggy and tucked him into my mouth. Sean roared his fury through the gag, but when I swirled my tongue around the pad and sucked it, his entire body went limp – except for Willy, of course, who swelled and darkened and wept shiny tears of joy.

What fun, I thought, delighted by his hypersensitivity. We couldn't massage his feet forever, though, not with so much lovely flesh to explore. Joe and I clambered on to the bed to work up his legs. His muscles were loose now, like clay beneath our oily hands. Straddling his knee, I pushed up and dragged down one heavy quadricep. By silent agreement, Joe and I skirted his genitals. We sneaked a few admiring looks at the twitching rod, but we didn't touch it or ourselves. Waiting was sauce for all our lust.

Sean's belly and chest occupied us for a good quarter of an hour. His moans faded to the occasional whimper of pleasure and his eyes had long since closed. For now, I allowed him this small escape.

His arms posed no challenge, such was his relaxation. His hands, however, required special attention. The palms in particular were rich in nerves. Sean squirmed as we teased our thumbs across the sensitive cup. His eyelids fluttered. Folding up like a Muslim at prayer, I kissed the curled backs of his fingers. 'Wake up, Sleeping Beauty. Time for the main course.'

His eyes opened slowly, dazed and dark with hugely

expanded pupils. His jaw worked on the gag. I reached behind his neck for the knot.

'Let's take this off,' I said.

The whites of his eyes betrayed alarm. Good. He knew the massage had lulled him. Now he feared what he might say in the heat of the moment. Once the cloth was free, he pressed his lips together.

I promised myself that would do him no good.

Joe crawled into the space between Sean and the headboard. Crossing his legs, he lifted Sean's head on to his lap, setting it off-centre to allow room for his own erection. He stroked Sean's hair and murmured something sweet. Joe had a perfect view of his face – until Sean screwed his eyes shut.

'Ah-ah-ah.' I straddled his waist and lightly slapped his cheeks. 'No hiding, handsome.'

'Screw you,' he said, the best comeback his trembling lips could manage.

'I intend to,' I said. 'Nice and slow and sweet. And you know why? Because I really want you to feel good, Sean. I never expected to like you so much but now that I do, I want to reach straight inside and press our hearts together.'

He clenched his jaw. His hazel-green eyes glittered under a thin film of tears. Ruthless, I pressed the tender knife home. 'You're a good man, Sean Halloran. Better than you know.'

He blinked and a tear spilt over. Joe bent to kiss it away. Sean flinched. 'You play rough,' he said, his voice like gravel.

I played my fingers across his sensual mouth. 'Don't be silly. I've barely started.' I tightened my thighs on his waist. Wary animal that he was, his torso shifted uneasily. Poor thing. He had no idea what he was in for.

'Here are the rules,' I said. 'You tell me what you want and I'll do my best to give it to you.'

His mouth twisted. I could see he thought this was a peculiar way to dominate someone. 'Would you untie me?' he asked.

'No. Although, if you really need to get free, you know the safe-word.' I ignored his huff of disgust. 'What I meant was you can tell me your preference – faster, slower, whatever.'

'And you'll do it?'

'Probably.' I propped my hands on his pecs and shifted until my labia hovered, plump and glossy, millimetres above his cock. He was so hard I'd have to pull the head away from his belly to take him, but he could feel my heat now, and see the wet gleam of readiness when he tilted his chin to his chest.

'Is this what you want, Sean?' I parted my lips with two fingers, spearing them to either side of my clitoris. Engorged with blood, the knot of flesh stood out full and red, twitching as the surrounding muscles contracted and released. Sean's mouth fell open. The tip of his tongue touched his front teeth. 'Or maybe you'd prefer something else?'

'No,' he said quickly. 'I want my cock in your cunt.'

Though the crude words were no stranger to his lips, they dissolved into a heavy breath, as though too loaded to utter. I was glad he wanted to take me that way, but surprised he wanted it so much.

We'd never done it vaginally before.

But, hey, I liked first times. Smiling, I lowered myself on to his upswung shaft. My flesh wrapped him, oiling his heat, sliding voluptuously up and down his length. His hips reared up, pressing harder, adding his undulation to mine.

'Oh, yeah,' he said. 'Oh, baby, get me wet.' He swallowed hard as my sheath released another flood. 'Take me, Kate. Take me now.'

Before I could move, Joe restrained me by the shoulder. His long, smooth arm flashed to the bedside table's drawer and rummaged through the contents.

'Aha.' He flicked a condom in Sean's face. 'Extra large, buddy. She must have bought these with you in mind.'

Sean's mouth quivered but he was too wired to joke back.

Intrigued by their byplay, I gathered Sean's scrotum into my palms and rolled the unstable weight across my finger bones. Sean's thigh muscles jumped. His eyes, however, never left Joe.

Carefully, Joe tore the wrapping and balanced the furled prophylactic on the ends of his fingers. 'Want a drop of lube in the tip?'

'Yeah.' Sean shuddered.

I bent closer to watch Joe squeeze the lubricant in. 'What does that do?'

Joe grinned. 'Increases sensitivity. Especially for those of us who come accessorised.' He skinned Sean's foreskin back with his thumb, demonstrating which accessory he meant. Then he seated the condom over his glans, squeezed the air out of the tip and rolled it down. 'There.' He patted Sean's juddering shaft. 'All dressed up and ready to roll.'

Sean and I laughed at his expression of fraternal pride. Sometimes Joe was too cute for words.

Just then a soft, feminine cry split the air. I didn't want to lose my concentration, but I couldn't help looking back. Neither could my partners. Lou had turned sideways on the window seat. With one leg crooked on the cushion, he held Amy by the waist and was lowering her on to his lengthy prong. The cry we'd heard must have been her reaction to the first fraction of penetration.

'Don't mind me,' she gasped, her face tightening as he eased her down another inch. 'We're just getting comfortable.'

Lou's hands looked spider long against her tiny waist. His arm muscles bulged. My eyes widened. I had to see her pubis meet his before I'd believe she could take him. The feat required a few angle adjustments, plus some hand work, but they managed. Lou's head fell back as she hilted him. His Adam's apple bobbed.

'Ah,' said Amy, a happy sigh. She wriggled closer and his hands clapped round her buttocks to hold her still. Awareness sizzled through my nerves. I knew they didn't intend to come until we did.

'They're fine,' Joe said, turning my attention back to Sean.

'And so are you,' I purred to our victim. I dragged my nails down his chest hard enough to leave eight faint pink trails from collar bone to hip. The trails faded even as I captured his swollen cock and tugged it to a more suitable angle. Sean's breath hitched.

'Wait,' he said. Beads of sweat sparkled on his brow. He hesitated before explaining, probably deciding whether to trust me. 'Don't put me in yet. Play the head around outside.'

'I'm not sure what you mean,' I said, even though I was. 'Shall I have Joe do it?'

He muttered something blasphemous. It sounded like a 'yes' to me.

'I'd be happy to help,' Joe said.

His hand skied down the slopes of Sean's chest, fingers spread until they caught the base of his cock. With his thumb he guided the shaft, tipping it gently between my folds. He had such beautiful hands: long, brown fingers and strong, oblong palms. Watching him handle Sean gave me as big a thrill as the slow circling of that fat red knob. Round and round Joe slid it, teasing it past my slippery clit, dipping it into the whorl of my vagina. Lush, wet noises rose from my sex. Sean struggled to get a better view by using his bonds to lift his upper body. When he saw what I saw, he began to pant with excitement.

A drop of sweat rolled down the side of Joe's face. 'Had enough yet?'

'Yeah,' Sean rasped, and Joe pressed his crown inside my entrance.

Fire shot up my spine. He was thick and full – and unfamiliar. That was a potent thrill, spiced with the slightest edge of guilt. The heat of him scorched me; the width entranced. I vowed I'd sample this treat again. Of course, I'd have to ensure Sean liked it enough to want to. With that in mind, I stretched my tender tissues around his bulk. His under-ridge was so pronounced, it rubbed me like a finger. Sighing with pleasure, I pressed down until Joe's forefinger and thumb were all that kept me from the hairy root. Joe would have let go, but I clasped his wrist.

'Stay. Let him feel both of us.' Sean's cock pulsed in agreement. I leant forward across Joe's arm, close enough for my breasts to warm Sean's chest. His eyes locked with mine, quivering with strain. 'Fast or slow?' I asked, not sure myself which answer I wanted to hear.

He bit his lip in indecision. I swivelled my hips once, a quick half-stroke.

'Fast or slow, Sean?'

'Fast,' he said. His pelvis jerked upward. 'Fuck me hard, Kate.'

I pressed up on my arms again, set my knees firmly for balance and proceeded to work us both, quick hard thrusts that kept him well inside me and slammed my jangling clit against the back of Joe's hand. Joe held him steady, so I rose higher and drove back faster. I pulled up to the flare, tightening inside and giving it a little tug. Sean cried out. His head thrashed in Joe's lap. Sensation gathered in my sex, centring on the velvet-wrapped steel inside. Images of everything I'd been through tonight bombarded me: the corset, the spanking, sucking Sean to the point of coming. My sex ached and throbbed. I wanted that release so badly, I forgot the reason I'd tied him to the bed in the first place.

'Come on.' I slung myself up and down that sweet, hard rod, rising higher and higher until the need to come was so urgent, it hurt. 'Come on, come on.'

My back stiffened. My sheath clutched his cock. Still the climax eluded me. Then fingers pinched my clit – Joe's fingers. Fireworks burst in the tiny shaft and roared upward. I closed my mouth against a scream, coming so hard my head flew back like a whiplash victim. Shudders rippled through me, honey-wet, knife-sharp spasms of rapture.

When I came to myself, Sean was still hard inside me and shaking with thwarted lust.

'I'm so sorry.' I dropped a penitent kiss to his lips. 'I lost control.'

Rather than complain, Sean jerked his mouth to mine. The pressure of his lips pulled me in for a deep, wet kiss. He tugged on his bonds. 'Finish me,' he said. 'Please, Kate. I need it. Please.' Again, he yanked at his ties, harder this time. 'Uncle, damn it, Uncle. Let me go.'

Joe freed his wrists in what had to be record time, but Sean was too impatient to wait for him to loosen his ankles as well. He sat up, flung his arms around me, and squeezed me so tightly I lost my breath. He showered my face with kisses, nipping the tip of my nose, licking the side of my cheek. His hands slid down to cup my bottom.

'Make love to me, Kate. Show me you want me. Let me feel how much you care.'

My throat tightened. Did he think I was lying before? I clasped his golden head to mine. 'I care, Sean. I do.'

He groaned as I moved on him, my body wet and soft, my eyes brimming. But Joe's eyes sparkled with mischief. He wrapped himself around Sean so that his front supported Sean's back and his thighs bracketed mine. He stuck his finger in his mouth and wet it. He winked at me. His hand burrowed under Sean's buttocks. Sean gasped as it found a home.

'Just a little deeper,' Joe said, twisting to get at him more easily. 'I'll be there in a tick.'

I knew the moment he found his target because Sean whimpered and his cock jerked inside me, twanging with eagerness. I thought his next instructions would be for Joe to 'rub harder, man' or 'push it in good'. But he surprised me.

He hugged me tighter. His lips grazed my ear. 'Say you love me,' he whispered.

My heart stopped. Sean's must have, too. He went board-stiff. 'I didn't mean that. It just came out.'

I threw my head back on a laugh and sank down on him again. I'd show him no mercy now. He knew it, too.

He sobbed for air, so close to orgasm he couldn't bear to pull out.

'I didn't –' He met my thrust with his own, more determined to reach his goal than to deny what he hadn't meant to say. 'I didn't – Oh, yes, like that. Do that again. Oh, sweetheart.'

'And now you forget to call me "babe",' I teased, repeating the motion he'd liked, a quick swivel down his rod.

'Fuck.' He panted hard, double-thrusting through my twist. 'I'll call you sweetheart if I wan– Oh, God, I'm going to come.'

With that he lost his powers of speech. He wrenched my thighs apart, then planted his hands behind his hips so he could pump deeper. Our bellies slapped together, sweaty and frantic. His face contracted in agony of suspense, mouthing some word he had no breath to speak. Aching with sympathy, I pinched his nipples. His breath whooshed out. His cock swelled. Lips drawn back in a snarl, he heaved into me once, twice, and then shattered.

'Y-yes,' he groaned, finishing the stroke with a slam.

He spilt hard. His cock twitched so strongly inside me I toppled over the edge in a swell of heat, a climax as comforting as swan's down.

A duet of sighs told me Lou and Amy had timed their crises to match Sean's.

When the last spasm faded, Joe helped me extricate myself from Sean, who had collapsed – limp and sighing – on the bed. Joe dispensed with his condom and I tidied his flaccid penis with a warm facecloth. A drowsy smile softened Sean's rough-and-tumble features. It seemed he liked being babied, after all. Spoilt brat, I thought fondly. His ankles were still bound and, too sated to worry about what he might have said, he let his legs fall open like a frog's. Joe untied the last two velvet straps and threw half the coverlet over him.

Then he turned and offered me a courtly bow, no less

graceful for his nudity or his phenomenal erection. 'Mistress,' he said in a tone of profound respect.

I laughed, but I liked the sound of it. 'Yes, Joseph?'

He straightened and spread his arms, allowing his dusky cock to make a mute request.

'Yes,' I said, beaming my approval. 'I believe I did save a little room for you.'

Dawn hadn't broken when I heard someone pounding on the front door. Joe was out for the count, but Sean and I sat up. We looked at each other, both pushing hair out of our eyes.

'Lou wouldn't come back at this hour,' he said. 'He's too polite. And Amy couldn't knock that hard.'

The pounding resumed and was joined by the buzzer.

'I better go see who it is.' My pulse skittered as I threw on my dressing gown. Had someone had an accident? Was my ne'er-do-well brother in trouble again?

Sean scrambled out of bed behind me. 'I'm coming with you.'

He didn't wake Joe, but he did grab my favourite fireplace poker.

When we reached the second floor, we heard the words that accompanied the pounding: 'Police. Open up.'

My gaze shot to the living room. Amy and Lou, bless them, had returned everything to its former innocuous state.

With a deep breath to steady my nerves, I flipped the mortice lock. Two uniformed officers waited outside the door, their hands on their holsters, their stance wary.

'Hello, ma'am,' said the nearest. 'We received a report of a racket here tonight.'

My fingers tightened on the door. 'A racket?'

'Loud noises. Shrieking.' He peered behind me and caught sight of Sean and the poker. 'Want to put that down, sir?'

'Sorry.' He set it against the wall. 'We didn't know who could be pounding on the door this late.'

The officer grunted. It was not an apology. 'Mind if we take a look around?'

I stood back as the policemen entered. Between them, they took two steps into the living room, three into the dining room, and one up the stairs. Thorough fellows, those Philly cops – but I was glad for their lackadaisical attitude tonight.

'You folks have a party here?'

'No-o,' I said, with a reasonable facsimile of confusion. I thanked heaven Joe hadn't woken. He couldn't lie to save his life. I nodded towards the VCR. A copy of *Silence of the Lambs* sat on top – Sean's pick, of course. 'We were watching horror movies, but I can't imagine it was loud enough to –'

'Some people are more sensitive to noise than others,' said the second cop. He was young and still fit. He tugged his belt higher on his trim waist. I hoped Sean wasn't ogling him.

'You said "we",' he continued. 'You and your boyfriend the only ones here?'

'Uh, yeah,' I said, startled to hear Sean referred to as my boyfriend. 'And our lodger. He's asleep now.'

'Hm,' said the younger cop, but I could tell he wasn't suspicious. 'Must have been the TV then. Next time watch that volume.'

'Yes, sir,' I said, and thanked them for coming round.

The door shut behind them. Sean scratched his head. 'We weren't that loud, and you certainly didn't shriek.'

'Maybe the neighbours –'

He blew a breath out through his lips. 'Your left-side neighbours are out of town, and old Mrs Perelli is so deaf she'd sleep through a hurricane. Believe me, I'd have found somewhere else to play if that weren't the case.' Yawning, he sat on the bottom stair and propped his shoulder on the banister. 'I think you've got an enemy, Kate.'

'Me?' I tightened the sash of my dressing gown. My scalp prickled. 'Who cares what I do?'

He pinned me with a speculative stare. Green flashed

in his hazel eyes – a cold colour, very self-contained. 'Your ex, maybe.'

'He's too busy planning his wedding to Marianne's teenage daughter. Besides, there would be no way for him to know. I don't blab about my sex life, not even to my friends.'

Sean cracked his knuckles. 'Neither do I, and neither would Lou or Amy. They're old hands at this scene. They know better.'

I sat next to him and sighed. 'Then who?'

'Someone who thought the cops would get here early enough to break up our fun.'

I chuckled at that. 'Whoever it was, they don't know Philly cops very well.'

Yawning again, Sean heaved to his feet. 'We'll talk about it tomorrow. Maybe Joe can think of an explanation. At any rate –' he offered his hand to help me up '– we'll find the spoilsport and squash him like a bug. Scout's honour.'

Scout's honour. That must have been some troop.

Sean slid the brown sugar to Joe's side of the table. With his speedy metabolism, Joe didn't believe in eating porridge plain. 'What about your uncle?' Sean asked. 'Can he find out who tipped off the police?'

Joe took a quick bite and swallowed. 'He doesn't work in this area, but I guess he could ask around.'

'Your uncle is a cop?' I offered him the raisin box. First a brother, now an uncle. What else didn't I know about Joe?

Joe shook some raisins into his bowl. 'Thanks. Good sex makes me hungry. And, yes, my uncle is a cop – a detective.'

I pondered the implications of his relative's career. 'How will you explain why you need to know who made a noise complaint?'

'I'll tell him the truth, or most of it. He'll understand.' Joe grinned. 'Uncle Joey likes to wear women's underwear. Strictly off-duty, you understand. He's happily married and has three kids. I was named after him.'

My spoon halted halfway to my mouth. 'Your parents named you after the family cross-dresser?'

'They didn't know at the time. He only told them two years ago. Ever since, my dad has blamed Uncle Joey for everything he thinks is wrong with me.'

Sean grimaced but Joe's smile shone with good humour. When God handed out bitterness, he must have skipped Joe. His father's bigotry didn't seem to bother him at all.

'Originals must run in the family,' I said.

Joe um-hummed around another mouthful. 'You bet. My Grandma Rose was a fan dancer. My mom's a pet therapist and my dad is a conspiracy-theory junkie.' Joe put on a fierce father face. '"Trust me, son, the government knows more than it's telling."'

'And then there's Al,' Sean added.

'Al?'

Joe rolled his eyes. 'Al is my big brother. He's a corporate lawyer. He married a nice Catholic girl. They have two normal kids, one normal dog, and a house in the suburbs. It's all very bourgeois. Of course, in my family, that is eccentric.'

'Does he know about –?' I glanced at Sean, wondering how to describe their relationship.

'Oh, sure,' said Joe. 'If I didn't tell my family, I'd have to worry about them finding out. Mom's cool with it, Dad flipped his lid, and Al leaves the room if anyone mentions Sean. He still loves me, though, so I try to be patient with him.'

Sean put his head in his hands and wagged it back and forth.

'What?' Joe shovelled in another spoonful.

'Nothing. I just wonder what planet you come from sometimes.'

'What's wrong with telling my family things? We're close.'

'There's nothing wrong with it. It's great. But most

guys would be afraid to tell their parents they're sleeping with another man.'

Joe shoved his empty bowl aside and slouched back, hands folded over his flat belly. 'Your family knows.'

'Yeah, but it took me four years to work up the nerve. Even now I haven't told them about Kate.'

Joe crinkled his forehead. 'Neither have I. I wonder what that means.'

I fluttered my lashes at the pair of them. 'It probably means I'm too special to share.'

'You know,' Joe said, 'you're probably right.'

I glowed for a minute, flattered as anything, then started upright in my chair.

'Larry,' I said, hardly aware my brain had been working.

Sean set down his spoon. 'Larry?'

'The obnoxious estate agent. The one you hung up on. Maybe he was skulking around last night to check out the competition.'

'You might have something there.' He smacked his fist into his palm. 'If it is him, I hope he's not too hard to discourage.'

I covered Sean's fist with my hand. 'Promise me you won't do anything crazy.'

'Who me?' He laughed. 'I never do anything crazy. At least, not if I can get caught.'

Chapter Seven
With Friends Like These

I'd forgotten all about my supposed enemy by the time
I reached work. Too many honeyed memories
crowded out the worry. I didn't even care that I was an
hour and a half late; my very joints felt oiled with
pleasure.

Regrettably, the scene that greeted me broke the mood.

I found Marianne berating Keith, our foot-fond assistant, for mis-shelving some books.

'How many times do I have to tell you? The big names
go cover out.'

'But I didn't know.' Keith's face was pink. He gripped
the sales counter as though it were his only shield.
Perhaps it was. He might be six foot something and a
competitive rower, but he was a nice boy, the kind who
would never hit a woman, no matter what. Unfortunately for him, Marianne looked ready to vault over the
counter and claw him – leather miniskirt and all.

'How could you not know?' she demanded, her voice
loud enough to turn customers' heads. 'Nora Roberts is
one of the biggest names there is.'

'Marianne,' I said, using the tone I reserved for misbehaving children and dogs. It wasn't nice, but it
worked. She spun around to face me, frustration written
in every line of her pale, skilfully powdered face.

'But he –'

I pointed towards the office. 'In private, Marianne. I'll join you in two minutes.' I turned to Keith, who fiddled with the cash drawer. Apparently, my intervention embarrassed him as much as Marianne's attack.

'Probably just PMS,' he mumbled.

'I don't care if it's a brain tumour. She has no right to snap your head off. You're our most reliable employee. In fact, I plan to promote you to day manager at the end of the month – assuming the hours fit your class schedule.'

Keith stared at me in shock. Then he smiled, revealing sparkling white but crooked front teeth. With his tousled brown hair and the smattering of freckles across his nose, he resembled an overgrown Mouseketeer.

'Are you kidding? I'll make the hours fit. Oh, Ms Winthrop, you won't be sorry.'

'I know I won't.' I patted his shoulder. Had I ever been that earnest?

When I entered our office, Marianne was crying over her keyboard, noisy, racking sobs. My anger faded. Crouching by her chair, I rubbed her slender forearm. 'Marianne, honey, what's wrong?'

She waved her arm with a jangle of sterling silver bracelets, too overwrought to speak. Her straight black hair curtained her face.

'Is my brother still arguing about the property settlement? Or did Brenda ask to borrow your wedding dress again?'

She shook her head and buried her nose in a tissue. 'It wasn't them. It – Oh, I don't want to talk about it.'

'That's a first.' I pressed my palm to her forehead. 'Should I call a doctor?'

'Only if he's well-hung.'

Reassured by her returning sense of humour, I pushed to my feet and tugged her black velveteen sleeve. 'How about me treating you to lunch today?' I wagged my brows. 'Le Bec-Fin?'

She sniffled and lifted her head. I noticed she'd barely mussed her make-up. 'We haven't got a reservation.'

Normally, she would have had a point. The exclusive restaurant had won so many awards, two weeks was not too long to wait for a table. Today, however, I had an ace up my sleeve. 'Remember that special order I filled for the *maître d'*, the Japanese pillow books? He'll find a corner for us. We'll kill a bottle of wine and you can tell Auntie Kate all about it.'

'Nice wine?'

I grinned. Marianne had a practical soul. 'I'll let you pick.'

She adjusted her silver Hermès scarf. 'All right. I'll get my coat.'

'But it's only 10.30.'

'So what? I need a drink now, not at noon.'

As soon as we arrived, the elegant French atmosphere put me at ease. The same was not true of Marianne. She fussed over a microscopic speck on her fork, and a draught, and then one of the chandeliers was glaring in her eye. The waiter, who'd gone beyond the call of duty to seat us well, satisfied every complaint with a bow and a smile. I resolved to leave him a generous tip and waited for Marianne to calm down.

The truth came out midway through the second bottle of Chateau Smith-Haut Lafitte.

'You knew I wanted them and you slept with them anyway.'

Trying not to choke on my trout almandine, I pressed my napkin to my mouth. 'That's what was bothering you? Come on, Marianne. We're not teenagers. I'm not obliged to avoid everyone you might have a crush on.'

'But you lied to me.' She threw back an angry swallow of the pricey wine. 'You told me they were gay.'

'I was trying to save you some embarrassment.'

'Hah!'

'Marianne, they showed no interest in you.'

Her mouth formed a bitter, red moue. 'They never had a chance. You kept them under lock and key.'

'That is not true.' Actually, it was sort of true, but I ignored the niggle of guilt. I leant forward and caught the calming scent of the white carnations that filled our table's vase. I lowered my voice. 'Joe was in and out of the shop for months before we started anything. Every time you saw him, you made a pass at him. He didn't respond to your overtures once. Face it, Marianne, you were this close to making a pest of yourself.'

She toyed with her salmon mousse. 'You don't have to be nasty about it.'

'But you don't listen when I'm nice.'

She pouted. 'It's just – You always get what you want.'

I collapsed against my chair's medallion back. 'You can't really believe that. Did I get what I wanted when my husband ran off with your daughter?'

This was not a good topic to raise. Marianne's eyes narrowed to glittering grey slits. 'Maybe you did get what you wanted. You certainly didn't fight very hard to keep him.'

'Christ, Marianne –' But I shut my mouth before I could say anything I'd regret. 'Maybe we'd better postpone this conversation until we're both thinking clearly.'

'Fine.' She tossed her hair over her shoulder. 'I know when I've struck a nerve.'

She made me so mad I ordered Triple Chocolate Torte for dessert, then ate so fast I barely tasted it. My sugar high crashed before the cab dropped us back at the bookshop.

Cursing myself for being so self-destructive, I returned Keith's cheery wave with half my heart. Depression weighted my feet; disillusion, my spirit. I wasn't like Sean and Joe. I didn't have so many friends I could afford to write one off.

I thought of all the things Marianne had done for me since she'd married my brother. Too many times to count, she'd been my sole family ally. At sixteen, she was my role model, then my drinking buddy, and now my business partner. I knew she wasn't perfect, but neither was I. How could I fail to admire a woman who

111

embraced life so fearlessly? Everything considered, her friendship had enriched me more than I could measure.

On the other hand, if she blamed me for all her woes, what sort of friendship did we have?

'Thanks for lunch,' she said, dropping an airy kiss to my cheek. 'I feel much better.'

I almost told her I'd promoted Keith then, so she could finish the day as crabby as I'd begun it.

The walk home worked off most of my anger and, I hoped, the chocolate torte.

Despite the nip in the air, I arrived sweaty. To my complete befuddlement, a construction crew was tramping through my house.

'Hey!' Joe bounded into the hall with a smile the size of Texas. 'You're home. Sean and I have a surprise for you.'

One of the big hairy guys grunted and tipped his fingers at me. Two others wrestled a board shrouded in bubble-wrap down the hall.

'I can't begin to guess,' I said.

Joe rose up on his toes. 'It's a exercise room! Or it could be. Sean's Uncle Mike owns a demolition firm. He salvaged this great cherry-wood panelling from a condemned mansion. And some fixtures, too. Victorian, I think.' He faltered at my uneasy expression. 'Don't worry, Kate. It's quality goods. You'll love it.'

'It's not that.' I stepped back into the dining room to avoid another pair of panel carriers. Joe joined me. 'I'm just wondering how much this is going to cost me.'

Joe looked hurt. 'Nothing. It's a present from Sean and me. His uncle's crew is bringing the stuff over for free, and Sean and I will install it. Sean knows all about building codes and renovation, and you know I follow orders well.'

That made me smile. 'You're right. It's a wonderful idea.'

'It doesn't have to be a gym,' he hastened to assure me. 'I just thought we could put a treadmill or something down there and then you won't have to walk outside when it's icy.'

'Very thoughtful.' I linked my arms behind his neck and tipped our hips together.

'You don't mind us, you know, making ourselves at home?'

His honey-brown eyes shot spears to my heart. I only wished this nesting urge could last.

'I don't mind.' I brushed his lips with mine. 'Making yourself at home by renovating my basement is much better than leaving the toilet seat up or throwing socks on the floor.'

Joe smiled and rubbed our noses together. 'You throw socks on the floor more often than we do.'

'True enough.' Happiness bubbled through my veins as we swayed by the dining room table – happiness, and a persistent prick of fear.

If my seventeen-year friendship with Marianne couldn't last, why did I think our fragile *ménage* would?

Partly because I love learning how things work, and partly out of camaraderie, I joined the renovation effort. From the start, I knew we were constructing an implausibly swanky gym. The cherry-wood panelling put me in mind of an exclusive gentlemen's club, as did the acid-etched art nouveau lighting fixtures. Once Sean cleaned and rewired them, their quality shocked me. I asked if he was certain his uncle knew what he'd given away.

Sean set the wire cutters aside. 'If you're worried, send his wife a basket of books. She loves that Maeve Binchy woman.' He scratched his rock-hard belly through his T-shirt. ''Course, my uncle will thank you if you include some goodies from the back room. Aunt Maire can roll when she's in the mood.'

I frowned. 'A basket of books isn't worth all this.'

'It is if Aunt Maire decides to treat my uncle to a hot weekend away from the kids.'

Well, I could see where Sean got his priorities.

He proved a finicky task master over the next few

months. I believe Joe and I pleased him, however. We did as we were told and only argued over important things, like meal breaks and sleep. Sean had a tendency to obsess over finishing a task. Then Joe and I would join forces to seduce him. We christened our gym many times before it held a single weight.

After a while, I developed a Pavlovian response to the sound of hammer hitting nail. One clanging blow and my pussy was awash.

But the project changed us in deeper ways. As we worked, we talked – about our childhoods, about our loves and hates, even our ambitions. I didn't want to think too hard about my future because I suspected they wouldn't be in it, but I liked hearing them dream. Sean wanted to start his own accountancy firm so he could work six months and play six months. Joe wanted to be the next Andrew Lloyd Webber.

'Only better,' he qualified. 'No one should roll their eyes at my musicals.'

The confession, and our failure to laugh at it, helped him overcome his inhibitions. He began to sing more around the house. The traditional shower-time warble was joined by cookery medleys and ironing arias. Some nights he even sang us to sleep. Fortunately, he had a beautiful tenor, just husky enough to remind me of sexy things like whisky and velvet or, better yet, post-coital hoarseness.

One day, I caught him singing in his room. He still studied and kept his clothes there, though by this time his cologne scented my room more strongly than his own. I watched him from the door. He sat with his broad shoulders bent over the second-hand desk, holding his hair off his face with one hand. He hummed each phrase a few times before scribbling it in a stave-ruled notebook. The pen didn't falter once.

I imagined real artists worked this way, with this furious concentration. I knew I held no part of his thoughts. I knew he inhabited a world entirely of his own making. Nothing but sex or a great book had ever caught me up so completely. I envied him even as a soft pulse of interest warmed my loins.

I wanted him, this private Joe, this independent Joe. But I held back and let the feeling simmer.

Finally, he pushed the notebook aside, ran both hands through his hair, and stretched the kinks from his spine. Unable to resist, I padded up behind him and buried my fingers in his gleaming locks. He jumped, then sagged back to enjoy the scalp massage. 'How long were you standing there?'

'A few minutes. I didn't want to interrupt.' I blew lightly in his reddened ear. He rewarded me with a shiver.

'I was just messing around,' he said.

I counted the stack of notebooks that sat on the metal shelving above his desk. There were six altogether, and every one was as dog-eared as the one he'd shoved aside. If they all held musical scores, he'd been 'messing around' a long time.

Smiling, I slid my hands down the front of his crisp blue Oxford shirt. 'You smell of starch,' I said into the smooth cord of his neck. His pulse thudded under my lips.

'Just a little.' His voice was thready. 'I like to use it when I iron.'

'I know.' I let my hands venture farther, down over his hipbones and on to the hard, slim muscle of his thighs. A knife-crease pleat bisected the front of his tan slacks. 'I like the way you iron. It makes me want to dishevel you.'

His laugh escaped on a choked exhalation. A hill was forming between his legs, lifting the neatly pressed cotton. As it rose, I measured it with my thumbs, testing its resilience and size. His legs fell open.

'Close the door,' he said, and I knew he meant for this to be one of 'our' times.

We hadn't had one in more than a week and I needed it, too. As exciting as our threesomes were, my nature craved the one-on-one intimacy Joe and I shared.

I had my sweater halfway off before the door swung shut.

Joe turned his chair sideways. He stared at my pink satin camisole, at the beaded tips of my breasts, then attacked his collar button. 'We don't have long,' he said. He watched me push my narrow, knee-length skirt down my legs. He moistened his lips. 'Sean's due home in half an hour.'

'Half an hour will do it for me.' I kicked my tights away and gestured to my camisole. *On or off?* asked my silent mime. We had our own shorthand now.

'On,' he said. His chest muscles flexed as he wrenched out of his shirt. 'But take the bra off, and the panties.'

I did as he asked, then fought a smile when he tripped over his feet trying to get his clothes off and watch me at the same time.

I bent to retrieve his trousers. 'You should fold these,' I said, but before I could save his ironing job, he scooped me off my feet and tossed me on to his neatly made single bed.

'Don't waste time.' He plummeted on to me wearing briefs and socks and nothing else. He nuzzled my neck. 'Once is not going to be enough for me. I miss having you to myself.'

His words liquefied inside me like sugar over a flame. I squirmed down until his hot, humid crotch met mine. Cursing sweetly, he pressed me into the mattress so hard the springs creaked. His cotton-covered cock delved between my swollen lips, its warmth catching, its firmness a powerful inspiration. Wanting more pressure, I gripped the sides of the bed.

'Mm, Joe.' I heaved my body towards his, my face level with his shoulder. 'This bed makes me feel like I'm seducing a teenager.'

'Does it really?' His hand slid up my silky camisole to capture one breast. He squeezed the nipple between finger and thumb. 'I hope you enjoy making love like a teenager, too, because all the condoms are in your room.'

I groaned in disappointment. 'I could run up quick.'

'No way.' He underscored his refusal with a forward roll of his hips. 'I want my full thirty minutes and not a second less.' Craning his neck, he kissed his way across my collar bones – feathery kisses interspersed with delicate licks that made me shiver with delight. 'Shall I try to remember how it was?'

'How what was?'

'To be a teenager, to see a naked woman for the first time.'

'That was so long ago, wasn't it?' I mocked, even as I tangled my hands in the thick, warm silk of his hair.

He hummed against my neck, a snippet of song. The sound vibrated through my nerves, tingling and pooling in the cache between my legs. I hummed back and he laughed. Then he lifted his head. His face, filled with humour a second ago, now held a look of tremulous expectation.

My breath caught. I always thought of Joe as vulnerable but this, this was the vulnerability of an adolescent boy, racked by unfamiliar desires, restrained by insecurity. 'Oh, my.' I fanned my cheeks, experiencing my own hormonal surge.

His bulging cotton briefs soaked up the sudden rush of moisture from my sex. The strength of my response embarrassed me. I would have hidden it, but we notched each other too intimately for that. I tensed.

'No,' he said, his breath puffing hot against my ear. His shaft rocked deep into my vulva and I soaked him again. He kissed my cheek. 'When we're alone, we can play at any fantasy we want. It should turn us on.' He drew back and held my gaze. 'We both know what you would and would not do in real life.'

I locked my ankles behind his hairy, sinewed thighs. 'Do we?'

'Yes,' he said, and slipped into character as easily as woman donning lipstick. He fanned shaky fingers across my upper chest, catching the spaghetti-thin straps, of my camisole on his pinkies. 'May I, Katherine? May I look at your breasts?'

117

'Where are your parents?' I whispered.

He went very still. He must not have realised I wanted to play at being the same age. 'They'll be gone all night. We have all night, Katie.'

'Then, yes,' I said, my eyelids heavy with desire, my sex thrumming against his. 'Look at anything you want.'

He caught his lower lip between his teeth and eased the lacy bodice down, baring my left breast, then my right. Light as air, he stroked the skin to either side of my nipples. They stood prouder at the touch, crinkling and flushing from areola to tip, so sensitive they hurt.

'Oh, Katie.' His mouth hovered over a lengthening crest. 'You're so pretty. May I kiss you here?'

My heart jolted as he took my nipple between his lips and teased it with the tip of his tongue, a gentle flicker, like a snake testing the air. I slipped my arms around him and cupped his shoulders in my hands, gentling the satiny skin that overlay his bunching muscles. He groaned against my breast and suckled harder, as if my reciprocation truly meant the world to him. His manner was so convincing – his breathless wonder, his hesitation – that I sank into the fantasy like a stone.

He would have been handsome at seventeen, a little skinnier, a little less graceful; sex-crazed, I'm sure, but too considerate to ask the girls he knew for what he wanted so badly. I wished I'd been his first time, his first girl. I stroked his shoulder blades, dreaming of how it might have been.

We'd start slowly, holding hands on twice-weekly dates, with maybe a hug and a peck at the end of the night. Months would pass before we'd progress to petting above the waist with all our clothes on. We'd live for the sound of each other's heavy breathing, live for our stolen moments alone. Afterwards, we'd masturbate like fiends and practise Frenching our pillows. Soon we'd be master tongue kissers, exercising our new skills under the stairwell at school, at the cinema, in the back of Joe's car. Or maybe Joe would forbid us the back seat.

He might consider having that much room too great a temptation.

Joe would worry about temptation. Going all the way would have to be my idea. Despite his rampaging hormones, I'd have to lead him step by step to this place, to the bed of his childhood, the bed where he'd had his first wet dream – dreaming of me perhaps. Had he clenched this pillow between his legs and pretended it was me? Had he thrust and groaned and left his hot young seed on the cotton that even now cradled my head?

I moaned at the image and his body shifted, restless with lust. His sucking slowed. I held my breath. As though he feared I'd stop him, his hand skimmed down my side to the crook of my knee. He massaged the tendon there, startling me with pleasure. Then he reversed direction, creeping up my thigh an inch at a time until he ruffled the curls that fringed my lower lips.

I twitched in response but didn't tell him to stop. Braver now, he parted the curls and began to explore, his movements tentative but thorough. The tip of his finger slipped into my sheath. He gasped when it clutched him.

'Touch me,' he said against my dampened breast. 'Please. I'm dying to feel your hands on me. I've been dreaming about it since the first day of class. You wore that tight navy crew neck and the short plaid skirt with the pleats. I got hard the minute you smiled at me. You wound one gold curl around your finger, kind of shy, and I thought I'd melt. When you took the chair in front of me, I pretended I was under you, that you would slide right down on my dick. I remember you couldn't sit still and I wondered if you could feel me staring at the muscles of your calves. I wanted to crawl under your chair and bite one. Every time you squirmed I got stiffer, as if I really were inside you. It wouldn't go down, either. I was hard all through Calculus and you weren't even there. I had to jack off in the men's before gym or the guys would have seen. I came so hard I thought I'd bust something.' His voice sank to a throaty rasp. 'I pretended you were doing it for me.'

'Like this?' I twisted my hand into his briefs so I could hold his velvety length, and ran my hand down his cock the way a girl would – a little nervous, and more than a little curious.

His body jerked. 'Yes. Oh, yes, slide it up and down. Ring it tight. I won't break. Yeah, that feels nice. Your hand is so soft. Oh, God, I can't believe we're really doing this.'

His breath came rougher as he suckled me, moving now to my second breast. He pulled me further into his mouth, circling me with the tip of his tongue, then laving me with the soft wet flat. The throb in my sex deepened to an ache. I groaned.

'Tell me what you want, Katie. Show me what makes you feel good.'

'Here.' I captured his hand and guided his longest finger in a circle round my clitoris. 'Rub me here. Steady. Yes, like that, but a little harder.'

I whimpered deep in my throat as he caught the motion, my own motion, pushing and pulling the soft hood along the tender shaft. Having him do it felt so good, I had to breathe hard to keep from coming.

'You're slippery,' he said, hushed with awe. 'You're wet and hot and I can feel your skin quivering. Does that mean you want me?'

'Yes.' I pulled his head up for a deep, tonguey kiss. 'I want you.'

He shuddered and his cock jumped in my hand. 'Say that again. Say my name.'

'I want you, Joey.'

'Again,' he demanded, then kissed me so hard I couldn't comply. I gasped for air when he finally released me. We stared at each other. He smiled, all boyish triumph and charm.

'I love you,' he said.

My jaw dropped. This time there was no mistaking the words. He sealed my gaping mouth with a kiss, this one a soft, swooning exploration. I found myself wanting to say it back: *I love you, too, Joe. I love you.* The words knotted in my chest like a physical pain. But how did I know what he felt today would last? Silenced by doubt, I held him tight, one hand steadying the back of his neck, the other stroking his cock. He gathered me closer, his body strong and sheltering, his caresses gentle. What had I done to deserve a lover as sweet as this?

Just say what you feel now, I told myself. Let tomorrow be. A moan slid through my throat, warming it for the declaration.

But, 'I'm taking off my briefs,' he warned, before I could tumble over the fence.

He wrestled them off and settled back with a heartfelt sigh. His hips lifted. His hand fumbled between us, pushing the head of his cock down between my legs. It sprang up at once, caught against my pouting folds.

'I won't put it in, I promise.' His buttocks clenched and hollowed as he shafted my vulva. 'I'll just rub up and down like this. Oh, God.' He gritted his teeth. 'Can you feel that, bare skin to bare skin? That is so good. I can feel everything. Lord, I wish I could slide inside you like this, with nothing between us. I've never done it, but with you – Can you feel it? Do you like it?'

I could only gasp and nod. His fingers slipped between us, parting my folds so that his long hot column slid directly over my clitoris.

I clutched his buttocks to hold him snug.

He laughed deep in his throat. 'You do like that. I want you to come for me. Can you, Katie?'

'Soon,' I promised, hitching against him faster, harder.

He bent to kiss me, swallowing my cries of excitement. His tongue flickered and probed. Sweat rolled down his neck. My tension wound higher. My thighs tightened on his narrow hips, mashing our curls together, ink and honey, until they rasped like static on silk. I half expected sparks to fly.

'Oh,' I cried, gulping for air. 'Soon, soon. Don't stop.'

121

His strokes lengthened. The broad flare of his cock-head brushed my gate. It dipped inside for an instant, making me clench instinctively to draw him in.

'No,' he gritted, sliding by more forcefully. 'I won't push it in. Just – Yes, do that again. Suck at me with your cunt. That feels so – You're so wet. The sound it makes – Oh, God, I'd kill to fuck you right now.'

He rubbed me faster, so fast the friction made its own heat. His glans flicked clit and sheath with every furious pass. He had my hips in a death grip. His teeth were bared in a silent snarl. The veins on his neck stood out. Lord, the sight of him made me hot. The train was coming. I could hear it chuffing, feel its rumbling vibration – down my spine, through my womb. My neck arched off the bed. I wailed at the unbearable tension. My nails bit his heaving buttocks, and then my climax broke in a long, shuddering wave that rattled me to the bone.

'Ah,' I sighed, collapsing back against his prim navy coverlet. 'That was good.'

Joe kissed my forehead with more energy than I expected. His jaw was shaking. That's when I realised he'd held back his own climax.

'Don't move,' he ordered, ignoring my whimper as he pulled away, taking all the heat in the room with him.

He backed off the bed, then stood at the foot staring at me with hungry gold eyes. I stretched, arms over head, showing off my sex-flushed curves, letting my thighs fall open. His cock strained upward from its thatch of black, shiny with my juices, dark with his blood. I ran my palms over and around my breasts, lifting them to his slitted gaze. He growled a warning. 'I've got to get inside you. I'm running upstairs but I'll be right back. You keep everything warm for me.'

'I will,' I promised, and slid my hand between my legs.

The sight of me masturbating snagged him a foot from the door. His eyes widened, then grew stern. 'Thirty seconds,' he said, and slipped out the door before I could distract him again.

As soon as he left, I leapt out of bed. I knew just what I wanted to do for him, but I didn't have much time. I rummaged through three drawers before I found his navy crew neck. The sleeves were too long, but other than that it fit. The wool scratched my breasts as I squirmed back into my narrow navy skirt. Neither pleated nor plaid, it was nonetheless a reasonably good match for his schoolgirl fantasy.

I had just enough time to smooth my hair and turn his sturdy ladderback chair towards the door. Joe skidded in from the hall. He scowled at his empty bed, then did a double take to find me dressed. He still wore his socks. God knows why, but he looked sexy as hell with his clean white athletic socks, his long hairy legs, and a hard-on fit to make a tart blanch.

'What are you doing?' he asked.

Fighting an urge to giggle, I wound a curl around my finger and smiled from under my lashes.

'Oh,' he said, recognising the image. A surge of excitement crimsoned his skin from flat, ridged stomach to sweat-beaded forehead. 'Oh, boy.'

I nudged the chair an inch forward. Joe shook himself and stepped closer. He sat slowly, his eyes wide, his breathing shallow, his cock bobbing high. He'd rolled a condom on already; he really didn't want to waste time. He smoothed his hands down his thighs. I glanced towards the door.

It was closed. The mirror on its back caught my eye. Though small, it still held possibilities. Humming one of Joe's melodies, I lifted it off its hook and set it at a tilt on the floor. I stepped backwards until my legs bumped his knees. Yes, we'd be able to see what we were doing – from the waist down, anyway.

A sharp inhalation told me Joe saw our reflection, too.

Without a word to break the spell, he gathered the hem of my skirt and bared my sex. I shifted my legs wider and reached back for the arm of the chair. He cupped my buttocks in his palms, both steadying me and kneading the muscles with lascivious intent.

Smiling, I lowered myself over him, stopping only once to adjust the angle of his penis.

Wet as I was, he slipped in like a charm, thick, meaty, and fantastically hot.

His breath scalded my ear as I engulfed him. He sucked the side of my neck hard enough to leave a mark, then crooked his chin over my shoulder to watch the image of our union.

His hands caressed my thighs, my belly, then centred on my mons. He pulled my labia back to expose the disappearance of his root into my body. The blade of my clit stood out sharply between his fingers and the pink convolutions of my sex glistened with secretions, visibly quivering as my body tried to pull him deeper. He exhaled softly and traced my stretched inner lips with one finger. His scrotum darkened.

'If I don't get deeper, I'll die,' he said.

He jerked his legs to the edges of the chair, widening my thighs in the process. I arched my spine. His cock slid a half-inch further. We both convulsed with a sharp throb of lust.

'Now,' he whispered, thrusting his second arm under my borrowed sweater. 'Move with me, sweetheart.'

He banded his arm beneath my breasts and lifted me, grunting with effort and longing before easing me back. I gripped both chair arms to help him, pushing up and sinking down. We found our rhythm and hastened it, all the while watching in the mirror the age-old in and out, the hungry tensing of our thighs, the ecstatic curling of our toes.

His angle of entry felt incredible. Every stroke compressed some sweet spot I hadn't known I had. I began to groan with pleasure, which made him shiver and swell. His arm tightened on my ribs. Almost before I knew it, he bore my full weight.

'Oh, man, I'm close,' he said. I couldn't believe how strong he was. Every motion was perfectly controlled and intense. He hit that sweet spot with the sleek, hot hammer of his cock until all that kept me from shattering was force of will.

I cried out, feeling him stretch inside me, feeling his thighs go rigid beneath my legs.

'Now,' he groaned, shoving upward with all his might. 'Come, baby, please.' But I was already there.

We climaxed as one, a rich explosion of sensation. Every time he jerked, darts of fierce, sweet pleasure showered me from his cock, and melted, and flowed like maple syrup through my veins. My neck sagged, my limbs went limp, and still he came. Finally, nothing remained but aftershocks, tiny spasms of sweetness like a ripe burst of fruit.

'Ah,' he sighed, long and low. He shifted me sideways and cradled me. 'Now that was good.'

I kissed his cheek. His self-congratulatory smile had to be the most adorable expression I'd ever seen. How could I not love him? Without warning, tears burnt my eyes.

'Don't worry, Katycat.' He hugged my shoulders. 'I know you'll say the words when you're ready.'

If he knew that, he knew a hell of a lot more than I did.

Chapter Eight
With a Song in his Heart

Sean and I took to wandering around the house humming Joe's favourite melodies. Sean mangled them worse than I did, but Joe was too flattered to care.

'You like that one?' he'd say, shyly pleased. 'You don't think it's too obvious?'

'No, no,' we'd assure him. 'It's just obvious enough.'

Then he'd attack whichever songbird was closest, backing us into the nearest wall for a big, wet kiss. Needless to say, we learned to listen carefully to his tunes.

One Sunday, contrary to habit, Joe tacked twenty minutes' worth of carpet in complete silence. Thanks to Sean's obsessive-compulsive leadership, our exercise room was almost done. The panelling was up, and the new ceiling treatment. We had a turn-of-the-century, wall-length mirror complete with gilded frame and barre. The barre was intended for my use, in spite of the fact that I could barely spell *plié*. In the opposite corner, Sean had constructed an 'L' of seating and storage space. Non-domestic that I was, I hired a seamstress to uphol-ster its cushions in muted rose and moss. All that remained was to finish the carpet, install the skirting board – which I was sanding to fit – and rescue Sean's weight-lifting gear from his parents' basement. I knew he was looking forward to that. He spoke of his body-building equipment with a warmth most men reserved for their first car.

'No more gym fees,' he'd crow. 'You have no idea the return I could be getting on that money.'

I didn't bother to ask. Our soon-to-be graduate could wax poetic on his first share purchase, too. I'm not certain he realised I knew how to invest my own money. His advice wasn't bad, mind you, and he meant well – just as he did when he dropped to his knees behind Joe, gripped his neck muscles and squeezed.

'Yo, buddy. You tired today?'

Joe's head swung around in surprise. 'What do you mean?'

'You weren't singing. Did we wear you out last night?'

'I'm fine.' He shook Sean off and returned to tacking the thick maroon carpet. 'I'm saving my voice.'

'Saving it for what?' I asked.

A blush stained the back of his neck. 'I've been composing some songs for a student musical. I thought I'd audition.'

Sean set down the glue gun. 'What musical?'

Joe mumbled something I couldn't make out from my post at the sanding bench. But Sean could hear. He sat back on his heels and smacked his forehead. '*Captain Blood?* Don't tell me it's that vampire-pirate thing everyone has been talking about.'

'I'm afraid so.'

Sean wrinkled his nose. 'I thought you didn't want people rolling their eyes at your stuff.'

Joe rubbed his temple with the heel of his palm. 'The story isn't mine, just the songs.'

Sean opened his mouth.

'I think that's great,' I said, before he could put his foot in it again. 'Is the audition tomorrow?'

Joe shot a wary glance at Sean and nodded.

'Well, I hope you get it. I can't imagine anyone else doing your music justice.'

'Of course, they could,' Joe said. 'I made sure the

songs weren't too hard to sing. I mean, not every person with a good voice can read complicated music.'

Sean pretended to strangle him. 'If they're that easy, maybe I should audition.'

Joe twisted free and looked at him. Sean couldn't sing his way out of a paper bag. Still, Joe was nothing if not polite. 'Um, well, sure you could.'

Sean slapped his shoulder. 'Just kidding. I'd rather watch you sing your heart out.'

'The director might not cast me,' he warned.

Sean dismissed that possibility with a soft *fft*. 'He'd have to be blind as well as deaf to pass you over.'

'I agree,' I said, and Joe gave us both a bashful kiss.

The call came through while I was up on the coffee balcony consulting with a publisher's rep. Four times a year the reps landed on Mostly Romance's doorstep, slavering to sell me the next season's releases. The process required many hours per salesperson, but I enjoyed it. The high-stakes gamble of it got my blood going – with the thrill of haggling thrown in for good measure. Plus, I loved seeing what my favourite authors had in store for me.

Consequently, when Keith tapped the balcony with our ivory-topped cane – the magic phone wand, Marianne called it – I told him to take a message.

'It's Joe,' he said, just loud enough for me to hear. 'It sounds important.'

My heart stumbled. Had something happened? Was he hurt? Barely taking time to excuse myself to the rep, I rushed downstairs.

Normally, I take personal calls in my office, but at the moment that was thirty steps too far. Instead, I joined Keith behind the counter, turned my back to the shop, and stoppered my second ear against a mixture of Latin jazz and happy customer hubbub.

'Joe?' I said, my palm sweating on the phone.

'Kate.' He sounded out of breath. 'How soon can you get off work?'

'I'm busy with a rep right now.' His groan of disappointment sank straight to my gut. 'Why? What's wrong?'

'Nothing,' he said, making me sag with relief. 'But I got the part and I –' His voice dropped a register. 'I really need to celebrate.'

I clamped my thighs together against a sudden flare of heat. I pictured him in a phone booth on campus somewhere, his muscular shoulder propped on the glass, his prick a painful swelling between his legs. He'd cup it in that way he had, squeezing the whole package hard, as if he could contain his lust by pressure alone.

'Oh,' I said. Now I was breathless. 'Congratulations. I wish I could get off but –'

'I wish I could get you off.'

I swallowed and clutched the receiver tighter. 'I'm tied up for at least a couple of hours.'

'I wish you were tied up,' he responded, not missing a beat.

Heat flooded my face. I covered one cheek with a trembling hand. Beneath my grey cashmere dress, my nipples grew erect with embarrassing zeal – and he was just warming up.

'Tying you spread-eagled against the wall would be nice,' he continued. 'I would like to go down on you first, but I don't think I can wait. I'll have to fuck you first, I think, real hard and fast, with long, thick strokes that go deeper and deeper until I'm lifting you off your feet every time I drive home. I'll try to last as long as I can. I'll clench my fists and grind my teeth, but it won't do much good. I'll need it too bad, need you squirming hot and silky on my dick, need your tongue in my mouth and your breasts in my hands. You'll want to hold me, to grip the small of my back and keep me close. But it'll be impossible. Your hands will be tied, and your ankles. You'll feel how badly I need to come and you'll wonder: will he last long enough to get me off? But I might not, Kate, because you'll feel so good and I'll have waited so long. It'll go fast at the end – real pile-driver thrusts.

That knot will tighten at the base of my cock, that ache in my balls that says, now, now, now. I'll pull back slowly, trying to hold on. I'll stop with the head clasped inside your beautiful cunt. You'll feel me shaking. You'll say, "Do it, Joe. Do it." So I'll ram back as deeply as I can. And then –'

He paused. 'Then I'll come so hard, I'll fill you with jet after jet, shooting straight for your womb, dribbling hot and thick down your thighs. I'll go down on you then, Katycat. I'll suck your little clit like a chocolate kiss. I'll savour the way we taste together. It's so good, salty and musky, like eating sex. Mm, I could suck you for hours. But I'll just wait until you start making those kitten cries in your throat. You know the ones: "Ah, ah, now, Joe, please."'

His mimicry was uncanny. I blushed harder. As though he knew, he chuckled wickedly. 'Then I'll give you everything you've been waiting for – everything.'

He paused to let the images soak in. I heard him breathing hard on the other end of the line. Oh my God, I thought, what I wouldn't give to have him inside me now.

'Kate?' he said, shaking me from my thrall.

'I'll finish as quickly as I can,' I said, my throat so tight I sounded hoarse. Evading Keith's knowing smile, I hunched closer to the phone. 'Unfortunately, there's no way I'll be done in less than two hours. I'm with a book rep and I simply can't delegate.'

'Hell.' I pictured his hand falling away from his crotch.

'Sorry,' I said, wanting to call him sweetie but constrained by Keith's big ears.

'No, I'm the one who's sorry. I know you've got a business to run. It's just I've got a stiff the size of New Jersey and I wanted to share it with you.'

'I want that too, honey,' I said, touched by his disappointment.

Keith stifled a snicker. I glared at him. 'Look, I'll come straight home as soon as I'm done. And I promise, I promise I'll make it up to you.'

'I'll hold you to that,' he warned.

'Good,' I said, and kissed the phone as discreetly as I could.

Keith's shoulders shook with amusement.

'If you laugh, I'll fire you.'

He turned his palms out in surrender. 'No, no, Ms Winthrop. I think it's sweet. But maybe you should train me to deal with the reps.' His grin bared his crooked front teeth. 'In case of emergency.'

'Pipsqueak,' I muttered, but my body sang with energy as I rushed back upstairs.

A trail of blood-red rose petals led me from the hall to the basement door. Over its cut-glass knob a white scarf was looped – a dashing silk scarf.

I tossed it loosely around my neck and rubbed the delicate fringe across my cheek. The scent of Aramis clung to its flowing folds: Joe's scent. Muscles humming with anticipation, I started down the stairs.

Halfway down, I found two sparkling goblets and a bottle of respectable burgundy, its cork partially removed to allow the wine to breathe. Tucking the booty under my arm, I descended the remaining treads.

'Joe?' I said, reaching bottom.

'Here,' he called softly, 'waiting for you.'

I rounded the corner and laughed. Joe was lounging like a pasha on our new red exercise mat. Naked except for a long black scarf – the companion to my own – he sat with one leg bent up and one bent down, his formidable jewels bared to the world. The trail of red petals ended in a puddle above his eager cock. The true *pièce de résistance*, however, was his rakish black eye-patch. Joe was definitely an original. I'd never known a man with the confidence to deck himself out so exotically.

Too bad the mirror still wore its protective plastic coating, or I would have enjoyed a back view, too.

'Well, hello,' I said, quickening with arousal despite my amusement. 'The vampire-pirate, I presume?'

Joe lifted his hips in unmistakable offering. Petals fluttered to the floor. 'In the undead flesh.'

'Tell me you're not wearing fangs,' I said, though I doubted even that could dull my desire.

He bared his teeth for me. 'The fangs only come out when I feel the hunger.'

I cast a suspicious glance at his sex. 'You look hungry now. Are you sure it's safe to approach?'

'As long as you bring the wine.' He waved me closer with two fingers, the picture of an autocratic male. I hesitated. His arm lowered and he stroked his cock with his strong, graceful hand. 'Come. I grow impatient.' His shaft lengthened at the treatment, demonstrating just how impatient he could get.

The sight of its swarthy glory convinced me to obey. I knelt beside him on the mat, and set the bottle and glasses down. Mesmerised, I extended my hand towards his petal-bedecked thatch.

'Pretty.' I toyed with a single petal, a single glossy curl. His erection jerked. He let go of his shaft, unable to bear even his own touch now. My gaze lifted to his and he smiled, his face shining so brightly with love a flower of pure happiness blossomed in my chest.

'Joe,' I whispered, touching his breastbone with one wistful finger.

He caught my hand to his lips and kissed the finger, and wrapped the soft curl of his tongue around the pad. My sex quivered with longing. I remembered his promise to suck me like a chocolate kiss. Joe had such a clever mouth.

'Do you still want a quickie?' I asked, game for anything at that point.

He released my finger and shook his head. A lock of hair fell across his silly, sexy eye-patch. 'Not yet. For now I want to anticipate how much I'm going to enjoy the quickie.'

He sat up and rubbed the front of his body against my grey cashmere dress. His erection stood far above horizontal. I could only imagine how good the downy knit felt against its stretched, sensitive skin.

'This is nice,' he purred, turning his cheeks from side to side across my breasts. 'Soft.'

A draught tickled my buttocks. He was gathering the dress up my legs. The feel of my lacy suspenders brought him up short. I wore stockings today, sheer white silk stockings.

'Kate,' he said with a quiet laugh. 'Have I mentioned you wear the best underwear?' Without waiting for a response, he pulled the stretchy dress over my head, pausing only to tug the white scarf back through the neck. When the dress was gone, he froze. My underthings were all of snow-white lace: my French-cut panties, my push-up bra, my suspender belt.

Like most men, Joe appreciated nice presentation. Now he stared, transfixed, and glided his hands down the nipped-in curve of my waist. 'Perfect,' he said. With the considering pucker of an artist, he arranged the ends of the scarf along my cleavage.

To my surprise, he turned away then and poured the wine, half a glass each, after which he recorked the bottle and set it out of harm's way.

'Just enough to relax you,' he said.

I wondered why he thought I needed relaxing.

He waited to enlighten me until the crimson liquid slid down my throat. He smoothed his palms down the fall of my white scarf, then tugged the ends of his black one.

'May I tie you up?' he asked.

My brows rose. He'd never expressed any interest in playing the dominant before and his request threw me off balance. I didn't want to say 'yes', even though I knew if Sean were asking I'd have complied without batting an eyelid. Then again, Sean might not have asked.

'I'd rather not,' I said carefully, unsure which aspect of the situation unnerved me the most. 'It's okay for fantasy, but in real life I prefer holding you.'

His mouth curved in a gentle smile. 'That's all right. I want you to feel comfortable.'

His ready acceptance disappointed me – and I couldn't explain that, either.

'I'm sorry,' I said, suddenly miserable.

'Shh.' He gathered me in his arms and kissed my hair. 'Whatever you want, sweetheart. That's what I want.'

But I'm not sure what I want, I almost said.

Dipping me back on the mat, he began to remove his eye-patch. I caught his hand.

His lips twitched. 'You like my disguise, eh?'

I nodded, feeling foolish. He kissed my embarrassment away with sharp, stinging kisses that travelled across my jaw and down my neck. The point of his tongue drew a cool trail down my carotid.

'I can smell your blood,' he murmured in an Eastern European accent too authentic to provoke laughter.

In truth, it excited me. I squirmed under his weight and gripped his back. His lips tightened on my throat. The suction of his cheeks drew my vulnerable flesh between his teeth.

'I'm going to mark you,' he warned, the words a dark rumble against my skin. 'Everyone will know you're mine.'

'I am yours,' I said, my voice tinged with melancholy.

He pulled back to search my eyes. I touched the stiff canvas eye-patch and wondered, without quite knowing why, which of us was blinder.

'I am yours,' I repeated.

He seemed to understand this was as close as I could get to saying, 'I love you.'

His breath escaped in a low, longing sigh and his hips surged into the cradle of my loins. He pressed the suede-soft skin of his cock between scallops of lace, its prominent veins a tantalising variation in texture. His eyes drifted shut, then opened, molten with hunger.

'Sweetheart.' His pelvis moved in slow, incendiary circles. 'I think I need that quickie now.'

But rather than rush straight in, he unsnapped my

suspenders one by one, soothing each tiny welt with a butterfly kiss.

'Lift,' he ordered, and slid my panties down my legs. My stockinged feet received their share of kisses, and my knees. He kneaded my thighs like a cat preparing to settle in, then deftly redid my garters. The lace now framed my naked sex, my lips pink with readiness, my clit peeping through the swollen folds. He pressed a single kiss into my honey-brown fleece, right above the rosy target.

'Later,' he promised, and shifted up to fit his cock to the mouth of my vagina. He rocked back and forth in tiny tormenting surges, not entering, merely testing the snug resilience of my sexual muscles.

I lifted my knees.

'Please,' I said, 'come inside.' But he continued to tease me, adding an upward slide to the motion so that my clit entered into the torture as well.

Frustrated, I hitched my legs higher still, lifting until my calves curved over his hard, broad shoulders. The position opened me so thoroughly the head popped inside at the next slight push.

Joe's mouth 'O'd at my unexpected flexibility.

Before he could regroup, I crossed my ankles behind his neck and pulled, swallowing three quarters of his cock at a single stroke.

'Oh, man,' Joe breathed.

He resettled himself to accommodate this change in posture, shifting his elbows and catching my hands in his. He laced our fingers together, locking them tight.

Determined to press home my advantage, I contracted my leg muscles one last time, forcing him the rest of the way inside. He filled me wonderfully, his cock thick and vital, his breathing harried. I could have stayed that way all night, but the warm, flickering depths of a woman's sex is one place a man has trouble keeping still.

Joe grunted with impatience. 'If you don't ease up, I won't be able to move.'

'Maybe I like you where you are.'

'Please,' he said, his pout a charming put-on. 'I've been waiting forever.'

I couldn't resist him. After all, I'd been waiting, too.

Once I'd relaxed my grip, he set a single-minded pace. Digging his knees into the mat, he focused his energy on the motion of his lower body. Straight and hard, he plunged. Firm and sure, he withdrew, tugging slightly each time his glans caught my brink. As we coupled, he spread my arms wider and wider until his chest weighted mine and a delicious pressure burnt in my thighs.

I guess his need for orgasm robbed him of his usual consideration. I didn't mind the discomfort, though. He hadn't been thrusting a minute before I was sighing at every stroke. I hadn't thought anyone could drive me so high so fast.

Slim as he was, he wasn't too heavy to bear, but he was bigger than me and most of his weight was muscle. With his ribs compressing mine, I couldn't draw more than half a breath. I hoped that was the reason my head was spinning, but I suspected not. The way his arms stretched mine, the way he bore me into the mat made me feel overpowered – trapped even – in a way no bondage *aficionado*'s tricks could equal.

The subtle edge of panic went to my head faster than the burgundy. I both loved and feared the hold he had on me. I knew I'd have to give him up someday, but I no longer knew how I'd bear it. Worst of all, Joe had no idea what he was doing to me, hadn't accessed even half his power to vanquish.

He could feel my response, though. He could feel me clutch his pistoning shaft with all my might and hear the growing wetness of our meeting. His rhythm accelerated.

'Ah, God, I needed this,' he said, shaking sweaty hair out of his face. His cheek caressed my stockinged shin where it crooked his shoulder. 'I thought I'd go mad when I couldn't have you right away. I can't stand to be without you, Kate. I could take you a dozen times a day and never have too much.'

'Fuck me then,' I said, desperate to drown myself in this libidinous sea, desperate not to admit how dearly I wished his words were true. 'Fuck me hard and don't slow down.'

His gaze flew to mine, but he wasn't put off by my language. His cock shimmied inside me and his lungs expanded like a bellows. 'All right, then.' He regripped my hands and drew a deep, bracing breath. 'Hold on tight.'

He pumped me smooth as silk, his way slicked by my lubricious enthusiasm. I bit my lip until I tasted blood, throwing myself over the cliff of feeling, sucking him inward so strongly he needed all his strength to withdraw.

'Jesus,' he moaned, pulling harder. Cursing with impatience, he shoved the eye-patch off with his upper arm. 'Sorry, sweetheart. I can't stand not seeing all of you. You don't know how fantastic you look.'

I laughed and whispered, 'Fuck me, Joe. Fuck me.'

His weight slammed into me, faster, faster, his intrusion increasingly full, increasingly greedy. His face contorted with need. It was sheened with perspiration, blotched with colour. 'Oh, no,' he said, starting to shudder. 'Oh, Kate.'

He gulped for air. His hands gripped mine with bruising strength. He drove in one last time, the deepest, thickest yet, and spasmed at the extremity of his downstroke. For a second, I revelled in the strength of his convulsions, and then I, too, crashed through the barrier. He cried out when he felt me quiver, coaxing out my orgasm with a swift churning motion of his pelvis until another climax, this one even more forceful, barrelled over the first.

I'm not certain, but I think he came again, too. His eyes snapped open and his cock contracted in a second vigorous series of pulses. He stayed that way, breathing hard against my neck, pressed tight inside me, hipbone to hipbone, cock-head to womb, until his softening penis precluded the intimacy.

'Incredible.' He rolled carefully aside and peeled off the condom. 'Thank you, Katie.'

With the breath that remained to me, I assured him he was very welcome.

Afterwards, I lay in Joe's arms, sweaty and sated. I stared at the plastic-blurred mirror, at the ghost-shapes inside, and thought about Tom, my ex. I hadn't done that in a long time, not really remembered. Tom was handsome and charming and the kind of liar who never believed he'd done wrong. I think he loved me. I certainly wanted to believe he did. I had a dream – I suppose everyone does – of starting a better, more loving family than the one I grew up in.

Tom wanted people to think he was good, wanted to think it of himself. To that end, he could be sweet as hell – attentive, well-spoken.

So I let him bamboozle me.

He cheated on me a month after we were married. I found out, of course. Tom wasn't good at subterfuge. Maybe he didn't want to be. Eventually, I confronted him in a big ugly scene with me screaming and crying and him pleading how it didn't mean anything. It just happened.

'Weather just happens,' I remember shrieking. 'But people choose to be unfaithful.'

In the end, though, I didn't want to admit to my family and friends – and myself – that, at the supposedly mature age of twenty-nine, I'd made the biggest mistake of my life. I didn't want to confess that I'd been a shitty judge of character and my dream of happy home and hearth was truly down the toilet.

So I forgave him.

But not completely. Part of me sat back, folded its cynical arms, and waited for him to knock the bottom out again. He knocked it out all right, more than once, but he never broke my heart like the first time – not even when he ran off with my seventeen-year-old niece.

He said my coldness killed our marriage. He may have been right. My only regret was that I hadn't killed it sooner. I wondered why I hadn't. Had I felt comfortable dancing that sick little dance with Tom, knowing all his moves, knowing he'd always live down to my new low image of men? And what about now? Was I over it? More grown-up? Sadder but wiser? Or had I lost a precious seed of faith I ought to be trying to recover?

'You're awfully quiet,' Joe said, stroking my curls as if I were a child.

I snuggled closer to his chest. We'd have to get up soon and dress. The basement wasn't as warm as the rest of the house.

'I love you,' he said, and kissed the top of my head.

The weight of expectation compressed the chambers of my heart. I knew I should say it back. I did love him. I just couldn't open my mouth. Was I still waiting for the next blow to fall? Did I intend to keep my guard up forever?

'I love you, too,' I said, to prove I'd escaped my past.

Joe sucked in a breath and hugged me close. 'Kate,' he whispered. 'Oh, Katie.'

I'd made him happy. But I didn't feel any better.

Chapter Nine
Captain Blood

Our days took on a new rhythm once Joe became Captain Blood.

Though he hadn't graduated yet, Sean obtained a part-time accountancy position at a law firm downtown. He loathed the stuffy my-cell-phone's-smaller-than-yours atmosphere, but performed his duties so brilliantly no one dared take him to task for breezing in late – in blue jeans, no less.

Actually, brilliance alone could not protect him. Brilliant people get fired every day. But Sean had an air that said only an idiot would refuse to let him have his way. He believed this in every fibre of his being and, as a result, other people believed it, too.

It seemed Sean was top in every arena.

Faced with some new and expensive desires, Joe left his job at the students' union to work for Sean's Uncle Mike, the demolition king. The work was strenuous, but the pay enabled him to hire a vocal coach and buy a second-hand piano – which we installed in our already eclectic gym.

Now that Joe had accompaniment, the extent of his talent grew clear. The first time I heard him play *Captain Blood*'s lush, humorous overture, the first time I heard him sing the catchy tunes he'd dropped into that beautiful net, the hair on the back of my neck stood up. This was no apprentice work. This was the creation of a genuine artist – not as mature as he would be in ten years, or twenty, but far from child's play.

When I stuttered out my amazement, he confessed – bashfully – that he'd been a child prodigy. Only his mother's insistence on a normal home life had kept his Aunt Florence from dragging him on tour.

'Your mother was right,' I said. 'You grew up modest and well adjusted. Now, instead of being burnt out and screwed up, you've got a brilliant career ahead of you.'

He rubbed the bridge of his nose. 'If I'm lucky.'

'Luck!' I shook his shoulder. 'Sweetie, talent like yours makes its own luck.'

I could see he doubted my claim. Pride swelled in my heart, and resignation. Joe might not know it yet but he was going places, big places. *Captain Blood* was just the start of it.

As for me, unlike my busy housemates, I had far too much time on my hands. Keith proved an efficient manager, eager to assume any responsibility I'd allow him. My overtime shrank to nothing, but now there was no one to greet me at the end of the day. Joe had rehearsals and Sean worked evenings.

Only bed remained sacred. Even if they stumbled home at midnight, the men would climb the final flight to my room. We were, however, sleeping a lot more than we used to.

I began to think more seriously about opening a second shop. Marianne, who did our books, said I couldn't afford to tie up our capital, but I didn't see the good in letting it stagnate. Our financial position was sound. We weren't in debt. Interest rates were low. It seemed to me that now was an ideal time to expand.

Of course, feeling neglected by my lovers probably was a lousy reason to do so. The problem was I'd become spoilt. I'd lost my knack for entertaining myself, by myself. Rather than recultivate my self-sufficiency, I moped.

141

Sean and Joe may have been busy, but not too busy to notice my gloom. They spoke to me in kinder, gentler tones. They made me breakfast and let me read the paper first. Eventually, shame for my behaviour jarred me from my sulks.

'I'm going to enjoy whatever time I have left,' I announced one night as we all lay in bed.

Snow fell outside the dormer window, like feather pillows bursting beneath the street lamps. In the pearly glow, my lovers struggled from their half-slumber to blink at me.

'What are you talking about?' Sean asked, his hair mashed to his head by the pillow. 'You contracted a fatal disease or something?'

That's when I realised only I could read the writing on the wall. Only I knew our days together were numbered.

Joe slung his arm across my belly. 'Don't worry, Kate. We'll have more time for love-making once these rehearsals are over.'

'I could use some more action myself,' Sean grumbled. He squirmed closer. He liked sleeping in the nude. His smoothly muscled chest warmed my side and, when he hitched one hairy leg over mine, his cock and balls warmed my hip. Voicing his complaint seemed to have broken his inertia. His penis twitched, slowly but surely assuming its full girth and vigour.

'Man, oh, man.' He insinuated his erection beneath the hem of my T-shirt so he could rub it skin-to-skin. 'How tired are you, Kate?'

I grinned. 'Not that tired.'

'Hey, Joe, toss me a condom,' he said, but Joe was snoring and I had to dig the prophylactic out myself.

That taken care of, Sean pushed me on to my side and entered me from behind. His cock slid into my sheath as if it were buttered, ecstasy after days of doing without. I arched back for more. When he gave it to me, I heaved a grateful sigh.

'Me, too,' he said.

He slipped his arm around my front to caress my sex,

then gripped the headboard for leverage. Soon his hips buffeted my backside. Every thrust pushed his warmth deeper, filling me with rich, animal sensation. I reached behind me to hold his flank. His breath rushed beside my ear, catching each time he struck home. I loved the simplicity of this act, the directness, the way his with-drawals grew shorter as his climax approached – as if he couldn't bear to leave his snug, warm mooring. Neither of us took long to come, but I still couldn't believe Joe slept through the whole thing.

'I'm still hard,' Sean griped, pulling reluctantly out.

'Pull the other leg, why don't you?' I pushed him on to his back and straddled him – and saw he wasn't kidding. He'd come long and hard, but his cock jutted upward along my belly, nearly as thick as when we'd started. I stripped off my T-shirt and used it to blot the remains of our exertions. When I threw it aside, his hands went straight for my breasts. He kneaded their soft weight with a gentleness I found as relaxing as it was arousing. Happy as a cat, I rolled my head luxuriously around my shoulders.

'One more as a nightcap?' I suggested, stroking his arms.

He grimaced. 'Why not two?'

'Greedy.'

'But I'm up now, and ol' Willy here hasn't got lucky in days.'

'Try a week, mister.'

He wagged his head at the horror of it. 'The working world sucks.'

'What if –' I bent to lick the rim of his ear '– I suck you instead?'

His shoulders hunched at the tickling caress. 'Later. When I need inspiration.'

'You find my humble skills inspiring?'

'Babe.' He chucked me under the chin. 'Your mouth is one of the seven wonders of the world.'

I was still preening over the compliment when he lifted me on to him.

Joe woke sometime during our third bout, probably when Sean pulled me out of bed and started rogering me over the squeaky footboard.

Joe rubbed sleepy eyes, then burrowed one arm beneath the covers. I followed its progress down his chest and between his legs. The sheets rustled. His left leg fell to the side. The hump that was his hand began an unmistakable pumping motion.

Sean laughed in my ear. 'He must be half-asleep. He never jacks off in front of people.' He reached for the rumpled chenille coverlet.

'Don't wake him,' I whispered. 'I want to watch.'

But such passivity was foreign to Sean's nature.

'Yo, Sleeping Beauty.' He lofted the covers. 'Wake up and join us.'

Joe screwed his eyes more tightly shut. His hand faltered, then resumed its steady masturbatory rhythm. I guess he wanted that release no matter who was watching.

'Too tired to get up,' he mumbled. 'Besides, it's cold out there.'

Not one to take 'no' for an answer, Sean reached around me, grabbed Joe's ankles and pulled him bodily to the foot of the bed.

'Hey!' Joe's eyes snapped open. 'I need my beauty sleep.'

Sean dragged the scrunched-up covers below Joe's waist. He wasn't fully hard yet and his erection wilted in the snow-chilled air, sagging back over the waist of his grey-plaid boxer shorts.

Joe groaned wretchedly. 'Now, look what you've done.'

'Too bad, pillowhead.' Sean smoothed my hair back from my face. 'Can you reach him?'

I gauged the height of the footboard and the distance to Joe's softening groin. 'Only with my hands.'

'On your knees then, Mr Capriccio.' He shook Joe's calf. 'No point wanking off when the mouth of the century can put you to sleep with a smile on your face.'

'Christ,' said Joe, hardly a flattering response, but he did grab the nearest post and heave himself upright. Sean tugged his boxers further down his hips.

Now that Joe was near enough to see what Sean and I were up to, his flagging erection rose. Encouraged, I cupped the weighty sac in my palm, following its curve back until I could press the firmer pad of his perineum. His involuntary jerk of response sent a thrill through my well-filled sex.

He touched my lips with his finger. 'Do you mind?'

Rather than waste time reassuring him, yet again, I bent forward and kissed him where it counted.

Being somewhat fresher than Sean or I, he came before either of us, then scrambled back under the covers to watch. He wore a contemplative look, his eyes quiet, his mouth softly curved. It made me wonder what he was thinking. Was he happy that Sean was happy? Was he memorising my response to Sean's personal repertoire of caresses? Or was he reviewing *Captain Blood*'s last rehearsal?

'I forgot to tell you,' he said as Sean began his final ascent. 'My Uncle Joe the cop finally got back to me about the noise complaint.'

'Uh huh,' said Sean, kneeing my legs apart so he could pump a little deeper. I doubted he had the faintest idea what Joe was talking about. He steadied my hip with one hand. 'Yeah, babe, that's it. Tighten around me. Man, you're good. You feel like you got a fist in there.'

'What did he find out?' I asked, though my concentration wasn't much better than Sean's. The outermost edge of an orgasm flirted around my cunt, there and then not there, there and then, oh, yes, it was definitely circling closer. I tilted back to take more of Sean's wonderfully fat rod. My hand slipped over his where it cupped my mons, urging him to work me harder. Our gathered fingertips brushed the place we joined.

'Sweet,' he gasped.

I heard Joe's next words through a fog of gathering need.

'Well, the estate agent is out. It wasn't a man. Uncle Joey couldn't get a name, but the switchboard operator said the caller was definitely an older woman.' Joe scooted close again and braced my shoulders for Sean's driving thrusts. 'I figure old Mrs Perelli must have had her hearing aid turned up that night.'

'Mrs Perelli. Right.' Sean gritted his teeth, his frantic pumping driving me to the brink. 'Right, right.' Coming hard, I bathed his cock in a hot flood of cream. 'Right, right, right. Ah, God.' He followed me with a groan of complete sensual exhaustion.

For the first time in a week, we all slept satisfied.

Finally, the day of *Captain Blood*'s opening performance arrived. Nervous as Tennessee Williams' cat, Joe had invited and disinvited us a dozen times during the previous week. 'You're going to hate it,' he moaned over the breakfast table, his hands shaking too badly to manage his bagel and coffee.

'We're not going to hate it,' I said. I spooned three teaspoons of honey into his mug. The honey was my attempt to reform Joe's sweet tooth. He permitted the interference, grudgingly, when I told him it was better for his throat than sugar.

'You might hate it,' he insisted. 'You can't be sure.'

'How could we not be sure?' Sean asked. Knowing Joe's preferences well, he spread a thick swathe of marmalade across a bagel half and tucked it into his friend's frowning mouth. 'We've heard most of it already.'

This was true. In the past two weeks, a parade of panicked cast members had snaked up and down my basement stairs, desperate for a few hours of coaching from their lyricist-composer. Joe agonised over the responsibility. He wasn't the musical director. He was still learning himself. What if he steered his fellow actors wrong? But the moment they arrived, he was patient and calm. The women, especially, gazed at him as though he'd hung the moon. Poor heartsick things. All he cared about was their grasp of the three Ps: posture, projection, and phrasing. Despite his worries, they improved under his tutelage. Plus, he spent enough time shoring up their fragile egos for them all to leave smiling. If only he could have done the same for himself. 'Basket case' was not too strong a term for Joe's current state.

'We'll love it.' I rubbed the back of his clammy hand. 'Partly because it's wonderful and partly because we love you. If you want an unbiased opinion, you'll have to ask someone else.'

He dropped his head into his hands. 'I can't do this. I'm running away to join the circus.'

Sean's palm slammed the table so hard my knife jumped to the floor. His chair scraped loudly as he shoved it back. 'Enough snivelling.' He strode around the table to stand beside Joe's chair. He put one hand on its back, one on the table, and stuck his nose in Joe's face. 'I trained you better than this, boy. Show a little spine.'

Joe sighed. 'Not now, Sean. I'm not in the mood to play drill sergeant.'

'Fuck if I care.' With an ease born of years of competitive wrestling, Sean plucked Joe out of his chair and slammed him, face front, into the refrigerator.

I gripped the table edge in shock, but I could see Joe wasn't hurt, only angry.

'Hey,' he said, trying to break free, an impossible task with his arms bent up between his shoulder blades.

'I can tell I've been neglecting your discipline,' Sean said in his formal master's voice. 'You know that kind of whining demands a good swift kick in the butt.' He planted his knee between Joe's cheeks as if to demonstrate where he'd land it.

'Piss off,' Joe said, his face plastered sideways against the freezer door. 'I told you I'm not in the mood.'

'Oh, really?' Quick as a flash, Sean had Joe's zip down and his cock out.

Joe growled in protest, but with two expert strokes his

penis stirred, and in six Sean had him as hard as I'd ever seen him.

'Not in the mood, eh?' Sean flicked the underside of the long flushed shaft with his thumbnail. 'I think you're dying to bend over and take me.'

Joe lost his cool at that. Luckily for him, the labour he'd been putting in for Sean's uncle had done his muscles some extra good. Gathering himself with a grunt of effort, he not only turned himself around but managed, inch by inch, to back Sean against the refrigerator.

'No more,' he said, panting but triumphant. The space between them shimmered with tension. Joe's cock stood out from his charcoal wool trousers like one of his pirate ship's guns. 'You fuck me face-to-face or not at all.'

Sure of his allure, whatever his position, Sean tilted his seam-splitting bulge until it tapped Joe's scrotum and set it swinging.

'Oh, really?' he cooed. 'Then you better make sure I enjoy it, big man.'

Joe reddened. A muscle ticked in his jaw. The overwhelming scent of testosterone had me squirming in my chair. I'd grown wet the minute Sean slammed his hand on the table, but now I was soaked.

Joe loomed over Sean, pressing closer. Before he could twist away, Joe covered his mouth and forced it open with the strength of his jaw. The instant their tongues clashed the two men melted, moaning and clutching each other as if they hadn't kissed in years.

I almost left the room then, but Joe caught the motion from the corner of his eye and waved me back to my chair.

Well, if he insists, I thought, hardly indifferent to the appeal of watching – especially when they were so into it.

Together, the heavy-breathing pair divested Sean – and only Sean – of his clothes. His powerful body gleamed under a coating of sweat. Joe wasted no time running his hands over every inch he could reach. But he soon ran out of patience.

Gripping his friend beneath the arms, he lifted Sean until their heads were level. Slowly, as if he couldn't believe he was allowing Joe to take the upper hand, Sean swung his legs around Joe's waist and crossed his ankles. His hips canted forward, positioning himself to be entered. Rapt, I watched the pucker of his anus flicker within its whorl of golden hair – with eagerness, I suspected, though trepidation might have played a part as well. Joe was no bantamweight.

'Kate,' Joe called, his voice reedy with strain.

I jumped to attention. By now, I knew how Joe's mind worked. I pawed through Sean's discarded clothes for the necessary accoutrements, finding what I wanted in the breast pocket of his plaid flannel shirt.

Joe paled as I rolled the sheath over his juddering erection, then whined through his teeth when I slathered KY Jelly down its length. I finished as quickly as I could.

'If you short-change me, I'll kill you,' Sean threatened, recognising Joe's I'm-about-to-die noises.

'Don't you worry,' Joe gritted back. 'I'm going to take my time and enjoy this.'

I wagged the lubricant in Sean's direction. 'Some for you?' I suggested gaily, feeling like a game show hostess.

'Why not?' Sean glanced down between their hard male bodies. Their cocks stood like crimson lances poised for battle. 'He's got a big piece of meat down there.'

Not fooled by his nonchalance, I knelt beneath him on the linoleum and squirted a generous dollop on to my fingers.

I took longer than I had to working it in. Whatever Joe claimed, I knew the heady novelty of playing top for once would preclude a long engagement. But if Sean were as primed as I intended him to be, brevity wouldn't matter.

I reached deeper, two fingers, then three, searching out his secret joy spot. The dark smooth passage clamped tight as I hit the walnut-sized swelling. Sean's moan sounded as if it were yanked from his throat. Gently, I massaged the hidden gland, awed by the power of this masculine mystery.

'Careful,' Sean said, even as his body curved to intensify the pressure I was exerting. 'Don't make me come.'

I reckoned he was primed enough then. I slid my fingers free with a tiny squelching noise. Both men quivered at the sound. I dropped a kiss on to Joe's shoulder and returned to my seat.

By that time, Sean required little coaxing to accept his burden. Joe nudged him once with the head of his cock, released a soft, wondering sigh, and pressed sleekly inside.

They kissed again when he hilted, open-mouthed and greedy. I felt that old sense of invading their privacy, though I knew they wanted me there. My discomfort was not strong enough to make me leave, however. I loved watching the rhythm of their thrusts. It was subtly different from a man and a woman's – because they were equals in strength, because different places wanted rubbing, and because they were hard and hard rather than hard and soft.

After a certain point, Sean lost control of his reactions. His eyes slid shut, his hands opened and closed on Joe's back, and his head lolled against the freezer door. He looked utterly debauched, flushed from head to toe and ravished with pleasure.

'Deep,' he said. The word came out slow as treacle. 'Fuck me a-all the way in.'

Joe shifted his feet, adjusted Sean's fit, and shafted him deeper. Even through his trousers, I saw his buttocks hollow with every stroke.

'How much longer?' he asked, his breath huffing between the words.

'Little longer,' Sean said in that same dreamy voice. 'Ah, Joey, that's good. You're so long. You're killing me.'

Joe laughed. 'Please die soon.' Though his face was red with effort, his eyes shone with affection.

'I'll come the minute you do,' Sean promised. His

head dropped back, exposing his throat. 'I'm floating . . .
right on the edge.'

Joe took him at his word and increased the pace. He
mouthed Sean's strong white neck and clutched his
buttocks until at last they both cried out, a harsh,
primitive sound, victory and surrender mixed as one.

A shadow of their pleasure jolted through my sex –
sweet but melancholy. What they shared between them,
I could never know.

I looked at the array of copper pots on the exposed
brick wall, at the bundle of thyme that hung from the
beam above my head. When I looked back, Sean had
both feet on the floor and was stroking Joe's head the
way a man might stroke a fierce, beloved dog. Joe bent
his neck to accept the caress, still mastered despite his
recent adventure.

'Better now?' Sean asked, his palm smoothing Joe's
glossy blue-black hair. 'Not so shaky?'

'Yes.' Joe clasped Sean's naked waist, leaning into him.
'Much better.'

Sean looked past his shoulder to wink at me. 'You
better go see to your sweetie, then. She'll think you
forgot all about her.'

Joe's head turned. Concern creased his sweaty brow.

'Later,' I said, reassuring him with a smile. I didn't
want to take away from their moment, their memory.

Joe's furrows deepened. 'Are you sure?'

'You know what the cooks say, Joe. Hunger is the best
sauce.'

Normally, I let Keith rule the roost on Fridays, but I
knew I'd chew my nails if I stayed home. I decided to
put in a half-day at Mostly Romance. Our new manager
seemed disappointed to see me – until I handed him the
company credit card and ordered him to Strawbridge &
Clothier to buy holiday decorations for the shop.

With both hands, Keith held out the shiny American
Express card, goggling as though it really were gold.

Then he dashed off before I could change my mind – or send him to Woolworth's instead.

Once he'd left, I parked myself behind our second cash register and prepared to schmooze customers. A few of my old faithfuls popped in to chat and before I knew it, an hour had passed without my dwelling on Joe more than a few hundred times.

Around ten, the man himself blew in on a gust of panic. He headed straight for me. 'Kate,' he said in a confiding, breathless tone. 'Do you know where I left my lucky eye-patch?'

I handed my customer her books and hoped she wasn't listening too closely. 'I wasn't aware you had an *un*lucky eye-patch.'

He jittered with impatience. 'The one I brought home the day I got the part is the lucky one.'

Of course it was. I thought for a moment. 'You checked the gym?'

'I turned it upside down.'

'What about the laundry room?'

He squinted in confusion.

'Remember last Tuesday?' I prompted.

His expression cleared. 'Oh, yeah. That was fun. Thanks, Kate. I'll run home and check.'

He turned to go but I called him back. I smiled at his worried, open face, more aware of his youth than I had ever been before.

Then again, my thirty-five-year-old husband had sworn by a lucky purple polo shirt. He never played squash without it, even when it started growing holes. Maybe what people say is true: men are always boys. I laid my hand on the shoulder of Joe's worn bomber jacket. 'Joe,' I said, judging his self-image too shaky right now for 'sweetie'. 'I hope you find your lucky eye-patch, but between you and me, you carry all the luck you need inside you. Your music is wonderful. Your singing is wonderful. Everything is going to be fine.'

Joe hung his head. 'I know. It's just a little extra insurance, to make me feel lucky.'

I was about to tug him across the counter for a kiss when Marianne strolled out from the back. I guess hope does spring eternal, because the sight of Joe perked her up at once.

'Hello, stranger,' she said in her best smoke-and-sugar croon.

She wore navy for once, a body-skimming, cleavage-baring velveteen dress. Her hips swayed with her approach and her heels clacked like gunshots on the hardwood floor. Joe winced when she grasped his jacket flaps and spread them apart to expose his nice charcoal suit.

'Don't you look professional?' She tapped the knot of his tie with her long red fingernail. 'Job interview?'

Joe shuffled backwards but Marianne followed without showing the least awareness of rebuff.

'Um, no,' he said. 'I've got my first performance tonight.'

'Of course! Your wonderful play.' She pressed her hands together in front of her full red lips. 'How silly of me to forget.'

I rolled my eyes at that. I hadn't told her the date – not because I wanted to exclude her, though that might be a good idea, but because every time I mentioned Joe or Sean she turned bitchy.

'Well, don't worry, Joey dear,' she said now, leaning close enough to whisk his jacket with her boot-black hair. 'I wouldn't miss your grand debut for the world.'

'Great,' Joe said weakly. He took a more determined step back. 'See you there.'

He didn't release his breath until she twitched her way back to the office. I noticed, however, that he was human enough to watch the seductive roll of her behind. He shook his head when she finally disappeared. 'I know she's your friend, Kate, but – yeesh – what a dragon.'

'She's got a crush on you,' I said, childishly pleased by his disapproval. 'And who can blame her?'

That brought a smile to his face. He pressed a wet,

smacking kiss to my nearest cheek. 'I'm the luckiest guy in the world to have a friend like you.'

Me, too, I thought, watching him bounce back out the door. Me, too.

I did not expect such a grand theatre. A buckled wooden stage maybe, or a student auditorium through which Joe's music would swirl like cognac in a plastic cup.

Stepping out of the cab, I looked about me in wonder. Beyond the modern silhouette of the Annenberg Theatre, I saw the softer brick and limestone of the older campus – Ben Franklin's campus. I hoped these privileged academics would be kind to my sensitive young lover. I had my doubts when I read the posters hanging inside the fancy glass displays. They all trumpeted well-known Broadway shows, featuring professional actors.

I turned to Sean with concern tightening my throat, a concern he didn't seem to share. A half-smile lit his handsome face. From the way he dressed at work, you'd never know he owned nice clothes, but tonight he'd trotted out his finery. He wore an up-to-the-minute Gianfranco Ferre suit, a red silk tie, polished shoes and – wonder of wonders – cuff links. With complete self-assurance, he cradled our opening night bouquet. The crinkling cellophane held three dozen red and white roses. I'd told him they symbolised desire and aspiration. He liked that enough not to balk at the cost. Of course, these days neither of us had to stint. Lawyers might be pond scum, but they paid him well.

Sean punched my shoulder. 'You've never been to the Annenberg Theatre, have you?'

I shook my head. 'Never. I had no idea. Look at this crowd. Some of those women are wearing evening gowns!'

Thank heaven I'd let Sean bully me into wearing my emerald shantung sheath. I had feared I'd be overdressed, but now I saw as much silk as denim.

Sean nodded towards a woman with her hair piled elegantly atop her head. 'Most of the dressed-up women are professors. Everyone on campus has been talking about *Captain Blood*. Our little Joe is about to make a big splash.' His own words energised him. He took me by the elbow and tugged me in the direction of the entrance. 'Hurry up, Kate. I want to find someone to take these flowers backstage.'

'My heels,' I protested with a laugh for his eagerness.

He looked down at my feet and paused for one gratifying moment to admire my ankles. Then he sighed and proceeded at a more gentlemanly pace. 'I don't know why you women wear those things. They're an accident waiting to happen.'

I smiled to myself. That brief, burning glance reminded me all too clearly why I wore high heels – now and then, at least.

The theatre was packed but, thanks to his position as composer and star, Joe had wangled us spectacular, centre-front seats. I could have kicked my shoes into the orchestra pit – though I doubted the musicians would have appreciated the contribution.

A mix of old and young students, the orchestra went about their business with an air of brisk competence. 'I know what I'm doing,' said their studious expressions as they arranged Joe's music on their stands.

I remembered how college could seem like the centre of the universe. Their seriousness amused me, but I was glad for Joe's sake. His score would get a fair hearing with these sober players and this big, acoustically sophisticated stage.

We hadn't been seated long when the lights flashed three times, then dimmed. Excitement rippled through me. Sean fumbled for my hand. People coughed in the darkness and rustled their programmes. Sean's fingers tightened on mine. The conductor – a shaggy, long-haired beanpole in a dinner jacket – lifted his arms. I forgot to breathe until they fell.

The orchestra launched into Joe's overture as if they had played it all their lives. I closed my eyes as the familiar strains washed over me, tart and sweet and intricate. Up until now, I'd only heard this music on a second-hand upright. How different it sounded wound together with the strings and the winds and the light poom-poom-poom of the percussion.

I'll remember this, I promised myself, no matter who fluffs their lines or trips over the stage curtain. I'll remember this moment when everything came together perfectly.

As it happened, no one fluffed their lines – not so the audience could tell, anyway. They were too busy drying tears of laughter.

Captain Blood told the tale of a vampire-pirate and the delectable young innocent who stowed away on his ship, tempting him to break his vow to drink no virgin blood. To my surprise, the play was hilarious, a melodrama pushed firmly over the edge into farce. The student actors played it straight as stone but that only made the awful dialogue funnier.

I hoped the writer didn't mind. I suspected he hadn't meant to be so comical.

The actors, on the other hand, knew exactly what reaction to expect – Joe especially. I shouldn't have been surprised, considering the role-playing he'd done for me, but the way he could milk a laugh with a tiny bit of business amazed me.

He looked at home onstage. He moved without self-consciousness. He spoke as if the words had come to him that very moment.

He had presence.

Whenever he appeared, he riveted all eyes to him and him alone. The curl of his lip got noticed, or a brief contraction of his fist. The other actors might not have existed. When he sang, women leant forward in their seats and pressed their hands to their throats.

'Good lord,' murmured the diamond-spangled woman next to me. 'Rod Stewart meets Pavarotti.'

'Hush,' scolded her bosomy partner. 'I want to hear.'

During the climactic scene, in which Captain Blood succumbs to his darker nature and brings the heroine across, Joe stripped off his pirate shirt and clasped the buxom ingenue to his breast. As he bent her tango-style over his arm, the muscles of his back rippled under the stage lights. A collective sigh issued from the female members of the audience, and a few of the males, too.

More than a little susceptible himself, Sean transferred my hand to his inner thigh, near his knee. His overcoat draped his lap, sheltering a pocket of warmth. My sex throbbed with longing. I wanted to measure his strong, swollen cock. I wanted to squeeze it through all that well-pressed wool while Joe seduced the girl onstage, while the audience squirmed in its seats and wished that they, too, had someone hot to hold.

Divining my desire, or perhaps just obeying his, Sean nudged my hand upward as Joe and the heroine plunged into a passionate duet.

'Don't make me take you,' Joe begged in fine operatic style.

Sean moulded my hand to his gargantuan bulge.

'Make me yours forever,' the heroine trilled back.

Oh, yes, I thought, and began massaging Sean's cock in time to the music. He pressed me closer, but not hard enough to make him come. Though no one paid us any heed, we didn't want to get caught doing something that might embarrass our pride and joy.

Up on stage, Joe sank his teeth into the heroine's neck and swore her blood was sweet as honey and ripe as spring. The longer he sang, the harder Sean got. The harder Sean got, the wetter I grew. The heroine warbled in orgasmic bliss, but down in the stalls I wondered how much more I could take.

The song ended just as I was sure a single touch would bring me off. Sean lifted my hand from him, his palm as damp as mine. He pressed a kiss on to the back of my knuckles and bent close enough to whisper in my ear.

'I'm going to fuck you both silly when we get home.'

I tossed my curls, feigning a coolness I did not feel. 'Promises, promises.'

He bared his teeth at me. 'Count on it, babe.'

My neighbour shushed us. We behaved ourselves until the final curtain fell.

As soon as Joe appeared, flowers rained on to the proscenium. Some of the ladies in the audience, professors included, stuck two fingers in their mouths and whistled. Joe took four curtain calls. He could have taken more but, after the fourth, he sternly refused to accept and summoned the rest of the cast.

He handed all his flowers to the heroine. She looked like a walking bouquet.

I'd never been prouder of him. He'd demonstrated a power and a self-possession I hadn't known he had, and he was still the same sweet Joe.

'You're crying,' Sean accused, and handed me the handkerchief from the breast pocket of his suit. It was silk and had a monogram. Now that was friendship.

He grimaced when I dabbed my eyes and blew. 'Women,' he said, but his voice was warm. He gave my shoulders a bracing hug. 'Come on, Miss Watering Pot. Let's see if we can shove our way backstage. I want to congratulate the star.'

Chapter Ten
Hell Hath No Fury

Shove was the operative word for our progress. With Sean acting as forward, we forged through the narrow corridor that led to the dressing rooms.

I spotted Marianne ahead of us in the crush. She slunk along in the same blue dress she'd worn to work, but a gleaming black chignon confined her flowing hair. A dangle of diamonds swayed from her ears, and her neck looked positively swan-like.

Heads turned as she passed, not simply for her sake, but for her escort's.

I caught a glimpse of his profile as they turned a corner. He was older than her usual, a good-looking man, though age had softened his jaw and good living had roughened his skin. I noted his high brow and hawkish nose. His silver hair was full and smoothly styled, like an ad for male hair products. He walked with his dark wool coat slung casually over one shoulder. Though Marianne held his arm, he did not glance at her, but scanned the crowd with sharp, restless eyes. He looked like he owned the world – or wanted to.

When they reached the student actors gathered outside Joe's dressing room, a flurry of whispers broke out.

'I don't believe it,' I heard one girl say. 'That's Desmond Gerrard.'

I didn't recognise the name, or the man, but that didn't mean anything. I wouldn't have recognised Walter Annenberg, either. What I did recognise was that Marianne had pulled off a dating coup and wanted to make sure everyone – especially Joe – knew she had what it took. I sighed to myself. I wouldn't have cared if Marianne had snagged Prince Charles for an escort. Now, if she'd found someone who made her happy for longer than a week, that would impress me.

'That was a fine performance,' Marianne's date was saying as Sean and I squirmed into the crowded dressing room. 'Very impressive.'

His voice was serious, professorial. It seemed a bit of a put-on. I wondered if he spoke that way because he was a pompous jerk, or because Joe was so much younger.

'Thanks,' Joe said. Still in costume, he sat before a grease-smudged mirror. Our bouquet of red and white roses brushed his shoulder, filling the small room with its scent. Pots of cold cream and crumpled tissues lay scattered across the vanity table. Beneath the remains of his stage make-up, Joe's colour was high. A chunky girl in flannel and jeans was helping him remove the heavy foundation. She clenched an orange-smeared tissue in her fist. Clearly, she resented the interruption. Another of his unwitting conquests, I presumed. It crossed my mind that no female under thirty should wear so much eyeliner – not that the girl would appreciate the suggestion.

Belatedly remembering his manners, Joe stood and extended his hand. 'It's a pleasure to meet you, Mr Gerrard.'

Desmond Gerrard gripped his palm. 'Please call me Desi.'

'Desi,' Joe complied, then cracked a huge grin. 'I know you must get tired of hearing this, but I'm a huge fan of your work.'

Desmond Gerrard ducked his head and scratched the smooth skin above his crow's feet. The gesture betrayed the shy teenager he must have been, once upon a time, before he became such an important personage. He recovered quickly, squaring his shoulders and clearing his throat.

'That makes two of us,' he said. 'Marianne tells me you composed the score.'

'That's right.' To his credit, Joe did not ask his idol if he liked it. In fact, before the man could volunteer a compliment, the sight of Sean and me stole Joe's attention. With a flattering lack of hesitation, he pushed through the crowd and swept me into a bone-crushing hug.

That he turned to me first made my heart soar with pleasure – and my conscience prick with guilt.

'Kate,' he exclaimed, loudly kissing my cheek. 'I'm so glad you made it.'

Grinning from ear to ear, Sean pounded his back.

I smoothed Joe's hair off his brow. 'It was wonderful. You were wonderful.'

He let out a throaty chortle that drew every eye in the room. Overflowing with excitement, he dropped a kiss to my neck, then my lips, then hugged me close again. Inside his black pirate's trousers, his sex had swelled to full tumescence. The ridge pounded my hip through the leather and I squirmed at the upsurge of lust this produced. The fact that I'd watched him seduce another woman for the last two hours did nothing to quell my hunger. I swivelled forward, pressing my softness against his leg. His erection pulsed more forcefully.

'Bad girl,' he whispered.

I squeezed his thigh between mine.

'Tut-tut,' he clucked and, before I could evade him, covered my mouth with his. His lips were soft, his jaw hard. Its muscles worked as his tongue breached me, thrusting deep to tease the sensitive nerves along my palate. He sucked my tongue on to the curve of his, a bold, possessive pull that drew me fully into his mouth.

Someone wolf-whistled. Blood flamed in my cheeks but I couldn't break free. Joe's arms wrapped me like

161

steel, flattening my breasts against his half-bare chest. Heat flooded my groin, inconvenient and unstoppable. His chest hair prickled my cleavage. In a motion too subtle to see – I hoped! – he dragged his pecs in tiny sideways jerks across my nipples. Oh, he made me ache. Moisture welled between my labia. A trickle quivered on the verge, then spilt over. I cursed my lack of underwear. With nothing to stop it, the trickle rolled down my inner thigh, threatening to tell Joe's fellow cast members a good bit more than they needed to know. Joe flicked his tongue back into my mouth. My lungs began to ache. When finally he released me, I was gasping like an asthmatic.

I tugged my hem down as far as it would go.

He laughed again, enjoying his taste of power. He slung one arm around Sean's back and the other around my waist. 'Come meet Desmond Gerrard.' He spoke close to my ear, *sotto voce*. 'He's a Broadway producer.'

I nodded, my face impassive even as dread knotted my stomach. Did Joe have to be discovered his first time out? With an effort, I ordered myself not to ruin the good impression he must have made.

'Desi,' Joe said, pride shining in his handsome face. 'These are my good friends, Sean Halloran and Kate Winthrop.'

Desi shook Sean's hand – a single manly jerk – then turned to me. I steeled myself to hide my instinctive mistrust but the twinkle in his eye disarmed me. He pressed my hand between both of his, almost bowing over it. 'You must be Marianne's sister-in-law,' he said. 'She speaks of you often.'

I wondered what Marianne had said to inspire that wolfish gleam. Then again, maybe I was better off not knowing.

'We're treating Joe to a celebratory steak,' I said, though in fact we'd planned nothing of the kind. 'Would you and Marianne care to join us?'

A tiny gasp from Marianne told me this was not the way she wanted the evening to unfold. A cosy circle

162

involving her, Desi and Joe, was my guess – with her queening it over both of them.

'We'd be delighted,' said her escort, without so much as a glance to consult her. 'But you simply must let me treat.'

'My cousin Frank has a steak joint across the river,' Sean said. 'You like pool?'

Marianne responded to that suggestion with a ladylike sniff, but once again Desi overrode her. 'I adore billiards,' he declared, and I almost believed he meant it.

He certainly was charming. I just hoped charm wasn't all there was to him. I'd hate to see Joe hurt by some smooth-talking New York power broker.

Joe was too euphoric to worry. He clapped his hands to get the attention of the crowd.

'Okay, everybody out,' he said. 'The star needs to change into street clothes.'

He earned a few cat calls for that, and a few offers to help, but the room cleared without much delay.

'Not you.' He caught Sean and me by the back of our collars. 'I have plans for you.'

He propped a cracked vinyl chair beneath the doorknob. Sean and I smiled at each other. Little Joe was ready to roll, and we were happy to oblige.

Sean walked his fingers up the gap in Joe's pirate blouse. 'I hope you've got something quick in mind. You don't want to keep Mr Broadway waiting.'

'I can't think about him now.' Joe shook his shoulders free of the shirt and yanked his hands from the ruffled cuffs. The white cloth hung over his waistband, draping the snug black leather. My mouth went dry at the sight of his perfectly honed torso. Dark hair circled his coppery nipples, then dived into the enticing shadows beneath his navel. I'd never seen him look so male, so dangerous.

Our eyes connected. Joe's colour deepened. He mouthed, *I want you*. A shiver rolled down my spine and he smiled, very slowly.

'Come here,' he said. His fingers brushed my wrist

before cuffing it and reeling me to his side. Greedy to touch him, I ran my hand up that silky line of hair, across his ribs and on to his pec. He jumped when I pinched his nipple.

'Mm, Kate.' He buried his nose in my powdered decolletage. 'I'm so horny I could scream. I kept thinking about the two of you sitting in the audience, watching me, holding hands, teasing each other.' Hunger rumbled in his throat. 'It's a wonder I remembered my lines.'

As he'd done with the heroine, Joe dipped me over his arm. The position arched my back and offered my nipples to his mouth. He breathed on them through the emerald silk, then mouthed them lightly. My eyelids drooped with pleasure.

The rattle of a belt buckle snapped me from my languor. With his free hand, Joe shoved Sean's trousers and briefs to his hips. As he continued to nuzzle my breasts, he ran his fingers over Sean's thick, ruby crested erection like a man reading braille.

Sean propped his hands on his waist. 'I guess you are hungry.'

'Starved,' Joe said, and tugged him, cock first, towards the make-up table.

Sean hopped up with a look of bemusement. The table was high enough that his feet swung inches from the floor. Except for the vigour of his erection, he would have looked child-like. Sean grinned, his sense of the ridiculous keen.

But Joe's intent wasn't humorous.

'Spread 'em,' he said, his voice rough – and not from singing all night. He turned me to face Sean, wrapped his arms around my waist, and pressed his cheek next to mine. 'Wider, mister, and get those trousers down. I want to see how much you need what's coming to you.'

Smiling faintly, Sean worked his trousers over his hips. They fell to his ankles and caught on his polished shoes. He spread his muscular legs. His sac hung between his thighs, its heavy contents resting on the

Formica table top. The surface must have chilled the delicate skin, but he rolled his bum from side to side as though he liked the sensation.

Joe pushed me between Sean's knees. 'Bend over,' he said.

I assumed he meant me to go down on Sean, but before I could do more than touch the swollen knob with my tongue he gripped my hair and pulled me back.

'That's mine,' he said.

I looked back at him, surprised and intrigued. Joe was really riding high tonight. He must have regretted his sharpness, though, because he released my curls with a soft stroking motion. His hands slid down my back, then reversed to push my heavy silk dress over my bottom. His hum of pleasure rewarded my fashion choice. I wore his favourite stockings, sheer beige silk with a sheen of gold. My suspender belt was satin, green to match the dress, and of course I wore no panties. His fingertips slid over my curves, smoothing the straps along my buttocks, then dipping gently into the well of moisture at the heart of my sex.

'This is mine, too,' he said, two fingers sinking deep.

His touch was heaven after all that waiting. Swallowing a helpless cry, I pushed back, working myself on his knuckles, drenching him with cream. Sean craned forward, eager to see.

'God,' Joe said. 'You're sopping.'

His hand left me. Buttons popped; cellophane tore. An instant later, his cock-tip travelled the length of my crease, my cheeks spread wide by his hands. He dipped the crown in my moisture, coating it generously. It slid more slickly then, leaving a cool-hot trail behind. My sex pounded.

'Please,' I said, angling myself to take him. 'I want you inside me. I need you.'

He corked the wet, waiting mouth, pressed the flare inside – and stopped.

'Don't tease me,' I begged. 'We haven't got much time.'

He didn't move. His hands covered my cheeks, massaging them in deep crease-parting circles. 'You are so fucking hot. It would take a saint to wait.'

'Don't wait, Joe,' I pleaded. 'Push it all the way in. Push it hard.'

Sean wagged his feet to either side of me. 'If you won't give her what she wants, I will.'

'Like hell,' Joe growled.

Bracing his arms on the table, he surged inside. That single push nearly sheathed him. Not satisfied with nearly, he bent over me, grunting as he worked himself deeper. The warm, drawn-up bulk of his scrotum squashed the undercurve of my cheeks. I shifted my legs wider. He leant closer. His chest was sweaty and hard. It pushed my upper body on to the table between Sean's legs until my arms draped his gold-furred thighs and my forehead rested on his hip. Sean's erection grazed the muscle between my neck and shoulder, sinking down and then bobbing off as the blood pumped intermittently through his shaft. Heat rolled off him in waves.

'Perfect,' Joe praised, breathless from his struggle. Reaching past my shoulder, he petted the upper slope of Sean's cock, slowly, gently, from lube-wet glans to thick, hairy root.

Sean's belly shivered. Joe craned closer, his mouth hovering over the head. Sean sucked in a breath and held it.

Joe's tongue curled out. With three leisurely strokes, he pushed Sean's foreskin back over the ridge. He drew back to inspect the results. He worked his jaw from side to side, loosening it, I imagine. His hips dragged back from mine until he almost slipped free. Then he took us both at once.

I felt Sean's twitch of response as intimately as my own. Our muscles tightened in tandem as my body swallowed Joe and Joe swallowed Sean. We moaned in chorus and I gripped Sean's buttocks an instant before his fingers clamped over my collar bones.

166

Luckily, Joe didn't take long to settle into a steady double rhythm.

'Oh, man, that's good,' Sean said, his hold on my shoulders gentling, becoming an unconscious massage.

'Mm-hm,' I agreed.

Joe chuckled and the sound vibrated through the skin of my back. He was so close. His hair brushed my cheek with every pass. I could feel his jaw stretch, hear him swallow. The wet sucking noise he made as he fellated Sean was indescribably arousing. I couldn't take my eyes off his mouth. It was bigger than mine. His lips slid easily to the golden curls that thatched Sean's pubis. The pressure he exerted was greater, too. As he sucked, Sean's vein-girded skin stretched taut and gleamed with saliva. The sight entranced me – to watch Joe's cheeks hollow, to see his tongue lap the purpled glans or dig greedily into the weeping hole, to hear Sean groan with pleasure – I doubted any act of voyeurism could crank me higher.

The fact that Joe's iron-hard prick was working me just as efficiently made the show all the sweeter. I couldn't hold back my pleasure. He drove in hard and I came with a deep, rolling shudder, milking Joe's cock with my spasms.

'No, no, no,' he said, pulling up to gasp for air, every muscle tightening in his quest for control.

'Don't stop,' Sean rasped. 'I'm almost there.'

Sean's buttocks clenched hard, pushing his hips forward until his balls nudged my cleavage. He was so velvety warm there and so male-smelling my hunger rose again. I had to touch him, had to help. Cursing Joe's weight, I worked one hand under my chest to knead the tender sac.

Sean squirmed into my caress. 'Say, Kate, have I mentioned what a sweetheart you are?'

I rolled him between palm and knuckles. 'Not lately.'

'Oh, man, hurry,' he said to Joe. 'This whistle's about to blow.'

'Do you know what she does to me when she comes?'

Joe said. 'I had to take a breather.' His eyes sparkled with laughter as his lips ringed Sean's cock again.

Sean sighed blissfully, then shook one fist in the air.

'Once more into the fray!' he cried, quoting *Captain Blood*'s big fight scene.

Joe chuckled around his bulging mouthful and I experienced a singular burst of contentment – champagne and sunshine, wobbling kittens, a book by the fire, and a three-hanky film wrapped up in one. We were happy. We were all happy.

'Once more, Kate,' Sean laughed, ruffling my hair. 'Push that cocksucker over the edge.'

As soon as he said it, I knew I could come again.

Joe did, too. His head bobbed determinedly and he kneed my legs wider. One hand slipped to my front, cupping and steadying my mons. His hard, choppy drives told me he wasn't far from peaking himself. I arched my back and drew him deeper, reaching for the sweet culminating pang.

Sean's laugh became a gasp. His thighs trembled under my arms. His hand knotted in my hair. 'Geez,' he said, twisting so hard tears sprang to my eyes. 'Geez.'

Joe sucked harder and thrust harder. His motions rocked my upper body into the table, into Sean. The mirror began to rattle. The ache between my legs intensified. A wail rose in my throat.

But Sean stiffened first, and shuddered, and pushed us all over the edge with his choked-back orgasmic cries. When the last quiver faded, he sagged over me, breathing hard. To my surprise, he pressed a tender kiss to the back of my head, then to Joe's.

'What a pair,' he panted. 'You guys can take me out for this culture stuff any day.'

Halloran's was a smoky neighbourhood restaurant with the sort of ambience that takes generations to develop. T-bones and beer ruled the tables out front, billiards the back. The scent of charred meat perfumed the air. My mouth watering, we followed the fragrance up a set of stairs. Black and white photos covered the age-browned walls, with well-known actors and politicians arm-in-arm with the original Mr Halloran.

'Isn't that a famous mobster?' Desi asked, indicating the dear, departed mayor.

'The man was a saint,' Sean declared. Joe and I laughed, but the man in question was a saint to some Philadelphians.

Once we'd reached the main dining room, a handsome waiter in a boiled white shirt and bow tie ushered us to a corner table. Dim lighting could not disguise the faded red carpet, but the tablecloths blazed like snow. Our beer arrived in huge frosted mugs. The steak was tender enough to cut with a fork.

That was sufficient to keep Sean and me happy. The others talked theatre while we devoured the carnivorous treat, blithely ignorant of almost everyone they named. No reference was made to Joe's ambitions or what Desmond Gerrard might do to further them. The few times Marianne tried to steer the conversation in that direction, the men ignored her. Sulking, she ordered a second manhattan. I didn't worry. I knew Joe and Desi were doing a man-thing; they'd get around to business once they finished sniffing each other over.

We'd reached the coffee-dessert stage when Sean's cousin Frank dropped by to say he'd reserved his two best pool tables for us.

'And when you gettin' married anyway?' the beefy restaurateur added, his eyes sidling to me as he cuffed his cousin's head. Sean had his arm around the back of my chair, so I guess Frank assumed we were together. He looked happy about it – too happy. He shook a meaty finger at me. 'Don't you let him squirm off your hook, Kate. Hallorans have great-looking kids.'

I assured him I'd keep that in mind. Sean could set him straight about our relationship later, assuming he wanted to. I wasn't sure how 'out' Sean was to his family. He'd told his parents, yes, but the rest of his relatives? People like the Hallorans probably didn't produce too many bisexual bachelors, or know what to make of them when they did. No doubt, plain old gayness would have been easier for them to accept.

Joe had a funny look on his face as he watched this exchange. I could not read it. It wasn't jealousy, but he was obviously entertaining unfamiliar thoughts.

As I'd expected, Joe and Desi paired off for a round of billiards. That left Sean and me coupled at the second table. I'd played exactly twice in my life and I was pitiful. I sent three balls in a row crashing over the edge. Sean howled with laughter. When Marianne offered to take my place, I was more than willing to let her, but Sean insisted I just needed a lesson from an expert.

'Relax, sweetheart,' he said, surrounding my body from behind. 'Let a master show you how it's done.'

For the next six shots, his hands covered mine on the stick, half-guiding, half-caressing. His hips spooned my hips; his knees nudged my thighs; and every so often his breath, warm and coffee-scented, stirred the curls at the back of my neck. At first, I thought the Casanova act might be for his cousin's benefit, but the healthy erection that brushed my bum with every shot suggested otherwise.

'Aim ze stick towards ze hole,' he said, making me giggle at his awful French accent – and his double entendre, which he underscored by sticking his tongue in my ear.

'Jesus,' I heard Marianne mutter.

Fearing she'd make a scene and ruin Joe's night, I insisted she take a turn. Unlike me, Marianne knew which end of the cue was which. Sean still trounced her – twice. Losing did not improve her mood, or the fact that whenever she was shooting Sean wrapped me in his arms and nuzzled my neck.

Refusing to play any more, she ordered a third manhattan, a pack of cigarettes, and lounged back against the billiard room's bar. The ice cubes tinkled in her glass as she tucked a Virginia Slim between her full red lips. She lit it deftly, then watched Joe and Desi amble and joke their way around the table. Each burst of laughter inspired a frown. Between puffs, her fingers drummed the elbow of the hand that held her drink.

Despite the miasma of vice that clung to her person, she looked more attractive than I could ever remember seeing her. She was always attractive, it was true, but tonight her eyes sparkled and her cheeks glowed with angry colour. Her high, apple-perfect breasts jiggled within the clasp of her short blue dress. Her nipples pointed straight out like tiny electrified points. Waiters ogled them. Customers licked their lips. Frankly, I didn't know where Desmond Gerrard found the strength to ignore her, unless this was how he maintained their balance of power.

Women like Marianne did not reward overt adulation. Look at poor Keith. Marianne hadn't had a kind word to say to him since he'd kissed her feet in Rittenhouse Square.

'Thanks for bringing Desi to the play,' I said, hoping to jolly her out of her funk. 'I know it means a lot to Joe to meet a big name so early in his career.'

'Right.' She blew a double stream of smoke through her nostrils.

Her acerbity made me wonder why she had brought Desi. If she'd hoped to earn Joe's undying gratitude, that ploy had failed. 'How did you and Desi meet?' I asked, suddenly curious.

She gazed across the room at her escort. Her eyes narrowed to black-rimmed silver slits. Desi sank a shot and shook his cue in a little victory dance. Marianne's upper lip curled derisively, as if she knew all his shameful secrets – but perhaps the sneer was the effect of her dangling cigarette.

'We have complementary interests,' she said, and beyond that I could not draw her.

Hours later, Sean, Joe and I lay sprawled before a crackling fire at my townhouse. Both men had discarded their jackets and ties, I'd kicked off my torturous heels, and we all sipped the Courvoisier Sean had bought to mark the occasion. Combined with the beer I'd drunk at dinner and the heat of the fire, the brandy had me nodding.

But I wasn't too sleepy to notice how quiet Joe had been since we left the restaurant. He hunkered before the fire, idly prodding a log with the poker, his eyes hooded with private thoughts.

Sean rolled on to his back and balanced the balloon glass on his breastbone. 'So,' he said, when the latest shower of sparks died down. 'What did Mr Broadway have to say?'

Joe replaced the poker in its stand. 'He says I've got charisma.'

'And?' Sean prompted.

Joe bit his lower lip. His chest expanded with a slow inhalation. 'He says he knows an agent in New York who'd be happy to represent me.'

'That's great.' I reached out to squeeze his knee.

Joe still looked glum. 'He says he'd represent me as an actor.' His nose wrinkled on the word. 'He says my music isn't mature enough yet.'

'Ah, what does he know?' Sean said.

Joe shoved his hair back from his face. Blue shadows smudged the hollows beneath his eyes, and the firelight picked out two faint lines radiating from the corner of each lid. The marks made my own eyes wrinkle in sympathy. 'Desmond Gerrard knows a hell of a lot more than I do,' he said, sounding as tired as he looked. 'In the last ten years he hasn't produced one flop. If he says my music needs more seasoning, he's probably right.'

I pushed myself upright and smoothed his tiny worry lines. Joe leant into the caress and closed his eyes. I knew I loved him then, with all my wary heart. I also knew I had to help him find the courage to pursue his dream. 'Would you really hate being an actor?' I asked, treading carefully. 'Because it could be a good experience. You'd learn more about the way theatre works, and you'd meet people who might be useful later on. Plus you'd be in

172

New York. If you're really serious, isn't that where you need to be?'

'Yes.' His head sank on to my shoulder. 'But I don't want to leave you.'

'Oh, baby.' Understanding his conflict all too well, I rubbed his back in slow, reassuring passes. I wished I could promise it would all work out.

'You gotta go see this guy,' Sean said, speaking for all of us. 'If you don't at least try, you'll never stop kicking yourself.'

Joe moaned a soft protest into my neck, then pushed back and shook off his melancholy. 'The agent might not even like me,' he said more cheerfully.

But I sincerely doubted that would be the case.

I woke before dawn, a sure sign I'd overindulged the night before.

Rather than lie in bed staring at the ceiling, I decided to leave for work early and get a jump on cleaning – maybe even buy a batch of sticky buns for my hard-working employees. Christmas was coming and, in this season of irate customers and overtime, a boss could never suck up too much.

With the sun barely up, the shop's interior remained a collection of wide, oblique shadows. It creaked and groaned like an old house, and smelled deliciously of coffee beans and ageing books.

Locking the street door behind me, I dumped my bag, coat, and the platter of buns behind the front counter. After a brief debate over whether I should nab one right away, I headed for the closet where we stored the vacuum. I'd burn a few calories cleaning. Then I'd misbehave.

The sound of muffled voices, a man and a woman's, brought me up short outside our office.

The female voice could only be Marianne's – and from the groans that interspersed the conversation, she wasn't going over the books.

Damn, damn, damn. I pinched my lower lip. As I saw

it, I had three choices: I could leave quietly; I could make a lot of noise and alert them to my presence; or I could barge in and demand to know why Marianne was using our office as a trysting place.

The final option tempted, but I wasn't up for a confrontation. Besides, I'd transgressed once myself. Memories of my back-room ball game with Sean flooded back. I remembered the way he'd manhandled me over to the ladder, the way he'd filled me so snugly, the sounds he'd made when he came. Worst of all, we had our tryst during business hours.

What if Marianne decided to throw that back in my face?

With that in mind, I opted for making noise. They'd pull themselves together as soon as I switched on the vacuum. I began to tiptoe past the door. Just as I did, the man's voice rose in volume – an over-enunciated literature professor's voice. No doubt about it, Desmond Gerrard was in there with Marianne.

'I simply can't, darling.' He heaved a sigh of deep carnal suffering. 'You're the best, the absolute best and it kills me to refuse you anything, but the boy has real talent.'

He groaned again, louder this time. I cursed the interruption. Was Joe 'the boy' and, if so, what did Marianne want Desmond to do to him? I strained to hear her response.

'You know no one does it like I do,' she purred.

'Too true, but – Oh, yes, a tad tighter, darling. Yes, that's perfect. The thing is, the boy is extremely good. You saw those women creaming in their pants last night – the men, too, truth be told. Someone is bound to snap him up and make a big deal of him. He's a young Mel Gibson, a new Brad Pitt –' His accolade ended on a sharp yelp.

'You promised,' Marianne said, low and dangerous.

I heard a loud, fleshy smack.

'No so hard,' he complained.

She's spanking him, I thought, but even that revelation couldn't prise my ear from the door.

'You've been very bad,' said Marianne. Another smack resounded through the office, and another yelp. 'Going back on your word. I ought to beat you bloody, little man.'

'No, no,' Desmond pleaded, his voice hoarse with excitement. 'I tell you, Joe Capriccio's going to be somebody. If it gets out that I lured him to New York on false pretences and then abandoned him, I'll be ruined. Even you can see that.'

If they hadn't been so engrossed in their game, they would have heard my gasp of outrage.

'So deny it,' Marianne said, punctuating her advice with a sharp wallop. 'It'll be your word against his. Who's going to believe some wide-eyed fairy from Philly?'

I'd heard enough. I slammed the door open so hard, a picture fell off the opposite wall. Despite my fury, the tableau that met my eyes temporarily shocked me speechless.

Desmond Gerrard was crouched doggy-style along the front of my desk, naked but for an assortment of metal-studded leather straps. What looked like clothes line secured his right wrist to one desk leg and his right ankle to the other. He didn't look as good without his power suit. His butt sagged a little, and his belly. Apart from the pink spank marks on his bottom, he was fish-belly pale. His erection, however, had to be the largest I'd ever seen – ten inches at least, and thick to boot.

He shrieked in horror at my intrusion. Kneeling up as well as he could with two limbs restrained, he tried to shield his scarlet monster from view. Even as he pressed the shaft down between his legs, it twitched violently and spilt a puddle of pre-come on to the floorboards. Intellectually, he might hate getting caught with his pants down, but physically, he was ready to explode with excitement.

My clit quivered with an inappropriate frisson of

interest. All I could think was that nobody would make a mouthful of that humongous beast.

'Like what you see?' Marianne drawled. 'Bet you'd like a crack at that swizzle stick.'

I turned to her for the first time and did my second double take. She wore a form-fitting latex dress, black and very shiny, with a long zip up the front, no sleeves, and a hem that failed to fully cover her fishnet-clad bottom cheeks. Five-inch heels encased her long, elegant feet and she gripped a ping-pong paddle in one hand. She smacked it periodically against her palm – keeping it warm, I guessed.

As usual, she looked great – hot as hell and completely in control. Even though I hated what she'd tried to do to Joe, I couldn't help admiring her balls. She hadn't turned a hair at my unexpected entrance.

Desi moaned, clearly inflamed by our battle of wills. Fat beads of sweat rolled into his cloud of silver chest hair. He clutched the shaft of his cock with his unbound hand, gripping it so hard his knuckles paled.

Marianne glanced at him and scowled. 'Bad!' She flicked him sharply across the chest with her paddle. Desi cried out as the blow stung the sensitive pinpoint at the centre of his pectoral. 'Did I give you permission to touch yourself?'

'No, mistress.' Desi bowed his head. He removed his hand from his cock. It sprang back against his belly. Struck dumb with fascination, I watched the huge phallus swell and contract with the pumping of his heart. Another trickle of fluid overflowed the winking eye. I expected him to come any second but – though he shivered like a wet dog – he managed to stave off that last crucial loss of control.

'Well?' said Marianne, returning her attention to me. 'I assume you overheard. Are you going to scold me now or ogle my slave?' She struck her palm with the paddle again, her eyes lingering coolly on my breasts. It didn't take a genius to conclude she longed to squash me under her five-inch heel as well.

I knew now why I'd always held back on forming an equal partnership with Marianne – despite her periodic requests to change our contract's terms. 'Pack up your desk,' I said. 'I'll mail you a redundancy cheque.'

She actually stomped her foot. 'You can't fire me. I'm the last friend you've got.'

'Excuse me?' I willed the telltale colour from of my cheeks, but Marianne saw it anyway. She tapped the paddle against her chin.

'Well, really, Kate. Who's come visiting since Tom ran out on you? Oh, forgive me, I'm forgetting your buddies here at work – your close, personal employees. Or do you want to count your little housemates as friends?' A mocking smile curved her scarlet lips. 'Trust me, as soon as the next kinky adventure rolls around, they'll be history. They're nothing but a pair of cocksuckers.'

I don't know what laughing devil whispered in my ear, but the riposte came effortlessly. 'I'm a cocksucker myself,' I said calmly. 'So I hardly count that an insult.'

My choice of words seemed to rob Marianne of hers. They also sent Desi over the edge.

'Oh, no,' he whimpered. He jerked so hard at his bonds the end of my desk lurched forward. 'I'm going to come, mistress. I can't hold back.'

'No!' Marianne smacked his shoulder back and forth with her paddle. 'I forbid you to come!'

But his cock darkened defiantly, the veins bulging, the shaft pounding like a rabbit's heart. The tiny slit in the head fluttered, desperate to eject its load. 'Agh, agh, agh,' he grunted, screwing his eyes shut.

A second later they opened and focused on mine, sharp as lasers. I couldn't look away. *Mistress*, he mouthed, sending a dark thrill to my core. Then he blasted off. His hips humped the air as streams of semen shot from his cock like water from a pressure hose. His seed spattered the floor boards from his knees to the opposite desk. I'd never seen anything like it.

All the while, Marianne rained blows on his shoulders and back, damning him to hell for coming without her permission. Impervious to her fury, Desmond held me prisoner with his hot, knowing stare. My hands shook; my vagina fluttered and wept. I knew what he was telling me: that Marianne and I weren't so different, that I got off on this dom stuff, too.

Tell me something I don't know, I thought. But the knowledge ran a little deeper now. Now I'd have to consider what it meant. I released my tension with a long, slow breath. 'I want you out before we open for business today,' I said once Marianne stopped swatting her rebellious slave.

She shook her head at me, off balance, but trying to hide it. 'You'll be sorry, Kate.'

'I already am,' I said, and tossed an empty book carton on to her desk.

The last thing I heard before I pulled the outer door shut was Marianne yelling for Desi to lick his jism off the floor.

Still fuming and shaken, I strode down South Street, oblivious to my favourite funky stores, to the early commuters and the bohemians out walking their dogs. In the seventeen years since she'd married my ne'er-do-well brother, Marianne had never stared at me so coldly, as if she loathed me. Then again, maybe I hadn't been looking for it. We'd been through so much together. We'd cried on each other's shoulders and toasted each other's victories. If Marianne got snappish, I reckoned she was just being Marianne. Friends put up with each other's moods, didn't they?

I hadn't known she resented me enough to strike at me through Joe. Her plan, flimsy though it was, had the potential to both rob me of his company and punish him for rejecting her – two birds with one stone. Except the plot had backfired. At the last minute, her instrument of revenge had developed cold feet. Chances were, she'd blame me for that, too.

Marianne never did get what she wanted.

Desmond Gerrard caught up to me four streets from the shop. I spun around to face him. 'What?' I demanded, more interested in walking off my anger than in anything he had to say.

'Please wait,' he said, then leant on his knees and panted. His breath puffed white in the mid-December air. He'd pulled his business clothes over his slave get-up, obviously in haste. The studded leather choker showed behind his half-buttoned collar. This reminder of what I'd just seen – and felt – unnerved me.

I wanted to leave, but my awareness of all he could do to harm Joe's career stopped me.

'I know how that looked back there,' he said, once he'd caught his breath.

I waited. He sighed, sounding more like a weary businessman than a slave.

'I admit, my hobby means a great deal to me, but my professional reputation isn't for sale. Not even to a –' his fingers searched the air for a word '– a paragon like Marianne.'

Some paragon! And some ethics. He'd had no problem going along with her plan before he saw Joe perform. I ground my molars rather than say this out loud, but my disapproval must have showed. Desi tugged his over-coat closed and buttoned it. The slave collar disappeared. His dignity had cracked, but not so deeply he couldn't pull it back together.

'Your friend is genuinely talented,' he said. 'I honestly believe I could help him get a solid start.'

'Why should I trust you?'

His thumb jabbed his chest. 'I'm Desmond Gerrard. My word is my bond.' My sceptical snort made him wince. 'All right, my word isn't always my bond. But I prefer it to be so, and I feel badly about what I almost did. I'd like to make amends.'

'I'm not going to blab about this to anyone, if that's what you're afraid of.' I shoved my hands into my pockets to hide my fists. 'I don't care what you and Marianne do in private. I just don't want Joe hurt.'

Desmond's eyes glittered. 'He's lucky to have a friend like you.'

'Don't try to charm me,' I snapped, my voice sharpened by my fear of how easily he could do it.

Desmond chuckled. 'Heaven forbid, Mistress Winthrop.'

I glared at him.

He shrugged philosophically. 'Sorry, dear. Wishful thinking. But if you ever consider getting into the scene ... No? Well, can't blame a fellow for asking.' He reached inside his coat to remove a business card. He held it out until I took it. 'Have Joe call me,' he said, 'and if you're concerned about my principles, feel free to tell him everything you discovered this morning. That way he can make an informed decision.'

I flipped the card against my fingers, sensing a gamble in his words. He was betting I'd keep mum because I wouldn't want Joe to doubt he'd truly earned the admiration of a bigwig like Desmond Gerrard.

Damn thing was, the bastard was right.

'I'll think about it,' I said.

He was smiling when I turned away.

Chapter Eleven

A Turn in the Road

'*I*'ll fill in for Marianne,' Sean said.

Wearing nothing but a pair of snug white briefs, he propped his shoulder against the frame of the open bathroom door. He appeared completely serious. When I failed to respond, he crossed his arms. His biceps swelled. Under the bright overhead light, the hair on his forearms glinted like gold dust, a light gilding that also bisected the muscular plane of his belly. My gaze trailed to the contents of his briefs, quiescent now but heavy.

This was not the best place to fix my attention if I wanted to gather my wits.

Nor did it help that I was naked. Fresh from the shower, I had one leg propped on the toilet cover so I could rub cream into my leg. Sean had seen me unclothed before. To cover up would have insulted him. It shouldn't have made any difference that Joe was staying the night in New York, that we were alone, or that Sean had just made an offer so generous it took my breath away.

Conscious of his gaze but trying not to show it, I squirted a line of moisturiser down my shin.

'You know,' he said. 'You should think seriously about opening a second shop.'

I looked at him sideways. He fiddled with the end of

the towel rail. Did he feel it, too – the sense of forbidden intimacy? The only rule we'd ever made was that none of us step outside the trio. But if Sean and I didn't feel guilty, why did Joe's absence make us edgy? Why didn't we jump on each other the way we would have if he were home?

'You've paid off the mortgage on this house, haven't you?' he pressed, ignoring the heightened tension.

'Yes.'

'And the South Street property?'

'Almost. But how did you know?'

He brushed the hand towel against its nap. 'I ran into your sales assistant, Keith, at the Campus India restaurant last week. We had a nice chat over our curry. He's hoping you'll keep him on full-time after he graduates, but I'm thinking a bright kid like that ought to have a shop to run by himself.'

I smiled at Sean's reference to Keith as a kid, but he hadn't finished making pronouncements yet.

'Another thing – your mail order business is getting too big for you to handle. You've either got to farm it out to a jobber or grow it big enough to make it worth the hassle. Buy ad space in a few women's magazines or, better still, establish a presence on the Internet.'

I tilted my head to the side. 'Congratulations, Sean, you've finally told me something that hadn't already occurred to me.'

He had the decency to flush. 'I guess I sounded cocky.'

'A bit.'

He grinned at the hem of the towel, then met my sardonic gaze. 'I am right,' he said, 'and I'd be happy to prove it to you.'

I shook my head and resumed creaming my leg. 'I can't ask you to help me. Between working for the lawyers and school, you've got enough on your plate.'

'I can handle it,' he said. His eyes followed my hands down my calf. 'Once the accounts software is installed, the computer does most of the work. Anyway, I know

Marianne's type. She'll take ten hours to do what ought to take one and then gripe about being too busy.'

The moisturiser bottle let out a startled *blat*, as though impressed by his insight. Marianne used to complain about her workload all the time. Sean had met her twice in his life. Why had he sniffed out her tricks when I hadn't?

'Don't you trust me to do a good job?' he said.

That brought my head up. 'Of course I do.'

'Then you don't want to owe me.' The words were flat, a bald statement of fact. He rubbed his thumb up the meeting of his ribs, the only indication that I'd hurt his feelings. My throat tightened.

He was right. I didn't want to owe him. To me, debts meant dependence and dependence meant vulnerability. I didn't want to owe anyone. Never mind that was already too late to avoid. Sean and Joe had given me more than I could ever repay: they'd given me back my confidence.

So why don't you act like it? I asked myself.

Unable to answer, I switched legs and started on my second foot. The position bared the outer curves of my sex, now pink and clean and fragrant. I wasn't trying to be seductive, but before I could work past the ankle, Sean plucked my foot off the lid and scooted on to the seat himself. When he set my sole on his hairy thigh, a carnal shock streaked towards my sex.

'I'll take care of this,' he said, and tugged the bottle of moisturiser from my nerveless fingers.

He squeezed a cool line up the length of my leg and massaged it into my skin with long, voluptuous strokes. His cock stretched as he worked, becoming a bold silhouette beneath his briefs. It might have belonged to a different person for all the attention he paid it. He murmured a compliment for my shaving job. I guess he thought that ankle-to-groin sweep was for his benefit – and maybe it was. I grimaced at the private admission, but didn't pull away, not even when his lips brushed my kneecap. The ghost kiss set off sparks in my clit, making

183

it swell and pulse within its warm, plump trap. His circling hands climbed my left thigh. One finger teased the edge of my towel-fluffed pubic hair.

I knew it wasn't an accident, especially when he wound a crisp auburn curl around his pinkie and tugged my labia apart. I couldn't hide what he'd done to me, what the whole evening had done to me. His middle finger stroked my frilled inner lips, slipping easily along the arousal-slicked channel.

'See what a good employee I'd be.' He cruised round the crucial delta and tickled the other side. 'I'm so good at anticipating your needs.'

'Well.' My voice came out an octave higher than normal. 'I'd appreciate your help – but only until I can find someone permanent.'

'Hire someone to input data,' he said. With an abruptness that startled, he set my foot on the floor and began rubbing moisturiser up my belly. 'I can handle the rest in no time. I'll even train the person.'

His creamy palms slid over my breasts. He splayed his fingers and pressed my bosom back against my ribs. My resistance weakened. I shifted my hands to his shoulders and inclined my body into the delicious pressure. 'You really want to work with me? Even though you know I can't pay what the lawyers do?'

'Of course, I do. Mostly Romance is a great shop. You've got satisfied customers, happy employees, and all the coffee they can drink. What more could a number-cruncher want?'

'A better salary?' I suggested, but his estimation of my business warmed me. Marianne's crack about my 'close, personal employees' had shaken me more than I cared to admit.

'I'm thinking of my future,' he said. 'You'll make me a partner a hell of a lot sooner than the lawyers will, and once Mostly Romance opens a few more branches, a partnership with you will really be worth something.'

I could feel my eyes bulge. He must have known how presumptuous he sounded because he wouldn't look at me. Instead, he focused his attention on the furled red tips of my breasts. They shone with cream as he plucked them. I found the sight a bit distracting myself, so much so that I could not formulate a diplomatic answer. Sean had such labourer's hands. Their calloused strength lent a piquancy to his gentle manipulations.

'I've been reading up,' he continued, as calmly as if he were discussing the weather. 'Romance is big business. I wouldn't be surprised if MR Enterprises went national one day.'

Finally, I found my tongue. '"MR Enterprises"? Sean, aren't you jumping the gun here?'

Satisfied with his handiwork, he dropped a kiss to one lengthened nipple. His golden lashes rose. He was smirking. I don't know why. I was reasonably certain I hadn't accepted his proposal.

'I'm not jumping the gun,' he said. 'I'm only jumping ahead of you. But I know you, Kate. You're too proud of what you've accomplished to rest on your laurels – and too smart.'

'Now I understand why no one says "no" to you. You're a bulldozer.'

'I'm a Halloran,' he corrected. 'Hallorans think big. Now let's hit the hay, Miss Kate. I've got you all to myself and I don't want to waste the opportunity.'

He didn't waste it, either. He took me vaginally first, a surprisingly intense quickie – to warm me up, he said. Then he positioned me face down with a pillow bolstering my hips and took me anally. If I'd ever doubted, I knew then that this was his favourite way to fuck. The way he lingered over every thrust betrayed him, the way he caressed my bottom and sighed and quaked and came like a man with a thousand volts running through his cock.

'Thanks,' he said when it was over and we lay spooned together in the big bed. He sounded more grateful than I thought he should. I rubbed the arm he'd draped around my waist.

'I like it that way, too, you know.'

He nuzzled the back of my neck. 'Good. 'Cause I'd hate to think you weren't enjoying it as much as I was.'

I smiled at this rare evidence of self-doubt. 'I'm not sure anyone could enjoy anal sex as much as you, Sean. But I suspect I come close.'

'Bitch,' he said, and playfully nipped my shoulder.

We fell asleep without once mentioning Joe, or the turn in the road he was even then poised to negotiate.

We didn't expect Joe until the next evening.

Without much effort, Sean convinced me to play truant from work and we spent the day alternately cooking and making love and napping. Considering our priorities, we kept the blinds closed and our clothes off. After a lunch of crisp potato pancakes – good energy food, Sean insisted – he slung me over his shoulder, fireman style, and carried me down the basement steps.

'Time to do the laundry,' he sang out. When I protested at being dangled upside down that way, he gave my bottom a sharp smack.

Luckily, my stomach had recovered by the time he bent me over the front of the rumbling dryer. 'Oh,' I said, because the vibration zinged straight from my nipples to my groin.

'Oh, yeah,' Sean agreed.

His thumbs parted my cheeks, baring me to view and tickling the fine, sensitive hairs around my anus. The light touch made me shiver, made the strong ring of muscle pucker and pull in. Sean sucked in a breath at my reaction. Was he wondering how that contraction would feel around his shaft? He shuffled closer and bent his knees until his erection nestled up against my mons. I could tell how excited he was. The turgid flesh jerked with impatience, eager to find a home.

I reached back to pat his hip, but Sean didn't want that sort of comfort. As if he couldn't wait another minute, he nudged my vulva with the full, round knob of his cock, then dipped inside. He sank deep, then withdrew and thrust again. Despite this activity, I felt a restlessness in him. His knees jiggled behind mine. His breath came in fits and starts.

He wasn't paying attention to me yet. This penetration, deep as it was, was merely preparation. When he'd wet the head and shaft sufficiently, he shifted back to his true target.

'May I?' he asked. Longing thickened his voice.

His politeness surprised me. But perhaps he thought two times in two days was more than the average woman would welcome. He needn't have worried. Even if I hadn't been game, seeing how turned on he got was worth the price of admission – so to speak.

'Please do,' I urged, equally polite.

With a luxuriant sigh, he eased inside. Yet again, I marvelled at the intensity of sensation as he filled me – over-filled me, rather. His cock stretched me to my limits, but agreeably so. I wriggled my front against the vibrating dryer and my backside against his velvety groin. He kissed my neck as my inner resistance melted and he slid inside that last delightful inch.

'I love this,' he crooned. His fingers burrowed through the auburn triangle between my legs, searching out my throbbing bud. 'You have the sweetest, tightest arse.'

I didn't have the breath to respond because he'd found my hooded jewel and was rubbing it back against my pubis with his thumb. His cock began to thrust – slow, shallow strokes that seemed to multiply every nerve transmission by a power of ten.

'Oh, God, Sean,' I said. 'Keep doing that. That's heaven.'

'What about this?' He eased two fingers into my vagina. Bending them slightly, his knuckles stroked the rear wall of my sheath. 'Is this good, too?'

I moaned my approval. He increased the pressure. His cock jerked inside me and a light went on above my head.

'Can you feel that?' I whispered. 'Are you stroking yourself, too?'

'Yes,' he admitted, and we both shuddered.

187

'Go slowly,' I said. 'Go as slowly as you can.'

'Yes,' he agreed, and then neither of us had the power to communicate beyond groans and wriggles of ecstasy.

We were wrapped in each other, in our aching, lazy climb to climax. We didn't hear the door open. We didn't hear him call out. We didn't hear the footsteps on the stairs. We didn't know Joe was home until he opened the door and spoke.

'Hey, guys, doing laundry? Oh –' He caught his breath with a funny gasp. 'Sorry, I didn't mean to – I'll wait upstairs.'

I tried to turn, but Sean's weight held me in place. He spoke before I could. 'Thanks, buddy,' he said, his voice froggy with lust. 'Give us half an hour.'

'Half an – Oh, sure. I'll just – I'll see you later.'

The door to the laundry room closed behind him. This time, I did hear his steps, faltering and heavy, as he trudged back upstairs.

'We should go up,' I said, then groaned. My body wanted to stay exactly where it was, especially when Sean resumed his shallow, maddening thrusts. 'We should find out what happened in New York.'

He drew his tongue up my nape. 'It'll keep. Anyway, he'll survive the boot being on the other foot for once.'

Did that mean Sean was jealous of Joe's closeness to me? Or of my closeness to Joe?

'I don't want to hurt him,' I felt compelled to say.

He pushed forward again, steady, unhurried. My traitorous body quivered with pleasure. I wanted to be here, with him. I wanted his tender, forceful presence in my bowels. My buttocks arched higher, seemingly by themselves. Sean slipped deeper. At the sound of his ravenous groan, my sex rained honey on his fingers. His soft laugh of triumph burnt the shell of my ear. 'Trust me, Kate,' he said. 'It's already too late not to hurt him.'

Joe was polishing off the remains of our lunch when we emerged from the basement twenty minutes later, hastily robed and sporting a glow no amount of towelling off could dim.

He looked up from his plate, but not long enough to meet our eyes.

The amount of sour cream he'd heaped on the potato *latkes* made me wince.

Sean headed straight for the fridge, removed a bottle of Evian water and chugged half of it down. If he'd spoken, he couldn't have said more eloquently that fucking was thirsty work.

He offered me the bottle, but I refused with a tiny shake of my head. Instead, I walked to Joe, kissed his cheek and laid my hand on his back. The knots of tension in his shoulders were impossible to miss. 'Welcome home,' I said.

He answered me with a grunt and forked another bite of potato pancake into his mouth.

Well, hell. I steeled myself to face a long sulk. I might feel guilty but, in strict point of fact, I hadn't done anything wrong. He wasn't going to con me into feeling responsible for his bad mood – the way my ex used to do. I let my hand fall from his back.

Joe caught it before I could step away. 'Sorry,' he said, and now he did meet my eyes. 'You took me by surprise. I was all excited to tell you what happened and then –' He made a sheepish face.

'So what happened?' Sean asked. He leant back against the sink, working on the second half of the Evian litre.

'I've got an agent.'

'That's great,' Sean said. 'We should celebrate.'

'Are you sure he's on the level?' I asked, wishing I'd told him the whole truth about Marianne and Desmond Gerrard, rather than merely warning him to be careful. 'Did you sign a contract? Did you get referrals from his other clients?'

Joe looked at me as if I were two years old and had just said a dirty word.

'No, I haven't signed a contract yet. I brought one home to read and I'm going to have my brother the lawyer go over it. I have a list of clients to call this week, and for your information, this isn't the only agent I met while I was there. This is just the one I liked best. And yes –' he forestalled my next question by poking his fork in my direction '– he is a friend of Desmond Gerrard, whom I gather you don't trust, though I don't know why. That's okay, though, because – from what I can tell – no one in show business is a hundred per cent trustworthy.'

'Oh.' I curled and uncurled my bare toes, feeling two inches tall. 'Well, as long as you're being careful.'

'I am being careful,' Joe said. 'I'm not some wide-eyed kid, you know.'

'I know,' I lied, because that was exactly how I saw him.

'So when are you gonna move?' Sean asked. His tone was casual, but he was picking the label off the water bottle.

'I haven't decided.' Joe squeezed my cold hand. He smiled at me as though he knew a secret, and I wondered what in the world it could be.

Joe picked me up after work the next day.

I wasn't expecting him, or the bouquet of baby pink roses he carried.

'Want to come for a walk?' he asked. 'The weather is crazy today. It's almost spring-like.'

'Sounds great.' I forced a smile. He was biting the skin beside his thumbnail, a sure sign that he was nervous. I supposed he intended to break the news about moving to New York tonight, and was trying to soften the blow with a romantic gesture. I sniffed the tiny budded flowers. My stomach tightened like an overwound clock. 'I'll just throw these in water and grab my coat.'

Neither of us was inclined to small talk.

We ambled in silence towards Independence Square, our hands in our pockets, our shoes scuffing the herring-bone brick of the old-fashioned pavement. The narrow streets, some of them cobbled, were an historian's dream.

If not for the cars, it might have been George Washington's time. Fresh paint gleamed on the wooden shutters of the two-hundred-year-old terraced townhouses. The marble steps were swept, ivy climbed the rich red brick, and small landscaped courtyards seduced both eye and imagination. I couldn't help wondering how many generations had set their wrought-iron tables beneath those gnarled oaks, breakfasting on scones or porridge or Pop Tarts.

I loved this city, and loved it best at times like this when the past hovered a breath away from the present. For all its energy, New York had nothing to match it. In Philadelphia, you remembered how the country began. You remembered the hopes and dreams, and you ached a little when they went awry.

I stifled a sigh. The unseasonably warm air brushed like pussy willows against my cheeks. To our left, a shimmer of scarlet fire trembled on the skyline, the dying embers of a breathtaking winter sunset. The twin art deco towers of Liberty Place glowed lime and gold and tropical blue – the best of new Philly looming over the best of old Philly. Here in the historic part of town, wreaths graced the doors of Library Hall – red-bowed reminders of Christmas.

I wondered if I were about to get my first, worst present.

When we reached the square, Joe hired a horse-drawn carriage. He helped me into the plush red seat like a fragile Victorian maiden.

'Just drive,' he said, when the man began his tourist spiel.

His instruction increased the pressure on my nerves. A quiet carriage ride around the prettiest part of town should have been romantic, but I knew it wasn't going to be. My pulse raced as we clopped past the clock and bell tower at Independence Hall. A gaggle of schoolchildren bounced in circles around their harried teacher.

'Thomas Jefferson was a wimp,' one little boy declared, obviously unimpressed by the story of how our constitution was signed. Under other circumstances, I would have laughed. Now all I could manage was a cough. Joe didn't seem to notice.

'I don't know how to say this,' he said. He pressed his temples as though they pained him, then turned sideways on the seat and pulled my hands into his lap. The evening was too warm for gloves. His palms were sweating. 'Kate.' He gripped me harder, apparently at a loss for words.

Dread trickled down my spine like icy rainwater. I knew he had to go, but I was going to miss him something awful.

He broke the silence with a shaky exhalation. 'Kate,' he began again. 'Would you marry me?'

My mouth fell open. I couldn't believe I'd heard him correctly. I was so shocked I did the absolute worst thing I could have done.

I laughed.

It wasn't a big laugh, but it succeeded in bringing a dull red flush to the tips of his ears.

'Well,' he said. 'Forgive me for suggesting something so ridiculous.'

'No, no, no.' My hands fluttered to his shoulders, patting uselessly. 'It's just you're so young.'

'Not too young to fuck.'

Our driver's head jerked but, to his credit, he didn't turn around. I smoothed the worn leather breast of Joe's bomber jacket. 'No. Just too young to marry. I'm not going to stand between you and your future – your future in New York.'

He must have heard the sadness in my words and found it cause for hope. He caught my hands and tucked them inside his jacket. His heart was pounding at marathon speed.

'I don't have to move to New York. I could commute. I could! It's only an hour on the train. I've got a cousin in the Bronx if I need to stay over.' He stroked the back of my hands, his eyes pleading for the mercy he feared

I'd withhold. 'I don't want to leave without a commitment between us.'

My fingers tensed with my urge to comfort him. Nervous sweat dampened his freshly-ironed white shirt, donned for the occasion, I'm sure. My heart ached, but I knew I couldn't afford to be soft.

'What about Sean?' I said.

'I'm not in love with Sean.'

I rolled my eyes. 'Trust me, Joe, the kind of love that friends share, that you and Sean share, lasts a hell of a lot longer than being in love. "In love" is just infatuation.'

His hands stiffened on mine. 'Don't tell me how I feel.'

'Fine. Maybe what you feel will last, but you're still too young.' The way his jaw clenched did not encourage me. I forged ahead anyway. 'Listen, honey, you went straight from your parents' house to college to postgraduate school. You don't know it, but you've barely started to live. You need to be on your own in the real world. You need to have a few adventures.'

'Adventures.' Joe's eyes narrowed. I hadn't known whisky-brown irises could look so cold. 'You mean if I fuck a few dozen New Yorkers, I'll be old enough then.'

'It's got nothing to do with how many people you sleep with.' I glanced at our driver. If ears could swivel backwards, I'm certain his would have done. I lowered my voice. 'What's important is discovering what life is about. What you're about. That takes time, and it's something you have to do for yourself, by –'

'– by myself.' He pushed my hands from his chest. Bookbinder's Restaurant rolled by behind him, the giant lobster over its entrance a comic counterpoint to our discussion. Joe studied his empty hands. 'I've never been good at being alone.'

'All the more reason.' I swallowed against the lump in my throat. I wished I wasn't so positive I'd given him the right answer, the only answer. I cupped my hand beneath his downcast chin. 'I know you're nervous, but you're going to take the Big Apple by storm.'

'And then I'll come back.'

My mouth softened with an almost-smile. 'I doubt you'll want to.'

Joe looked up. Tears shimmered in his eyes, but his gaze held steady. 'You don't know me as well as you think.'

I shook my head. I didn't share my other fear, the one that shadowed – and deepened – all my reasonable protests. If Joe denied half his sexuality, would he live to regret his choice? I had no doubt he would deny it, either; a man like Joe would honour his marriage vows.

Joe would not let the matter drop. He waited until Sean fell asleep, then hauled me out of bed and down the stairs to the sitting-room.

I plopped on to the sofa, my limbs heavy with interrupted sleep. Joe knelt in front of me and gripped my legs just above the knee. Bleary or not, I could scarcely bear to face his stubborn hope.

'Kate, I love you. More than my family. More than music. I want to spend my life with you. That's why I want us to marry. Not because I'm afraid of being alone – and I know you love me, too,' he added, the one statement I could not debate.

'I just can't do it,' I said. 'It wouldn't be fair.'

He growled, a sound of anger and frustration words could not express. His head rolled back and forth across my knees.

'You're afraid,' he accused, the words muffled by the leg of my paisley silk pyjamas. 'You're afraid I'll turn out like your ex. But he was an idiot. I know what I've found with you, and I'm smart enough to hang on to it.'

I said nothing. The urge to succumb to his arguments was so strong I dared not open my mouth. Already, the pain of losing him was physical. My chest ached with stifled sobs and my throat felt raw. I hugged my waist to hold myself together.

He lifted his head. 'Would you marry Sean if he asked you?'

I started. 'What?'

'You heard me.'

'He wouldn't ask me.' I resettled my arms, folding them beneath my breasts.

'But if he did ask, would you marry him?'

'No,' I snapped, but for one weird second I wasn't sure it was true. Joe saw my hesitation. The skin around his eyes tightened.

'No,' I said more firmly. 'He needs too much control and too much freedom. I couldn't live in a way that would make him happy.'

Joe's mouth twisted. 'But he's not too young.'

'Sometimes I think Sean is older than I am,' I said, without considering how that would sound.

He blinked at me, absorbing the implied insult: that he wasn't too young in years, he was too immature.

I squeezed his forearm. 'Being young is not a bad thing. God willing, you'll never be as old as Sean.'

He turned his head to the cold, ash-strewn grate, getting older – or at least more haggard – as I watched. 'I'm wasting my breath, aren't I? You don't believe I really love you. You don't believe anything I feel is going to last. No matter what I say, you'll have an argument against it.'

'I'm not doing this to hurt you,' I said. Even I could hear the plea in my voice, but it did not move him.

'You could have fooled me,' he said.

For six long months those words would haunt me. *You could have fooled me.*

Chapter Twelve
Birds of a Feather

When Joe jumped ship, I thought Sean would, too. I couldn't imagine he enjoyed my brooding company. We weren't having sex. When he started sleeping in his own bed, I assumed he was halfway out of the door.

But, apart from the switch to private sleeping quarters, he made no move to leave. Every morning he stumbled downstairs in time to pat my bottom out through the door, and every evening he parked his bulging briefcase beneath the Queen Anne side table in the hall.

The first thing I did when I came home from work was look for that briefcase. I couldn't relax until I saw it. To tell the truth, though, I almost wished the territorial marker would disappear – so I could get used to being alone again.

One Friday, weeks after Joe's departure, we sat in the living room watching TV – with me curled up on the couch and Sean on the floor, both in sloppy tracksuits. The evening news served in place of conversation as we delved for our dinner from an assortment of takeaway cartons.

Sean had swung by Susanna Foo's in Chinatown on the way home. He'd brought me pheasant dumplings with *shiitake* mushroom sauce – real Chinese comfort food. The chocolate-covered fortune cookies weren't bad, either.

Feeding me was Sean's way of proving he cared. I'd lost weight since Joe left. He'd gained it. I left him grapefruit halves for breakfast. He brought me dumplings for dinner. The perverse symmetry of it made us both chuckle.

Feeling more content than I had in weeks, I tucked my feet into the space between the sofa cushions. Maybe we could survive as housemates.

But Sean's next words blew that fantasy out of the water.

'I've been thinking of moving out,' he said. His gaze darted between me and the TV. 'It's not that I don't like living with you. I do. In fact –' he struggled a moment for words '– I like you more than just about anyone I know.'

The dumplings had turned to lead in my stomach, but I smiled at his backhanded compliment. 'Thank you, Sean. I'm touched.' His head swung around to see if I was being sarcastic. A crease appeared between his straight, fair brows. 'I'm serious,' I said. 'I am touched.'

He set his carton on the coffee table and scooted around to face me. 'I won't leave you in the lurch. My big sister Louise owns a security firm. I'll make sure she wires you up before I go. Her employees will keep an eye on you.'

'But will they drop by for coffee when I'm lonely?' I teased, not to make him feel bad, but to let him know he was more than a guard dog to me.

The implication seemed to confuse him. 'Do you want me to stay?'

I trailed my finger down the slope of his nose. 'No. I know it's awkward for you to be here without Joe. It's awkward for both of us.'

'But if you need me –'

I covered his lips. 'I'll miss you, but I'll be all right.'

'I like you, you know,' he said, as though I might not have heard him the first time.

'I know.'

'Really, I mean it.' He shifted to his knees and caged my legs between his arms, his whole body intent on asserting what must have seemed outrageous to him. 'I really like you. You and Joe are the best friends I've ever had.' His voice broke. 'I just can't believe it's over.'

I put my hands on his shoulders and spoke as gently as I could. 'I'm sure Joe still wants to be friends with you. As for us, our friendship is only over if we want it to be.'

He buried his face in my lap. 'I don't want it to be over, but people always promise to keep in touch.'

I bent closer, letting my warmth blend with his. I stroked his cotton-covered back down to his waistband and kissed the wavy hair at the nape of his neck. I wondered how many broken promises it had taken to make Sean the man he was today. 'I try very hard to keep my word,' I said, pulling my hands up again.

His shoulders hitched under my caress. I thought he might be crying, but he didn't make a sound. When he swallowed, his Adam's apple knocked my thigh. 'I called him an idiot,' he said. His hands clenched on either side of me. 'I said he shouldn't cut you dead just because you wouldn't marry him.'

'Shh.' I kissed the rigid line of his vertebrae. 'Joe did what he felt he had to do, and I'm sure he'll forgive you for expressing your honest opinion.'

Sean snorted at that, but his tension did ease. 'You sound like a shrink, and I sound like a big, blubbering baby.' He pushed back from me and wiped the moisture from his cheeks. One side of his mouth twitched. 'I don't know why, but pouring my troubles into your lap is making me horny.' He drew his thumb down the onset of an erection, a small hummock now, but growing. 'Are you up for something rough?'

The hungry glow in his eyes sent blood sluicing straight to my groin.

'Um,' I said, temporarily dumbfounded. I knew he needed to reestablish his tough guy stance, but how rough was rough – and after two celibate weeks, did I really care?

I pressed my thighs together and measured the trapped tango beat of lust, the soft, wet pulse of tissues longing to be stretched. Six simple words and I was raring to go. *Are you up for something rough?* Those words implied he would take care of me – his show, my pleasure. I needed that tonight. My nipples tightened beneath the stretch lace of my bra. Sean licked his index finger and touched its tip to one aching point. Even through my clothes the contact felt like a shock from a live wire. I couldn't restrain a gasp.

He laughed. 'I'll take that as a "yes", Ms Winthrop.' He pulled me off the couch and up to the second floor, to his room.

From the door I watched him rummage through his walk-in wardrobe, muttering to himself until he found a dark grey suit bag. He held its hanger out to me.

I hesitated – to be difficult, perhaps, but also because I didn't yet know what I was getting into. My gaze drifted to his crotch. Beneath the black tracksuit, he was fully hard, standing out a clean ninety degrees from his belly. He wasn't shy about it, either. Even as I stared, he shifted his free hand to his erection, cupping it back against his body and giving it a hard, shaft-stretching pull. Whatever that suit bag held, it really blew his horn.

He thrust the bag closer. 'Take these clothes to the bathroom and put them on. Then come back and knock on the door.'

I couldn't resist his voice of authority, or the prospect of letting his horn blow me. I collected the hanger with two bent fingers and swung the bag over my shoulder. 'No problem,' I said. 'But do me a favour. Don't start without me.'

With a taunting leer, he treated his shaft to another tug. He stopped beneath the head and waved it at me through the cloth. 'Don't worry, Miss Kitty. I'm as hot to trot as you are.'

That stung my pride a bit, but it was true. My quim

was swimming and my palms tingled with adrenalin. I could hardly wait to have it off with him. I prayed his game would be a short one. Knowing Sean, though, I expected he'd torture us both as long as he could.

In the privacy of the bathroom, I unzipped the suit bag. My eyes rounded. It held a Catholic schoolgirl's outfit: a prim white blouse, a pleated navy skirt and twinset, and short white socks with lacy hems. Everything, down to the utilitarian cotton bra, was my size. He hadn't bought these things for some nameless playmate. He'd bought them for me.

I didn't know whether to be flattered or amused. In any case, I wasn't too amused to dampen the virginal white panties as soon as I pulled them on.

All dressed and buttoned and tucked, I knocked on his closed bedroom door. After a moment, during which papers rustled, he told me to come in. His voice sounded strange – crisper than usual, but also kinder. *Come in, Kathryn,* he'd said, the way a teacher would.

A tiny shiver chilled the back of my neck. I opened the door. Sean sat behind his desk, flipping through a fat manila folder. He'd made good use of my absence. Not only had he turned the desk away from the wall, but a picture of a saint hung where his print of Edvard Munch's *The Scream* used to be.

'Close the door behind you,' he said in that same soft-spoken manner. He rose slightly to scoot his chair back from the desk.

That's when I saw he was wearing a cassock and dog collar. Though I wasn't Catholic, the costume took me aback. Scenes from *The Thorn Birds* raced through my mind.

Sean made a very sexy priest.

He folded his hands on top of the open folder. Frowning gently, he shook his head at me. 'I've been receiving some disturbing reports about you, Kathryn, very disturbing.'

The words, the tone and manner in which they were spoken, had a strange effect on me. I put out a hand to

200

catch the balance I'd unaccountably lost. I knew he'd attended boarding school, and – without being told – I knew that, once upon a time, someone must have spoken to him just like this.

I touched my soft navy twinset and studied the scuffs on my trainers. For a second I smelled blackboard chalk. I knew just who I was supposed to be: a misbehaving schoolgirl, a bit of a smart alec, but far from fearless – and normally a pet of the good father. He was a favourite of mine, too. Despite my rebellious nature, I didn't like disappointing him.

'How old are you now, Kathryn?'

I thought for a moment. 'Sixteen.'

'Sixteen,' he repeated. Was it my imagination, or did his eyes linger on my breasts? 'I'd expect such behaviour from an ordinary sixteen-year-old, but not from a Saint Demeter's girl.'

Sweat prickled between my shoulder blades at his sad reproof. Oh, if only I'd been good. My mouth was dry. I bobbed in a curtsey I'd only seen on TV. The pleated skirt tickled my knees. 'I'm sure I can explain, Father.'

'I don't see how. Sister Mary Francis says you've been inciting the other girls to lustful thoughts.'

My good intentions dissolved. 'Sister Mary Francis is a jealous hag!'

My passionate outburst inspired a smile that threatened, but did not destroy, the sober set of his mouth. Regretting the slip perhaps, he assumed a more lawyerly demeanor. 'Did you or did you not instruct both Ellen and Beth in onanistic practices?'

I stared blankly at him. He pursed his full, sensual lips. Not for the first time, I imagined how he'd kiss. Ellen and Beth said he wouldn't ever. He was a good priest, not the sort who caused a scandal and got sent to the back of beyond. That might be true, but it didn't explain the things I felt when he met my gaze in lectures, as if a current were surging between our deepest parts. In my daydreams, I told him the secret things I wanted, things I'd never heard of anyone wanting. He always understood. He was still young, he'd say. It was hard to give everything over to God. In my fantasies, he was afraid to touch me but once he started he couldn't stop. He made me his secret lover. I wasn't certain what that involved, but I knew I wanted it.

'Kate?' His frown deepened as if he sensed my sinful thoughts. 'Did you teach your friends to pleasure themselves? Did you, in fact, crawl into their beds after lights-out and put your hands on their private parts?'

I hung my head. 'Yes, Father, but it was only to keep them from trying it with boys.'

His palms smacked the surface of his desk. My hand flew to my chest. The anger that darkened his handsome features seemed entirely real. 'Do not compound your sin by quibbling,' he shouted. 'And where on earth did you learn such a filthy habit, anyway?'

'From you, Father,' I said, without pausing to think.

He goggled at me. 'How dare you even suggest –'

'But I saw you. Remember the day I left my hanky in your office, the one my nanna embroidered specially? I went back to get it, but I didn't know if you were there so I just opened the door a crack. You were standing by the window with the blinds closed. You had your cassock pulled up in front and your, your thing was in your hand. I couldn't believe how big and hard it was. I couldn't look away. It seemed so strange and beautiful – the way it moved, the way the veins wound around it, all blue and strong.'

I took one step closer to the desk. He stared at me with a mixture of fear and fascination, his mouth slack, his flush extending from clerical collar to hairline. He knew his future was on the line, and only I knew I'd never, ever hurt him – even if it meant abandoning all my dreams.

'You rubbed it with my hanky,' I said. 'You had my nanna's hanky in your hand and you rubbed it up and down your thing. The big knob at the end looked so red I thought it must hurt, but you were humming the way

I do when they serve chocolate for dessert, so I thought you must like it.'

'I did like it,' he whispered, a man in a dream.

'I thought so.' I leant on the edge of his blotter. Sweat glistened on his forehead and upper lip. My nostrils flared. Vocation or no, he could not quell the most primitive evidence of his maleness. I drank his scent in quick, shallow breaths. It dizzied me. My voice darkened. 'You'd been rubbing so long, I think you'd polished it,' I said. 'The part on the top was shiny. It looked so smooth, I wished I could put it in my mouth and suck it. Just as I was thinking that, you moaned my name and started rubbing faster. It made me feel all squirmy inside. "Kate," you said. "Katie, Katie, Kate." On the last "Kate" you made a face as if you were going to scream, but nothing came out – except down below, from the tip of your thing, a spurt of, of seed came jetting out. It made a noise when it hit the blinds. I guess you didn't want to make a mess because you shoved my hanky over the end. There must have been a lot, though, because some dribbled on the floor.

'I wanted to touch the little puddle. I'd never seen a man's seed before. I wondered what it felt like. Was it creamy or sticky? Was it still warm, and how would it taste? Things like that make me curious. I can't rest until I find out.'

Sean gasped like a fish out of water, too breathless to respond.

A little weak-kneed myself, I sat on the corner of his desk and hugged my waist. 'I got the idea to touch myself from you. You liked it so much I thought I would, too. I guess you know a girl's thing is really little, but it's between my legs right where yours is and it gets wet and slippery when I play with it. It feels good, but I've never felt what you seemed to be feeling. Beth was like I was, but Ellen was like you. Beth played with her breasts while I rubbed her thingie. It made these loud squishy noises. She got so excited at the end we had to put the pillow over her mouth so she wouldn't wake the others.'

Sean covered his face.

'I know priests aren't supposed to do it,' I continued. 'In fact, I know I'm not supposed to, either. But since I've already decided I'm going to, I may as well learn to do it right. I hoped you'd tell me what I'm doing wrong. There isn't anyone else I trust enough to ask.'

Sean muttered something I couldn't hear.

'What?' I said.

He lifted his head. His lips were pressed together, the flesh around them pale. 'You're too curious for your own good.' His heavy-lidded gaze dropped to my breasts, long enough for me to be certain about it. 'And too grown up for your age. You tempt me just as you tempted Beth and Ellen – with your beauty and your spirit. You make everyone you meet long to possess you. I understand why you enjoy it, Katie, but it's a dangerous game.'

'I didn't mean to hurt anyone, Father. I only wondered –'

'Hush,' he said.

'But I love you, Father. I would never –'

'Hush,' he repeated. He showed no awareness that I'd just spilt my deepest secret. He steepled his hands before his mouth. They were shaking.

I waited for him to collect himself. After a few deep breaths, he rolled his chair back until it hit the wall. He smoothed the black robe over his knees. The gesture drew my attention to his tented crotch. A small damp spot told me he must be naked under the cloth.

My sex fluttered with longing. Waiting for him to play out the drama took all my self-control. I almost wished he'd made this more of a caricature. I could feel the young priest's torment. I wanted him as much as if I truly were his backsliding pet.

'Come here,' he said, in a low, quavering tone. 'I think you need correction.'

'I do,' I agreed and circled the desk to his side. 'Shall you beat it out of me, Father?'

'Is that what you want, Katie?'

The look we exchanged was eerily intimate. He seemed to see straight into my soul, or my character's soul. We recognised each other. Our desires were equally dark, our hopes equally tremulous. We were birds of a feather – whether we liked it or not.

'I believe I need it,' I said. 'I believe it would do me good.'

What I really meant was: I know this is the only bridge you'll let me cross to get close to you.

'Very well.' He searched my eyes a moment longer. 'Come here and bend over my lap.'

He arranged me over his armless chair. Both my hands and feet touched the ground. He braced his legs to keep the chair pressed firmly to the wall. His thighs were warm, his erection hot. My shirt had ridden up and the damp spot over his cock met the skin under my navel. I allowed my weight to settle closer. A muscle twitched in his leg. He touched the hem of my pleated navy skirt.

As though reluctant to touch me, he lifted the skirt to my waist, folding it neatly as he went. He paused. 'You're almost too beautiful to spank.' The heat of his hand hovered an inch above my buttock. 'It must be done, however, and nothing must shield you from the blows.'

His fingers slipped under the waistband of my panties and slowly, slowly, he pulled them down my tingling curves. He could not avoid touching me then. The back of his fingers slid over my haunches and, after a moment, his thumbs joined them, gently following the crease where my buttocks met my thighs. I heard him groan as the panties dropped to my ankles.

'Like dove's breasts,' he murmured, his hand hovering again. He swallowed hard. 'Prepare yourself, Kate.'

The blows began before I could, cracking upward on to the underside of my buttocks – brisk, quick smacks that stung just enough to make me squirm.

'Oh,' I cried, wriggling forward until his erection prodded the curls of my fleece. 'Oh, Father, it hurts.'

'Be still,' he ordered through gritted teeth, but he liked

me where I was. He spanked me from the top now, lifting his hand high and driving it down, jolting me into his cock with every blow. The vibrations rippled through me to him and through my sex as well. My pussy felt huge and swollen, swollen tight like ripe, juicy plum. The blows were all the relief I had for my cravings. I began to lift myself in anticipation.

'Want more, do you?' he said. His next smack caught the division between my cheeks, driving them apart and baring for one instant the aperture of both our dark desires.

Again and again he spanked me this way, warming my crack until it seemed to sizzle under his hand. He panted with exertion. Warm drops of sweat flew from his skin to mine. I wondered if his palm stung as badly as my bottom. Did he like the aftershocks as much as I did, the way the memory-pain throbbed in tandem with my pulse? He liked having me at his mercy, of that I had no doubt. His erection stretched beneath my belly, solid as stone. The noises he made grew distinctly pre-orgasmic, the war between self-control and intense excitement apparent in every grunt.

I wanted him inside me when he came; I wanted it so badly I could hardly keep from begging.

'Lord have mercy,' he gasped and – with a suddenness that made my stomach swoop – lifted me up and around and sat me facing him on his lap.

The starched black cassock burnt my paddled buttocks, but I didn't care. The pain heightened every sensation, tightening in on itself and then flaring out. I'd long since soaked through my panties. I'm certain he felt the moisture because his hands tightened on my hips, setting off a ricochet of pleasure-pain. The kernel of flesh around which all my ecstasy centred was so engorged it poked through my swollen lips like the trigger of a gun.

'No,' he said, when I tried to press closer. 'You'll make me spend, Katie.'

'Spend inside me,' I pleaded. 'I want to know what it's

like. I need to know. You made me ache so I can hardly bear it.'

His face twisted. 'Damn you for liking this.'

'I can't help it.' I mouthed the strong line of his jaw. He sighed and tilted his head towards the caress. His lips brushed mine. 'I'm made that way, Father. Just like you. My body needs things, dark things, and you're the only one who'll give them to me.'

He let himself smile, a wry, self-mocking smile. 'Hardly, little Kate. You and I both know men will queue up in droves to give you whatever you want.'

I cut a glance from under my lashes. 'But who will help me now, Father? Who will love me the way you do?'

He had not meant for me to guess his feelings. His expression darkened. 'Very well.' He set me gently on the desk and spread my thighs as wide as they could go. 'Let's see if I can show you what you've been missing.'

He parted my lips with his thumbs, tracing the wet channel between inner and outer. His hastened respiration brushed my skin. His golden hair tickled my thighs. His thumbs travelled higher, catching the soft hood between their pads. He smoothed it back to reveal the rosy jewel within.

I tensed. I did not like to be stimulated bare. I was so sensitive there.

But, 'I'll be careful,' he said and, with a greater delicacy than I knew he possessed, he laved me ever so gently with the tip of his tongue.

I couldn't hold back my cry of startled pleasure. The sensation was so sharp and hot and penetrating. The dozenth flick of his tongue brought me off, and the second dozenth tipped me over the edge again.

'Better?' he asked as he helped me on to my feet again.

'Yes,' I said, breathing hard – and I was better, but not satisfied.

Before he could stop me, I bent down to grasp the hem of his cassock and flung it all at once to his hips. As I'd expected, he was wore nothing under it. The black cloth settled about his hips in feminine abundance, but the treasure I'd revealed was supremely male. Knotted calves led to hard slim knees and bulging thighs, all of which shone pale but vibrant against the dark backdrop of his robe.

The sight of his black socks and shoes made me smile, but his sex – the stout mauve shaft capped with a crown of shining burgundy – that sight struck a blow to my solar plexus.

His cock vibrated with the pressure of his need, swollen to the limits of its skin. His foreskin clung to the grossly flared rim, catching up the rich, silky tears that flowed from the tiny cock-mouth. I could have wept myself at the taunting, potent image.

This was forbidden, I reminded myself, for the sheer thrill of the word: forbidden by his vows, by my youth, and by the power disparity between us. Forbidden like the first apple – and just as red and firm.

With the tip of my little finger, I traced the slippery moisture that ringed his cock, gently pushing the taut covering back until it snapped down of its own accord. The good Father bit his lower lip so hard a drop of blood appeared.

'Have you ever had a woman?' I whispered, circling him now beneath the rim.

'Never,' he whispered back. 'But I've dreamt of it – too many times to confess.'

'Did you dream of me?' Unable to wait any longer, I straddled his lap.

His eyes drifted halfway shut. Now bare thighs met bare, simmering buttocks. His hands settled uneasily on my hips, on top of my skirt. 'I dreamt of you,' he admitted. His thumbs ventured round to stroke my belly where the skirt's smooth pleats were sewn together. 'I spilt my seed on the sheets dreaming of you, and when I prayed – in my heart – I prayed to dream of you again.' I grasped his hands and eased them under the finely woven wool to my naked skin. He sighed, his fingers lighting and un-lighting like a wary bird. When they settled on my hips, I rolled the front of the skirt up over itself and tucked it into the waistband. He stared at what I'd uncovered and licked dry lips. Then I cocked my hips forward until my fleece tickled the underside of his shaft.

'I cannot put it in you,' he warned, his voice gravel and smoke. 'You're a good girl. I would not deprive your husband of his marital flower.'

I tossed my head and took hold of his root. 'My husband will take what he can get and say "thank you".'

He clucked his tongue. 'Such arrogance.'

Unrepentant, I tugged the crown closer until it slipped between my plump, wet lips.

'Ah-ah-ah,' he scolded, and pried my hand from him. 'I don't trust you, little Katie. You must take what I give you.'

He steadied his under ridge with four curled fingers and pressed the upper with his thumb. Firmly in hand, he manoeuvred the head against my clit and gave it three firm taps, each of which sent a shock of feeling down the tiny stiffened shaft. As easily as that, I wanted to come again.

I whimpered when he eased away.

'You must promise to behave,' he said, 'and if you make me believe you, I'll slip just a bit inside you, so you can feel what it's like.'

I promised, of course, and pretended not to see him roll the condom on.

We both made small, hungry sounds when he pressed the head inside.

'How lovely,' I marvelled, all wide-eyed wonder. 'It's like satin, so warm and full. Does it feel as nice to you, Father? I wish I could make you feel as wonderful as I did when you kissed me between my legs.' I petted the shaft where it entered my body. His penis bucked. 'Look how it moves under my hand. I think it wants to shoot like it did before. See how red it's getting.'

When he looked at the place where our bodies met, sweat popped out on his brow.

He lifted my hand from him and ordered me not to touch him there. He said he wouldn't come and I mustn't try to make him. *Yes, Father,* I said and kissed a drop of perspiration from his temple. He said I mustn't squirm like that: it made him want to push, and he couldn't push. It wasn't safe. Priest or not, he was still a man. He only had so much control. *Yes, Father,* I said, but when his buttocks clenched, driving him a fraction deeper, I couldn't help squirming a bit. He muttered a prayer and said maybe a little further would be all right and then a little more and then he groaned and said he knew it must hurt but couldn't I take all of him just for a moment? Only just a moment, because he'd never felt anything so heavenly and he promised on his mother's sainted memory that he wouldn't spill inside me.

I wriggled on to him, girl-tight, woman-wet. My lips kissed his thatch.

'Mother of God,' he swore, and caught me in a crushing embrace. 'Yes, that's – just a little more. I'm almost in. Just one more push. I promise I won't – Ah, ah, yes, that's all of it. Bless you, Katie. Bless you.' He shuddered from his belly out. His cock swelled. He paled. 'Oh, dear God, help me not to –'

'Come,' I whispered.

He held my hips immobile, locking me tight to the cradle of his loins, fighting the inevitable with a strangled moan.

'Come,' I said. I licked the spot where he'd bitten his lip. He gasped and I flicked the red wet tip past the edge of his teeth. 'Come with me. I'm almost there. A push or two is all it will take. Don't you want to feel it around your thing? Don't you want to feel how a woman quivers when you show her a glimpse of heaven?'

'A glimpse of hell,' he said, shaking all over with need.

'Heaven,' I insisted. I kicked my feet, forcing the chair to rock. The spring squealed.

'I'll pull out,' he warned.

I laughed and rocked again. 'Is this how you want it to end? Rocking like a baby? Or thrusting like a man?'

His growl was unintelligible. With our bodies still connected, he rose and slammed me back on to the desk. Papers fluttered to the floor. I winced as my head hit the edge. He reached up to cradle it, exclaiming in distress.

'I'm fine,' I insisted. 'Take me. Hurry.'

'Have it your way then,' he said. 'Might as well be hanged for a sheep as a lamb.'

He grabbed my thighs beneath the knee and pushed them back towards my chest, bracing them with his shoulders. The position opened me completely to his first deep thrust. He held himself inside me at the utmost end of the downstroke, sweating and trembling. The tendons in his neck stood out. I thought he'd explode then and there. He must have thought so, too, because he pulled back gingerly, gritting his teeth, then drove in hard. This time I felt the jolt through my womb. A warning tremor made my sheath dance around his shaft.

'Not yet,' he growled, freezing again.

But I couldn't wait. The need for release cramped deep in my sex, too insistent for delay. Vowing I'd make him come with me, I reached under the cassock to grip his tight round buttocks. I burrowed between his cheeks until I found the dark sensitive pucker. He jumped when I touched it and moaned when I pinched it.

'Put it in,' he ordered hoarsely. 'Shove your thumb inside me.'

His sweat eased my way but it was a rough, partial insertion. Just what he wanted, apparently. The responsive ring of muscle flexed and clung as I rimmed him from the inside. His hips writhed with pleasure, then began to pump in earnest – deep, long strokes that drove me quickly to the edge of orgasm.

'Oh, Lord, Katie,' he said, his voice jolted by the force of his thrusts. He spread my legs wider. 'I can't stop it. I can't. I've got to come. Take me. Jesus, take me.'

With that, we both caught a glimpse of the ultimate. My heart slowed. A fist of pure hunger clenched and released between my legs. Almost – almost – Grunting with effort, he slung in to my utmost limit and, finally, the body-wrenching spasm of sensation broke, jetting through me hot and tight and then warm, wet, loose, like mulled wine through my belly – spicy, drunken pleasure. I remember our mingled cries, harsh and sweet, and the strength of his climactic pulses meeting mine.

I don't remember him lifting me off the desk and settling me on his bed, but he must have. He must have taken off our clothes, too, because when I came to myself we were snuggled under the covers in our birthday suits. He had a queen-sized futon, perfect for the pair of us – perfect for him and Joe, as well, I supposed. Limp as an overcooked noodle, I didn't have the energy to mind the reminder.

'Are you back?' he asked, pressing a kiss to my sweaty brow.

I hummed a mild affirmative.

He hugged me closer. 'When you do come back all the way, remind me to explain about topping from below.'

Pleasantly drowsy, I ran my hand down his ribs to his hip. I was always amazed by how narrow men's hips can be. Sean had an inch-long scar I'd never noticed before, right behind the bone.

'Is that some sort of S and M code?' I asked, tracing the raised flesh with my finger.

He moved my hand to his chest. '"Topping from below" means the supposedly submissive person takes control of the scene.'

'Oh,' I said, then digested what he meant. 'I'm sorry, Sean. I thought I was following your lead.' I hid my face in the valley of his chest. 'Guess I ran away with things.'

His chuckle soothed my embarrassment, as did the hand that stroked my hair. 'That's okay. Your way was fun – a little more intense than I'd planned, but fun.'

Since he seemed so jovial, I thought I'd push my luck.

'Sean –' I flattened my palm over his right nipple. 'I was wondering. I know you attended boarding school.

Did you ever – Did anyone try anything like what we played out?'

A near-silent sigh lifted his rib cage. 'There was a priest at school who I wished would try. Father Mike was his name. I had a terrible crush on him: my first. He coached the soccer team. He was a good guy. He took an interest in me even though I was a hell of a smart-mouth back then, if you can imagine that.'

I smiled and petted his chest.

'Father Mike was the youngest priest there. He had a great body – tall, slim – and a funny, friendly face. Once in a while they'd let him handle Sunday service. I'd get an erection before the first hymn was done, which made all that kneeling and rising a challenge.' He laughed through his nose. 'Man, I had it bad for him. That's how I knew I liked boys as much as girls.'

Or more, I thought, but I kept the comment to myself. 'Did he ever try anything?'

Sean shook his head. 'No. But I think he knew. I think he felt sorry for me. My second year, he threw me together with an older boy named Dave Woodbury. A real loser, I thought. He was a maths genius, and gay as the day is long. He didn't even try to hide it. Turned out he was one of the coolest people at the school. He knew who he was and didn't give a damn what anyone thought. He became my mentor – for sex and mathematics. I lost every friend I had when I started hanging around with him, but even then I knew he was the best thing that ever happened to me. He moved to Arizona after he graduated, though, and we lost touch.'

'Was he into games?'

'Nah. Dave was kind of conservative. I got involved in that later. Some of my friends at college were into it. They'd drag me along to some scene and all I'd think was: this is so lame. I could do better than this. So one day I tried.'

'And the rest is history?'

He laughed. 'What can I say? I have a gift. I have to admit, though, if the person I'm mastering doesn't

213

interest me, I get really bored, really fast. I like to deal with a bottom who's strong, who won't get fucked up over it. People can, you know. They let it take over their lives. They use it as a way to avoid real interactions. I steer clear of people like that. On the other hand, if I do find someone who interests me between the ears, mastering them doesn't seem so important – like with you.'

I looked up at him, surprised and flattered. His eyes twinkled as he tucked a stray curl behind my ear. He seemed pleased to have taken me off guard. 'I don't want you to bend to me,' he said, 'even supposing I could make you.'

'What do you want?'

'Damned if I know.' The covers rustled as he tried to get comfortable. 'No. That's not true. I know what I want. I'm just afraid I won't get it.'

I hugged his ribs. 'What do you want?'

He stared unblinking at the ceiling. 'I want to be free, but I don't want to be alone.'

'That's a tough one,' I said, helpless to hide the rush of emotion in my voice.

He knuckled the top of my head. 'Don't you worry about me, Miss Kitty. Some people never discover what they want. I'm one step ahead, this way.'

Despite his words, he sounded sad. I rubbed my cheek against his shoulder. He was a good person. He deserved to live his dream. I was sorry I couldn't be the one to help him.

'I'm glad I know you,' I said, my throat still too tight for comfort.

'I know,' he said. 'So am I.'

Two weeks later, Sean moved into one of the tower blocks on Rittenhouse Square. It was an exclusive place with lots of room, but he left his weight-lifting equipment in my basement. That's how I knew I'd see him again.

He dropped by relatively often, sometimes to work out, and sometimes for a more interesting form of

214

exercise. We probably had more sex than some married people. Despite this, we behaved more like friends than a couple. I never asked who else he was seeing and he never took exception to my infrequent dates – my very infrequent dates.

We also became business bedfellows. A month passed before I was sure in my mind, but I did make Sean my partner. He walked out on the lawyers the very next day, which scared me, though he expressed no doubts whatsoever. Together, we opened a second bookshop, this one called Mostly Mystery. Like Mostly Romance, it became as much meeting place as shop, a space where people went to see and be seen. Sean's business savvy proved invaluable, along with his Halloran work ethic. Both shops did so well I increased his power-profit share to 60/40 – in my favour, of course, but he didn't complain.

Then we went on-line.

Sean and I both bit our nails over that. Would people buy from a cyberspace genre bookshop? Could we give it the same cosy feel we gave our real-world sites? Actually, the real question turned out to be: could we keep up with all the orders?

One morning I woke up, rubbed my sleepy eyes, and realised I had nearly half a million dollars in personal assets. The idea floored me, along with the fact that, if business continued as it was, I might be a millionaire before I turned forty.

Philadelphia Magazine plastered me on their cover for an article on the city's Top Ten Female Movers and Shakers. There I stood, looking dazed, as I wondered why they hadn't put the new mayor on the cover. Sean said she wasn't as photogenic as me but, I don't know, I thought she looked pretty good for a sixty-year-old.

A week after the article hit the newsstands, I caught a piece in the *City Paper* on Marianne, or 'Madame M' as she called herself now. It seemed she'd set herself up as a dom-cum-sex therapist and quickly scaled the heights of the local S-and-M-for-hire community. She informed the reporter that she had a number of international clients as well. 'The Japanese find bondage very therapeutic,' she confided.

Trust Marianne to land on her feet. I was glad her current victims considered the abuse she doled out a privilege. I even felt, strange as it sounds, an urge to call and congratulate her on her career move. I quashed it, but it told me I was over my bitterness.

And then there was Joe.

For a while we heard nothing and I told myself: well, he's a struggling actor, we're not likely to hear. If he's lucky, he's off-off Broadway and waiting at tables, and so much for Desmond Gerrard's high-powered agent friend.

Then I saw him in a sweets commercial. He played one rowdy teenager in a crowd of rowdy teenagers. He looked skinny, but it was definitely him. He even had a line. 'Tastee-licious,' he said with a heart-stopping grin. The ad ran every five minutes, it seemed, and my pulse jumped every time.

'They have to pay him residuals whenever they run it.' Sean nodded sagely. 'So we know he's not starving.'

We also know he's in touch with you, I thought, giving him a sideways glance. Words like 'residuals' weren't part of Sean's normal vocabulary.

I assumed Joe had sworn him to silence. While I admired Sean's loyalty, I resented it, too. After all this time, I could have been trusted with a lousy postcard. I wasn't going to stalk Joe, for goodness sake. Our relationship was fun while it had lasted but now it was over – end of story. What I felt was the concern any woman would feel for a former lover, no more and no less. If no one else made the stars shake in my firmament the way Joe had, that was only because lady tycoons didn't have much time for dating, or sex, except with Sean – and Sean didn't want to shake my stars.

The sweets commercial, apparently, was just the start of Joe's brilliant career. Over the next month, we watched him hawk soft drinks, gardening implements, and a call screening service for the local phone company.

Then he got the Big Break, a juicy part in a torrid night-time soap. *Manhattan Nights,* they called it. Before the show even was aired he popped up on *Good Morning America* and *Entertainment Tonight* – the newest, hottest, flavour of the month. The tabloids had him engaged to three different actresses in a week.

Sean found the latest scandal sheet stuffed in the bin beneath my kitchen sink. 'You'd be an idiot to believe that crap,' he said.

I agreed, but crumpling the paper into a ball made me feel better.

We watched the first episode together. Neither of us cooked if we could help it, so Sean brought a goody hamper from his mother. It held roast chicken, mashed potatoes and a tiny green salad – which Sean ignored. Mrs Halloran had let it be known she considered me prime daughter-in-law material. Sean insisted she was barking up the wrong tree, but mothers will hope.

Eating her chicken seemed dishonest, under the circumstances, but it smelled too good to resist. Besides, I needed sustenance to face Joe's national debut.

I sat up as the opening credits rolled. Joe appeared first thing, striding down a bustling New York street in a natty double-breasted suit. He'd gained back the weight he'd lost before the sweets commercial. His walk radiated health and strength and single-minded purpose.

'Wow,' I said.

'Yeah,' said Sean. 'He looks good.'

He acted well, too.

Joe played a chameleon-like stockbroker, the black sheep businessman in a family of cops. He was courting the daughter of a wealthy magazine publisher – the second patriarch of the saga. Between the script and Joe's natural acting ability, deciding whether his character was good or bad was impossible. Without a doubt he was dangerous, not to mention sexy.

Sean hooted as the camera panned lovingly over Joe

taking a phone call in the shower. 'Do you think they could make him spend any more time with his shirt off?'

I noticed he didn't look away. Of course, neither did I.

'This is going to be a big hit,' I predicted, impressed with the look of the show, with the quality of the actors and the chemistry between them.

Sean leant back against my knees and pointed his fork at the screen. 'Big with a capital "B".'

He sounded happier about Joe's prospects than I did. I guess he was the bigger man. But it was hard to be big when you'd been dropped like a stone for doing what you knew was right.

'He'll come round,' Sean assured me, reading my frown. 'People don't forget someone they're so crazy about.'

Maybe not, I thought, watching Joe gaze soulfully at the publishing magnate's daughter. But they certainly could get distracted.

Manhattan Nights's record-breaking first season was just wrapping up when one of the producers made the mistake of bragging publicly about the astronomical sum he expected to earn by selling the show worldwide. Joe and four of the other central characters promptly refused to re-sign unless their salaries were tripled. To my surprise, Joe was the reputed ringleader. *People Magazine* said so, in the same issue they splashed him on their cover as the Sexiest Man Alive. Even seeing the rumour in print, I didn't believe it until one of the quintet, an older actor who hadn't worked in a while, broke ranks and signed a contract for less.

'This doesn't alter my position in the least,' a very self-contained Joe told the roving reporter for *Entertainment Tonight*.

The reporter had collared Joe outside Café Tabac with a stunning redhead clinging to his arm. She wore filmy aqua chiffon. He wore jeans and a neatly pressed dress shirt. I wondered who did his ironing these days. He and his partner seemed comfortable in the eye of the camera, though Joe did refrain from batting his eyes.

After a brief, bosom-inclusive shot, the camera ignored Joe's date and focused on the clean, resolute lines of his face.

'I, personally, will not agree to return for a second season until these demands are met for every member of the group of five,' he said, 'including Mr Sandoval.'

'But Mr Sandoval has already signed a contract,' the reporter pointed out. 'What makes you think the producers will renegotiate on your say-so?'

Joe's mouth curved in an expression just short of a smile.

'Believe me,' he said, 'the producers read more of my fan mail than I do.'

That one soundbite proved tasty enough to air on national news. Each time I heard it, I wondered at the change in Joe.

'Now that's chutzpah,' Sean said admiringly, as we watched a dignified anchorman stoop to report on the drama.

I plumped a pillow behind my back. 'Joe's agent must be having fits.'

'Unless it's his agent's idea.'

I wanted to believe that, but I couldn't. Joe's confidence – Joe's *cojones*, some might say – sat too easily to belong to anyone but him. The whole affair knocked me back. Despite the fact that Joe's balls were no longer my concern, I didn't like seeing him change from the sweet, unassuming boy I'd known.

'I guess he's Mr Big now,' I said.

Sean patted my thigh. 'And you're Ms Big, Kate, so pull in your claws.'

I knew I deserved that but I didn't like it – any more than I liked the sight of the slinky redhead whispering in Joe's ear.

Sean was too sharp to miss my scowl. 'Poor pussy,' he mocked. 'Someone else is drinking from your bowl.' He cupped my trouser-covered mound in his broad, callused hand. He squeezed roughly and laughed to find me wet. 'Why don't you take your frustration out on me, Miss Kitty?'

So I did. We both felt better afterwards – except I dreamt of Joe, again. In the dream, Joe and I faced off in the centre ring of a circus, our audience invisible, our sole illumination provided by a single spotlight. Joe held a lion tamer's whip. He cracked it over my head, skirling it out like a snake as he drove me towards my cage. I snarled at him, but I couldn't get away; I couldn't even move except on my hands and knees. Closer and closer he backed me to the open door. Faster and faster I crawled, my knees grinding painfully in the sawdust. The dream was so vivid I could smell the shavings and the sweet-sharp scent of my own humiliation.

Joe's amber eyes caught fire as I gave way before him. Blue glints shone in his straight black hair and his lips were a stern red slash in his handsome face. I'd never seen him look so beautiful – or so heartless.

'How can you do this when I love you?' I said, but he cared nothing for the words.

'Get – in – the – box,' he ordered, swinging the long whip between the words. 'You know you won't be happy until I've caged you.'

I hated that dream. I didn't believe it. I didn't want anyone to cage me – ever.

But I couldn't deny I woke up wet every time I had it.

Chapter Thirteen
The Prodigal Returns

A huge bouquet arrived the day we opened MR Enterprises' new administrative office. Sean and I had
purchased a narrow, three-storey building in Philadelphia's Old City neighbourhood. The building was in dire
need of renovation, but the price was right and the view
could not be beaten. From the little rooftop garden, we
could see the gleaming white spire of Christ Church and
the slow brown roll of the Delaware River. Inside,
sunshine bathed every corner. At our request, the archi-
tect left the beams and pipes exposed and knocked two
skylights through the roof. The infrastructure we painted
teal. The skylights we filled with ferns. Framed cover art
decorated the exposed brick walls, and the combined
effect was lush and fresh.

My admiration could not, however, unpack my boxes
any faster.

Seizing on the arrival of the floral messenger as an
excuse to wander out, I leant over the second-level
railing to watch our twenty-year-old receptionist sign
the delivery slip. She turned to call across the sun-
dappled space.

'They're for you,' she said.

Sean must have sent them, I thought as I clanked
down the painted metal stairs. He was at the warehouse

221

today for an efficiency meeting with the company who handled our on-line orders. He was good with the managers, most of whom had worked their way up from the loading bay. They admired a man who'd earned his living with his hands – and could still heave a crate with the best of them.

I smiled as I scampered down the last few steps. The men at the warehouse didn't know that these days Sean kept his calluses in shape by heaving dumbbells, not crates. Fortunately, what they didn't know wouldn't hurt our service, including the fact that Sean could be awfully sweet when he put his mind to it. Imagine – sending me flowers for opening day.

At my approach, the receptionist clasped the fat hand-blown vase and slid it towards the centre of her C-shaped counter. The heavy iron and glass told me this was not a standard arrangement.

'Shall I carry them up, Ms Winthrop?' asked the wide-eyed girl.

I laughed. 'They're bigger than you are, Cheryl. No, I'll just read the card and leave them here to impress the movers.'

The profusion of roses was impressive. Three dozen red and white American Beauties spilt from the vase. The air conditioning wasn't up to scratch yet and their perfume overwhelmed the reception area.

The scent triggered a flash of déjà vu, more the memory of an emotion than an event. Unaccountably, my pulse began to race.

'Here's the card,' said Cheryl, extracting it from the mass of dark green leaves.

I opened it with unsteady hands. 'Prepare yourself, Kate,' it said. 'J.'

My mind blanked. Then I recognised the handwriting. My heart leapt before I could stop it. 'J' for Joe. Joe was sending me flowers? Joe was in town? I touched the bold, swooping initial. He probably was if he'd written the card himself.

But what did he mean by 'prepare yourself'?

Whatever happened to 'How have you been?' or 'Congratulations' or 'Sorry for being such an uncommunicative toad!'?

I glared at the heavy cream-coloured paper. I guessed earning a hundred thousand per episode gave a person airs.

'Bad news?' Cheryl asked, practically quaking in her teeny-tiny combat boots. She was an adorable slip of a thing, bright as a new penny, and for some reason I scared the pants off her.

I patted her narrow shoulder. 'Just a note from an old friend. But I remembered something I need to do at the South Street shop. Can you handle things while I'm gone?'

'Sure,' she said, looking worried but staunch.

'You'll be fine.' I suppressed an urge to pinch her cheek. 'Shall I say "hi" to Keith for you while I'm there?'

She fiddled with the last of the three gold rings that pierced her right eyebrow. 'Oh, well, if you think he'd want me to say "hi".'

I grinned. She had no idea what her diminutive tootsies did to our otherwise conservative shop manager. Keith's freckles practically melted the day he met Cheryl – and her perfect size twos. Too bad he didn't have the nerve to speak to her.

'I'm sure Keith would be delighted to know you were thinking of him,' I said, 'assuming you want to delight him. He has a wild side, you know.'

'Does he?' she breathed, sounding intrigued enough to justify my matchmaking.

I left assured that she'd have better things to mull over than what might go wrong in my absence – because absent I was determined to be. If Master 'J' decided to follow his flowers into my office, he could bloody well lord it over someone else.

'"Prepare yourself",' I fumed, not stopping to wonder why those words sent me into a fury when they came from Joe – and would have made me chuckle if they'd come from Sean.

* * *

The normally quiet Cheryl was bubbling with news when I returned that afternoon.

'You'll never believe who was here,' she said, her elfin face as pink as the proverbial English rose.

'Joseph Capriccio?' I suggested, pretending to flip through my mail.

'Yes!' she shrieked, then covered her mouth with both hands. I couldn't help smiling as she bounced on the balls of her feet. 'I can't believe you know him, Ms Winthrop. That is, like, way totally cool. He is so hot on *Manhattan Nights* and even better looking in person. Did you know he had the same voice coach as me? And he's nice. When he heard you were out, we just talked and talked.'

I looked up from the mail.

'Talked about what?' I asked, more sharply than I'd intended.

Cheryl's smile faltered. 'About you, mostly, and MR Enterprises. But I swear I didn't tell him anything that isn't in our brochures. Except –' She drew a circle in the condensation from Joe's huge vase of roses.

'Except?' I prompted.

'Except I sort of let it slip that you didn't have a date tonight.'

I sighed heavily, rolling my eyes behind closed lids.

'I'm sorry, Ms Winthrop. He seemed kind of sweet on you and I know it's none of my business but I got the impression that you and Mr Halloran aren't, like, joined at the hip. Mr Capriccio was just so nice and he smelled so good, the words popped out of my mouth.'

She looked so miserable, I gave in to impulse and tweaked the tip of her nose. 'It's okay. You didn't know.'

'He left you a present,' she offered in a forlorn voice. 'I carried it up to your desk.'

'Thank you,' I said, and waited until she met my eye. 'Don't worry, sweetie. I'm not mad at you. This is something I have to handle myself.'

I refused to open the big, bowed box until everyone had left for the night. My office, like Sean's beside it, had no front wall. We planned to buy some Japanese screens to preserve our privacy without blocking the great light but, until we did, our every move was gossip fodder.

I was glad I waited. The box contained a long sequined evening gown in cobalt blue. Heavy as hell, its back swooped so low I suspected it would flirt with more than one sort of cleavage. Beneath the dress lay a neatly folded pile of accessories. One by one, I discovered white evening gloves, creamy suede Ferragamo shoes, silk stockings, a lacy suspender belt, a minuscule G-string – and no bra.

Under the pile of goodies lay a second message. The fact that Joe knew I'd dig far enough to find it infuriated me. Six months without him had not dimmed my passion for provocative lingerie.

'Eight o'clock. Tonight. Halloran's,' said this equally curt note. 'Wear the dress.'

Halloran's. I fanned the envelope against my chin. That was Sean's cousin's place across the river, which meant Sean was an accessory to whatever scheme Joe was cooking up.

Great, I thought. They join forces and I lose the one person I could complain to – or ask for advice.

Was avoiding Joe childish? Would I kick myself later if I didn't at least hear what he had to say? I had to admit I was curious, even if his invitation did put my back up.

I stroked the sleek, fish-scale surface of the dress. The blue sequins winked at me and threw sparkles off the rough brick wall behind my desk.

Heat curled through my centre as I pictured myself pulling on the long white gloves and the panties and the stockings. I could almost feel the heavy gown draping my breasts and buttocks, the mermaid cling at waist and ankle, the cool expanse of skin along my back. I knew I'd look like sex on the half-shell in that dress.

I also knew I'd look a fool if I traipsed into a steak joint like Halloran's wearing it. Joe was playing games with me. I wasn't sure why, but I damn well didn't have to play along.

To hell with dressing up, I decided. Mr Big could take me as I was or not at all.

When the cab dropped me off beneath Halloran's green awning on the dot of eight, I found a CLOSED FOR PRIVATE PARTY sign on the door.

The music and laughter drifting out the windows told me I wasn't the only guest.

What now? I thought. I swung my linen jacket over my shoulder. The evening smouldered, though the sun was just a sliver of mango and lime on the horizon. My bra showed through the light crocheted top I wore, but it was a nice bra, so who cared?

Throwing caution to the winds, I yanked open the unattended door and headed up Halloran's stairs, loud jazz music buffeting me all the way.

As soon as I reached the dining room I saw that I was, in fact, severely underdressed. Men in dinner jackets sat at every table, accompanied by women who were poured into gowns much more elaborate than the one I'd refused to wear.

I looked down in dismay. I wasn't even wearing a skirt. Hell, I had my trainers on. Heads turned towards me from the nearest tables. My face heated.

'May I help you?' asked a man in a slightly worn dinner jacket – presumably a waiter.

'Yes.' I strove not to act like a gatecrasher. 'Joe Capriccio asked me to meet him here.'

The waiter stared at me. Did he think I was lying? I lifted my chin and stared straight back, determined to brazen this out. The waiter's expression cleared. 'Ah, yes, Ms Winthrop. Follow me, please.'

He led me to a table in the very centre of the room. It held two place settings. More heads turned as I sat in the chair the waiter held for me.

'Where's Joe?' I asked, before he could slip away.

The waiter tucked his hands together like a Chinese

Mandarin. 'Regrettably, Mr Capriccio has been detained. We expect him shortly.'

Somehow that did not surprise me. 'What about Sean Halloran? Is he around?'

The waiter cocked his head. 'We're not expecting young Mr Halloran this evening.'

'Fine,' I said, close to grinding my teeth. 'Would you mind bringing me a drink while I wait then?'

The waiter gestured towards a bevy of satin gowns. 'We have an open bar tonight. Please help yourself and, as I said, we're expecting our host presently.'

Of course you are, I thought. I immediately weighed and discarded the option of running the diamond gauntlet to the bar. To make matters worse, the jazz quartet took a break – as if my arrival had been a signal. Resigning myself to a dry, painful wait, I looked around the glittering crowd. I recognised a councillor, a sax player, a local record producer, and a respected African-American author. I didn't know any of them to talk to, unfortunately, and no one talked to me – though I suspected some of them were talking about me.

Twenty minutes of standing out like a sore thumb changed my mind about assailing the bar. Forty minutes – and two vodka tonics – later, my capacity for martyrdom was completely exhausted.

Joe wasn't the Joe I'd known if he could play a rotten trick like this, luring me here only to stand me up. He made sure I'd feel as uncomfortable as possible while I waited, too. But I had too much self-respect to tolerate it any longer. Besides, the liquor was making me maudlin. I'd be crying in my tonic before long, and God knew I didn't want to give Joe that satisfaction.

Giving up, I threw my napkin beside my plate, donned my jacket, and went in search of someone to call a cab.

I was trying to find a waiter among the sea of black jackets when I heard a familiar voice. Its rich, brandied tones sent heat prickling across my scalp. 'There you are,' it said.

I turned slowly, girding myself. Despite the warning,

the sight of my former lover made my stomach do the foxtrot. He was tucking a wafer-thin cell phone inside his dinner jacket. A slim gold watch flashed at his wrist. He seemed taller than I remembered, and broader. He'd put on the kind of flesh you get from working out, and his skin – always fine – had the smooth, buffed look that comes from regular facials.

The sheer force of his beauty intimidated me. I could hardly believe I'd once been intimate with such a creature. Cheryl was right. He was better-looking in person.

He met my gaze calmly, seemingly unmoved by our reunion. Of course, I didn't look as if I'd just stepped off Mount Olympus – or the pages of a fashion magazine.

'Yes, here I am,' I said, praying my face didn't betray the wild palpitation of my heart, 'right where I've been for the last forty minutes.'

His face winced in apology. 'I am sorry, Kate. The limo broke down and had to be towed. It'll take days to fix, according to the garage. I caught a cab here as soon as I could.'

The two vodkas combined with six months of hurt to make me lose all self-control. 'Liar,' I said.

'Kate.' His hands lifted, palm out, in the age-old gesture of innocence.

'Liar,' I repeated. This time I smacked his chest and, when that failed to satisfy, stomped on the toe of his thin Italian shoe.

'Ow,' he complained, jumping back. He held me off with both hands. 'Jesus, Kate, get a grip on yourself.'

The supreme rationality of his voice pulled me back from making a scene – even if I did doubt his veracity. I wanted to doubt it, really, because if he was telling the truth, I'd just made an even bigger fool of myself.

'Look, Kate.' He pulled a folded yellow paper from his pocket. 'I've got the garage receipt to prove it.'

I snatched it from his hand and read it. 'Well, it looks real,' I grudged, and handed it back.

He laughed. 'Of course, it's real. Now can we have a nice dinner and talk?'

Seeing I'd calmed down, he tucked my arm through his and led me back into the dining room. Before he could guide me to the Table of Doom, however, I dug in my heels.

'No way. I am not sitting centre stage in my trousers and trainers while people stare at me as if I'm a circus freak.'

He lifted one dark brow. I expected him to tell me I should have worn the dress he sent, but after a brief silence he switched direction and escorted me through the crush towards a table in the back. People hailed him as we passed, slapping his shoulder, lifting their glasses in salutation. Two of the women winked. I might have been invisible for all the notice anyone took of me.

'Later,' he said, when his guests tried to ask him questions. 'After everyone's had time to enjoy the food.'

He held my chair for me, leaning so close a whiff of Aramis tickled my nose, not to mention my hormones. I felt his hand gather up my curls for an instant before he withdrew, as if touching them was a temptation he couldn't resist. I tried to hide my shiver of response.

'Your hair is longer,' he said. He shrugged out of his jacket and draped it over the back of his chair. 'I like it.'

'It grew,' I said brusquely, sensing danger in his flattery. A waiter whisked two covered silver platters to our table. Amazing. I'd waited forty minutes and no one asked me if I wanted to eat. Limo breakdown or no, I suspected that wasn't an accident.

Joe ignored my prickly attitude. He rolled his sleeves to his elbows and tipped the lid off the first platter. Clouds of fragrant steam billowed out. He sighed with pleasure.

That sigh I recognised. Joe must have been sighing like that since the very first time he blasted off. Annoyed with the sharpness of my memory, I flipped my napkin into my lap. 'Do you want to tell me what this is about?'

He set the lid aside, revealing medallions of veal and steamed asparagus, both swimming in juice. He slid a portion on to my plate. My stomach growled.

'I'm thinking of establishing a recording studio,' he said, serving himself just as deftly. I watched the tendons shift in his forearms and the fine, dark hair that veiled them. 'This party is to take the local temperature, to find out who else would use the studio, who'd back it, and who'll help me get a permit. Now that my career is somewhat established, I plan to return to serious composing.'

'And you wanted me here because . . .?'

'Kate.' His eyes sad, he covered my hand with his and caressed my wrist with a flush-inducing sweep of his thumb. I couldn't help noticing what nicely manicured nails he had. 'I asked you to come because I haven't seen you in half a year. I thought it was time we made peace.'

I tried to retrieve my hand but he wouldn't let go. My thighs were sweating. 'I didn't make war on you,' I said. I didn't want it to happen but my eyes filled with tears. Damn those vodkas, anyway.

'Kate,' Joe said again. He tugged my hand closer and turned the palm for a soft, lingering kiss.

Unfortunately for my composure, he didn't stop with one kiss. Over and over, he pressed his warm, mobile lips to the sensitive skin, travelling the length and breadth of my palm as if its print held not just my future, but his. Chills broke out in waves along my limbs. My lungs stalled. When he reached my wrist, he closed his eyes and ran the tip of his tongue slowly, sinuously up and down my veins. The longing that tautened his face was so intense, I could have sworn it wasn't feigned.

'I know you didn't make war on me,' he said, his voice whisky rough. 'I'm the one who needs to make peace.'

I didn't trust myself to speak; I didn't dare caress the smooth line of his cheek, mere inches from my hand. If he wanted to punish me for rejecting him, if this was all a trick . . . I curled my fingers back towards my palm.

He set my hand down, on his thigh this time, and leant so close his cinnamon-scented breath warmed my ear. His lips whispered down my hairline. 'I haven't slept with anyone for the last two months.'

I shivered. 'Is that supposed to impress me?' I said, though in truth it did. This was Joe, after all, the fellow who could take it two, three times a day and still be up for more.

Then the emotional half of my brain ticked the other way. Why only two months? He'd been gone for six.

Joe spied my involuntary frown. He chuckled, a sexy, confident sound, then caught the back of my neck so I couldn't pull away. The way he massaged the knotted muscles made me forget I'd wanted to.

'For the first few months I did what you expected,' he said in that same intimate murmur, 'or what I thought you expected. I slept around – young and old, gorgeous and plain, women I liked, women I didn't like, plus a few men for variety's sake.' His shoulders lifted and dropped philosophically. 'Some of it was fun. A lot of it was awkward. None of it was the same. I didn't love any of them. And I still loved you.'

I pressed one fist to the sudden ache in my chest. I reminded myself how deeply he'd hurt me, and how changed he was from the boy I knew. 'If you loved me so much, why did you stay angry so long?'

He stroked my cheek the way I'd wanted to stroke his, following the curves and hollows with the back of his fingers. 'I wasn't angry.' He smiled. 'Well, maybe at first I was. Mostly I was humiliated. That's why I left the way I did and broke off all contact. Call it the Heathcliff Syndrome. I couldn't come back until I'd made something of myself. Problem was, back then I didn't know what that something was.'

'And now you do?'

Fine lines crinkled around his eyes, brought to life by an infinitely gentle smile. His expression mesmerised. I saw the old Joe in it, and the new. I couldn't decipher all the separate parts, not in my current state of mind, but I knew the combination frightened me in some deep, atavistic way. I put my fork down, certain I'd never swallow the bite it held.

Joe drew his fingertip down the valley beneath my nose, then continued across my lips and over my chin. 'Now I know I don't have to make myself into anything at all. Now I know everything that really counted I had all along. I just wasn't smart enough to see it – and neither were you.'

I tensed at the sureness in his eyes. 'That sounds like quite a revelation.'

His smile turned wicked, a thousand' watts of devastating Capriccio charm. Even though I'd seen that trademark smirk a hundred times on *Manhattan Nights,* I found I was not immune.

'Believe me, darlin',' he drawled. 'The revelations are just beginning.'

But there weren't any more revelations over dinner. The quartet began to play again, more softly this time, romantic saxophone pieces – plus a decent cover of an old Robert Cray tune, 'Little Boy Big', I think. I hadn't listened to his music since Joe left. Some of the guests stepped on to the dance floor. Joe and I had never danced together.

I wished that hadn't occurred to me, and that I really were relieved he didn't ask me now.

With music greasing the wheels of nostalgia, Joe told me about his work and asked about mine and made me laugh and kept my wine glass consistently topped. Now that he'd backed the pressure off, I warmed to him. I couldn't help it. He wasn't the old Joe, but he was still a man who knew me well and liked what he knew and obviously found me attractive. Of that I had no doubt. The banked heat of his gaze proved it, the way he used any excuse to touch me, the way he hung on my every word.

He kept my palm cupped to his inner thigh, urging my little finger against the solid swell of his cock. I quickly perspired through his trousers, or he did, but he didn't seem to care. His seam-straining erection never faltered, not for the whole hour-long conversation. Nor did he seem to mind that all I did was press the outer edge. I was the one squirming in my chair.

Anyone who saw us would have thought we were lovers. By the time I swallowed the last sip of coffee, I almost wished we were.

'I have to work the room now,' he said, with seemingly genuine regret. He lifted my hot, damp hand from his lap and kissed my fingertips. 'I'm afraid it'll bore you. Why don't I get my driver to take you home?'

My driver. What a funny thing to hear Joe say. Not so long ago his primary means of transportation had been a ten-speed bike. He escorted me down the stairs to the car park. Even in my trainers, I wobbled a bit. I'd drunk more wine than I realised – enough not to care very much, or to remember why a shiny Cadillac limo should not be idling in front of the awning.

Joe helped me into the passenger compartment and leant on the open window. We stared at each other. The streets were quiet. Halloran's was the only place open here. I looked at his lips and remembered how soft and gentle and clever they were.

He muttered something under his breath.

'What?' I asked.

'Lean out so I can kiss you,' he said.

Amazingly, I did.

He clasped my face in his hands and brushed his nose against mine. Our breath mingled, silent and warm. His tongue touched one corner of my mouth, then the other, then the centre. He pushed lightly, delicately penetrating the barrier of my lips until we both moaned low in our throats. Our mouths opened to each other, then closed, commingled. Oh, his reined-in hunger tasted so good, his heat, the assurance he'd grown like a sleek new skin. I ran my hands over his shoulders, testing the hard, rounded muscle. I wished I could rip his shirt off and ravish him where he stood.

The kiss grew deeper and wetter. Our tongues slid together like lovers coupling, quivering with six months of unassuaged yearning. My emotions seethed like heated oil as my desire for him fought my need for self-protection. Was this kiss merely one of a long procession of kisses, or did it mean what his half-choked moans implied it meant? Was it special? Did it make him sing from soul to sinew?

Ultimately, my sinews didn't care. I clutched his shoulders. My nails pricked him through the starched cotton of his shirt.

At the tiny injury, he exhaled slowly, as if he'd set down a heavy load. He turned his head and kissed me harder until the back of my head met my own shoulders. His hand bracketed the arch of my throat. He swept it lower, crossing my collar bones and dipping into the warm, scented valley between my breasts. He counted the ribs there with the pad of his thumb, up and down, down and up, as though he dared not stray from this track but could not force himself away.

Touch me, I thought, my nipples a stony pain, my blood thundering in my ears. The strength of my attraction to him dizzied me.

Then he broke away.

My only consolation was that he was breathing as hard as I was.

'Now.' He gave my cheek an little smack with the flat of his palm. His eyes glittered coolly under the street-lamp. 'That wasn't so bad, was it? Maybe next time you'll do what I tell you to.'

He couldn't have shocked me more if he'd slapped me senseless. I closed my gaping mouth with a snap. In a flash I remembered the supposedly broken-down limo, the very limo whose engine purred so smoothly through the quiet night.

He'd lied – about everything – and I'd fallen for it.

'Don't hold your breath,' I said.

He stuck his hands in his pockets and grinned. 'Take the lady home,' he instructed the impassive driver, 'and make sure she gets safely inside.'

* * *

234

Joe didn't even try to convince me to see him again. My mind boiled with fantasies of tossing huge, thorny bouquets in his face – but I never got the chance.

Every time I tried to talk to Sean about what Joe had done, he remembered a meeting he was late for or a call he had to make.

I knew his defection was Joe's doing. He was rubbing my nose in it, demonstrating in no uncertain terms the power he exerted over the man who – in his absence – had become my best friend.

The betrayal hurt so badly I spent days on the verge of tears. How can he do this, I'd ask myself, barely knowing whether 'he' was Sean or Joe. How can he be so cruel?

The fact that I was looking for an explanation bothered me. Part of me believed there must be a reason. Part of me remembered the longing in Joe's face when he kissed my palm, and that part believed – even in the teeth of the evidence – that Joe still loved me.

I fought a primitive urge to call my mother and cry on her shoulder. With her middle-class, homemaker's propriety, she'd be the last person to understand. She hadn't forgiven me yet for divorcing Tom.

On Friday I claimed boss's privilege and left half an hour early. I strode down Front Street towards Society Hill, dodging skateboarders and grimacing at the couples taking in the balmy river view.

Ice cream, I thought. I'd sweat for an hour on the stairclimber, then drown my troubles in a big, fattening dish of double-chocolate chip, and maybe I'd have a glass of wine on top of that!

I stomped two streets farther before I noticed the limousine crawling behind me. As soon as I did, I knew who sat behind the tinted glass. The big black car stopped when I did. Folding my arms beneath my breasts, I faced my reflection.

The window rolled down like butter.

'Get in,' said Joe.

'Go to hell,' said I.

He opened the door and stepped out, his length unfolding with the grace of a ballroom dancer. He buttoned his stylish Armani jacket and smoothed it straight. In my head, I damned him for looking so temptingly prosperous.

'Get in,' he said, gesturing me ahead of him. 'I can see you want to give me a piece of your mind. In there is the only place I'm prepared to listen.'

As incentives went, it was pretty thin. Even so, I couldn't bring myself to turn away. 'I don't trust you,' I said.

The skin around his eyes tightened. The response could have signalled anger or hurt. The stupid part of me chose hurt. 'Please,' he said more humbly. 'Don't you want to know why I behaved the way I did?'

I did want to know why. The stupid part of me thought he might tell me. I climbed inside the plush grey cave. Joe slid in beside me. The automatic locks shot home as soon as he closed the door. The sound startled, but Joe distracted me by taking my hands in his and gazing into my eyes. His mood seemed very serious, like a doctor about to break some bad news.

'I'm sorry to have to do this,' he said.

'Do what?' I asked at the very moment a pair of intricate velvet cuffs slid over my wrists. They tightened almost before I registered what they were.

He covered my eyes next, then bound my ankles together. I didn't fight any of it. He was stronger than I was, and I feared he'd enjoy subduing me too much.

Let's see if he likes this game when only one person plays, I thought. I vowed he'd get no response from me: not anger and not fear.

But those weren't the responses he really wanted – just the ones I could control.

Chapter Fourteen
Mind, Body and Soul

*A*fter a fifteen-minute drive, the limo stopped. Joe scooped me up and hustled me from the car to a lift, a freight lift by the sound of it. Since I was blindfolded, my ears were all I could go by. Once inside, he set me on my bound feet, steadying me when I would have teetered.

He said nothing, but I heard him breathing – deep, deliberate breaths, in through his nose and out through his mouth, like an athlete preparing for a race.

A strange calm settled over me, as though I weren't really involved in this drama. So be it, I thought. If Joe wants to alienate me for good, so be it. At least I'll stop pining for him.

But those thoughts flowed like ripples on the surface of a river. Other feelings ran beneath them, too murky to acknowledge. Despite my outward passivity, my skin tingled with energy and I hovered on the verge of arousal. My womb was heavy, my awareness of every sensation keen. It's the blindfold, I told myself. But I knew it wasn't.

As the lift rose, Joe wrapped a wide velvet collar around my neck. I brought my arms up – wrists together, of course – to touch it. A long leash led off from its front.

'Honestly,' I huffed. 'You couldn't come up with something more original?'

Joe proved better at keeping silent than I. The lift clanked to a halt. He lifted me in his arms again and carried me down a long, quiet corridor. My neck ached from trying not to let my head rest on his shoulder. We must have made quite a picture – he in his suit, I in my black velvet bonds. Someone gasped as we passed, but did not try to stop us.

I could have cried out then, made it clear I was being held against my will. For a moment, the possibility excited me. Adrenalin surged through my veins. But I did not act to save myself.

This was Joe's first victory.

'Good girl.' He nuzzled the baby-fine hair at my temple. 'Now you begin to understand.'

I did struggle then, but silently, and it was too late anyway. Ignoring my squirms, he shifted me to free one arm. Seconds later, I heard a door open. He set me down inside and closed it. My struggles died. I waited, bound hands clasped before my sex. The door shut. The bolt turned. A silence fell. I imagined I could feel the weight of Joe's eyes as clearly as I felt the weight of the slave collar.

Watch me then, I thought, my skin twitching with awareness. Watch me and weep.

He circled me with slow, measured footfalls. As he did, the leash cinched under one breast and over the other. A pulse beat in my nipples, tapping my skin from the inside out. Because I refused to give way, the leather bit into my arm, crossed my back, and trussed my other elbow to my side.

The circuit complete, he covered my breast with his hand, squeezed, then smoothed a burning path up my neck and over my jaw until he reached the blindfold. His fingers brushed the edge, stroking both velvet and skin from my cheekbone to the bridge of my nose. The gentle touch spurred a soft explosion in my groin. Warm, creamy pleasure spread outward from my core, up my belly and down my thighs. I pressed my lips together to still their trembling.

'You've been good so far,' he said, his voice another caress, 'and I know you don't like having your eyes covered. Shall I reward you by taking this off?'

He did not wait for my answer but eased the blindfold away. I blinked. I knew this place. We stood in a penthouse suite at The Four Seasons hotel.

No other hotel commanded such a view. The Swann fountain in Logan Circles plashed beneath the veranda and in the distance, at the end of a long grassy stretch of Benjamin Franklin Parkway, I spied the 'Rocky' stairs at the museum. I'd put up a few business contacts here, ones I wanted to impress. I knew for a fact it cost two hundred a night, and that was for a standard room. Lord only knew how much this suite cost.

Probably enough to buy Joe a lot of privacy.

He knelt before me, untied my ankles, and pulled off my trainers. I don't know why, but I immediately felt more vulnerable. As he rose, he untangled the leash and wrapped the end around his wrist. 'Now you can walk like a proper slave.'

I tried to laugh but it came out strained. He spoke without melodrama and with utter, unshakable confidence. My mouth closed on my pitiful attempt at mockery. When he tugged the leash, I followed.

The plush navy carpet could not steady my shaky knees. He led me past a well-stocked bar, an alcove with a built-in library, a formal dining room, and a bathroom big enough to host an orgy. Then we entered the bedroom.

The bed itself was huge. Like the rest of the furniture, it was an eighteenth-century American reproduction, carved of good quality mahogany with shells and eagles forming the primary motifs. Solid head- and foot-boards framed either end. It struck me as a particularly serious bed. I pictured Joe lying naked on the navy counterpane, his cock dark and hard, his muscles drawn tight with anticipation. I would straddle his narrow hips, take him delicately in hand and lower myself. He would moan as I swallowed the crown. He would –

My daydream broke. Something gleamed on one of the pillows. Something that shouldn't have been there – a pair of tailor's scissors.

What did Joe want with those? What could Joe do with those? Unless he'd changed more than I believed a person could change, he didn't have a physically violent bone in his body. But the scissors were there, cold and sharp, and they had to hold some threat. Troubled, aroused, and not wanting to be either, I forced my eyes away and found an image of peace.

A large picture window, curved to follow the hotel's distinctive U-shape, overlooked the sea of greenery around the courtyard café. People would be gathered beneath those trees, enjoying the late summer sun, drinking a tall cold one after work – innocent pleasures.

I sighed at how inviting it sounded. If things had been different, Joe and I could have sat down there. We could have held hands across the table and gazed into each other's eyes. Painful as it was to admit, I wanted that stupid, bourgeois fantasy. Except maybe, just maybe, I wanted this, too.

'Pretty, isn't it?' Joe said, then grabbed me and tossed me on to the bed.

Before I could regain my balance, he pulled a tie from his pocket and lashed my bound wrists to the eagle at the centre of the headboard.

'Hey!' I said, but he was done almost before the word was out.

I'd never seen him so aggressive. He dragged my legs apart, ignoring the aborted jerks that signalled my desire to kick him where it counted. Long velvet straps dangled from opposite ends of the footboard and to these he secured my ankles. He laughed when I couldn't resist a tug to verify their strength.

'Feels good, doesn't it, Katie? Feels good to meet your master.'

'You wish,' I muttered, but the bindings were working their insidious magic.

I was helpless now, entirely at his mercy. Cool air drifted between my spread legs, emphasising the heat of my groin. Welling, swelling, it lapped outward in thick, feverish waves. I could not deny I wanted him or that, in some secret corner of my soul, I wanted him to overpower me.

He knew it, too, damn him.

'I'll take you to your limit,' he promised, in a silky growl. 'I'll take everything you gave to Sean and more.'

'Is that what this is about? Besting Sean?'

He did not dignify my accusation with an answer. Smiling like the Mona Lisa, he stepped back and loosened his tie. My pulse jumped in my throat. Our eyes connected and held. His smile deepened as he slid the knot down. He threw the tie across the room.

I watched it hit the window, the huge, bare window. Did he intend to strip off without drawing the curtains? What if those tower blocks were close enough to see in?

'Don't.' Though he did not speak loudly, the order rang through the stately room. My gaze snapped back to his. 'Don't look away or it will go harder for you.'

I wasn't sure I believed him, but I didn't really want to look away, not when he removed his jacket and pulled his shirt-tails free. The stark white cloth quickly covered his erection. Not that it mattered. The instant I saw the stupendous bulge, the image was engraved on my retinas. His left trouser leg had trapped the fat knob, pulling the shaft off true. Such a personal thing to know, which way a man liked to hang his goods.

He undid a cuff link without breaking eye contact.

'As I recall,' he said, 'you like to watch. That was part of the thrill, wasn't it? Seeing Sean and me take it in the arse, seeing us suck each other off or steal a little feel in the middle of fucking you.'

I squirmed on the satiny bedspread. Why waste my breath denying it? 'Are you going to talk or take off your clothes?' I said, my voice too breathy to count as flippant.

241

His hands rose to his collar. One button popped free, then another. Sheer black curls appeared at the base of the 'V'. Button by button, he widened the alluring gap, then reached inside to massage his flat male nipples. When his hands withdrew, tiny points lifted the smooth Egyptian cotton. I remembered how he tasted there, how he felt on my palm.

His clever hands worked the last button free.

'I like to watch, too,' he said.

I didn't know why he said that. Tied up this way, I couldn't put on a show. He could, though, and did. He cupped the shirt-tails between his legs and rubbed himself through the added barrier, a roving, thorough exploration that told me – beyond a shadow of a doubt – how much he wanted touching. He kneaded the imprisoned head, a circling pinch between fingers and thumb. I knew he loved that. He used to love it when I licked him there. Was he thinking of that now? I swallowed. He was swelling even more. His hip swivelled forward. His voice turned rough.

'I like watching the way you watch my hands,' he said, 'the way a flush crawls over your cheeks, the way your hips roll a little – as though you're imagining how I'll feel inside you. You know I'll be big. You know you'll have to stretch to take me.'

I opened my mouth to catch a clear breath. He pushed the shirt-tails behind his hips and bared his glory. Its size distorted the fall of his elegant slacks, pushing out the zip, creasing the crotch.

'I'm imagining it, too,' he said. 'I remember how wet you'd get, how you'd drench me when I pushed inside you. I especially enjoyed the way you'd squeeze me with your cunt like you wanted to trap me there all night, like you wanted to milk the life out of me.' He leant over the footboard, sharing a secret. 'I hope you'll do that today, Kate.'

Fat chance, I wanted to say, but all that came out was a pitiful whimper. My nice Christian Dior trousers were halfway to drenched already. They grew more so when he shrugged each shoulder free of his shirt. I'd always thought Joe had the perfect physique, but this was ... That hair-covered wall of hard male muscle affected me so strongly, so primitively, I felt embarrassed, almost disloyal to my memory of the younger, smoother Joe.

Heavens, he was gorgeous – a Greek statue in warm, living flesh. I wanted to touch him, to rub myself all over him like a cat marking its owner.

My desire must have shone on my face. He grinned and flexed for me. His pecs flicked up and down. He slapped the rippling six-pack at his belly. 'What do you think, Kate? A hundred thou a week pays for a lot of gym time.'

I could not respond. My throat was too tight. His hands fell to his belt buckle. The distinctive clank of it opening, the hiss of leather through the belt loops, made me shiver. Those sounds meant sex to me: meant the imminent approach of relief. But not today. Today, relief was no sure thing. I should have been enraged. Instead, I lay spellbound.

He undid the waist catch and drew down the zip, inch by rasping inch. He paused, holding the edges together. My body tensed from toe to scalp. Let go, I thought. Let me see. His fingers opened. The trousers slid to the floor in a sibilant, silk-lined rush.

He wore nothing beneath them, just himself, springing upward now from a nest of shiny black curls. He planted his hands on his hips and widened his stance. His balls swung free between his thighs, heavy and full. I couldn't laugh at his machismo. He looked too good. In any case, he was laughing at me, silently, his eyes dancing with triumph. Somewhere I found the strength to frown.

'Now, now,' he said. 'Let's see if we can't make you more comfortable.'

I discovered what the scissors were for then. He cut the clothes off my body, piece by piece, skimming my limbs with the back of the cold, sharp blade. To my shame, I hadn't the presence of mind to regret the loss of my designer outfit. I was too elated at the prospect of being one step closer to intercourse. With a flourish that suggested he knew my expectations, Joe reserved the final snips for the sides of my panties. He pulled them from beneath me as smoothly as he had the rest, then sat beside me with one leg bent on the mattress. The smooth skin of his hip warmed my thigh, the hairy skin of his thigh, my side.

He cupped the rise of my mound, surrounding it, squeezing it. The tip of his middle finger slipped into my pooling warmth, just grazing my clit. My hips surged off the bed, but as soon as I moved he withdrew. I couldn't bite back a groan.

'You want me a lot, don't you?' He pulled his fingers lightly up my meridian, bisecting my belly and breasts.

Silence was my only defence, a thin one, considering how badly I was shaking.

His fingers ghosted back to my fleece. They drew an outline around its periphery, an arrow of lust. 'That's all right, sweetheart. You don't have to answer. Yet. I'm looking forward to torturing it out of you. I know you need to give yourself completely to a man, not the separate parts, but the whole: mind, body and soul. You want mastering, Kate. You need it.'

He didn't see me grinding my teeth because he turned to the bedside table and opened the drawer. Instead of the small foil packet I expected, he removed a calligrapher's brush.

I stared at it, bemused.

'We're going to play a game now – an ancient Chinese game, one I learned from a Nepalese sex guru in New York. No, don't laugh. The Asian world has made an art of sex. They understand that sometimes even foreplay is too purposeful. Sometimes teasing is its own reward. So close your eyes, Kate. Imagine yourself naked in the sun on a warm spring day. You're lying on a blanket in a beautiful field of flowers. Hear the bees, Kate? Feel the balmy, velvet breeze?'

I did hear them. I did feel it. My eyes flew open. 'You're hypnotising me.'

'Shh.' He smoothed my lids shut with the flat of his palm. The calming singsong continued. 'No one can be hypnotised against their will. In your heart you know you're safe with me, and very relaxed, so relaxed that all your awareness centres on the pleasant sensations in your body. The sun is warm. Your body melts like honey under its rays. That's right, sweetheart, breathe deeply. Breathe in the scent of the beautiful flowers.'

'I love when you call me "sweetheart",' I said, stupid and stuporous, drowsing under the spell of his words. I could feel the hairs on my arms prickle as his movements stirred the air. I wanted him to touch me, but between my languor and my bonds I couldn't budge an inch.

'Now a butterfly comes,' he said. 'It's fluttering above you, looking for a place to light. You're nice and warm, Kate. Butterflies like to be warm, but it wonders if you're a safe place to rest.'

My lips curved at the silly story. Still, I could see the butterfly, an iridescent, sapphire angel, hovering against the clear spring sky. Something soft brushed the arch of one foot, then the other, then skittered to my toes. I knew it was the calligraphy brush but, in my mind, shimmering blue wings fanned the air. I gasped at the intensity of the gossamer touch, at the trail of tingling nerves it left behind.

The butterfly skimmed my ankle, my calf. It lingered for a moment on the warmth of my inner thigh. My buttocks tightened with longing and it took flight, alighting on the areola of one nipple. The centre erected at once, painfully. I moaned and it fled to the other breast.

'Oh, God,' I whispered as it circled there, a caress as light as air, but so potent it brought tears to my eyes.

The touch flittered to the sensitive skin beneath my upraised arm, then darted back to my toes, my belly. I never knew where it would land or how long it would stay, and the anticipation aroused as much as the moments of contact.

I heard Joe breathing hard and deep. I smelled the musk of male arousal.

He touched a point midway between my navel and pubis that almost made me see stars. Energy rushed out from my centre. My back arched off the bed.

'Ah,' he whispered, 'we're getting closer to the warmest spot.'

He drew the brush up my clitoris, a light, glancing stroke. He repeated it. The sensation changed as the brush grew slick with dew. I felt it more, needed it more. The brush lapped me like a tiny tongue. My thighs trembled. My head thrashed back and forth on the pillow. I tightened my inner muscles, trying to pull myself to climax but the delicate stroking held me on the edge – pushing me up but not over.

'Please,' I groaned, forgetting all my promises to myself. 'Please, Joe, I need to come.'

'Do you?' His lips tickled my earlobe, setting off a new set of sparklers. The brush continued its ethereal torture. 'I wonder if you need it enough to do me a favour.'

'Anything,' I said, and meant it.

'How you tempt me.'

The wistful answer made my eyelids flutter open.

'Anything,' I repeated.

His eyes darkened, pupils swallowing up the glowing gold. 'I don't want what you think I want – not sexual favours, not a night of fucking.'

'What do you want?' I sounded drugged. I couldn't help it. He'd never stirred me this way before. No one had.

The brush dipped for one aching moment into the well of my sex. 'I want you to marry me.'

My mouth dropped. I tried to summon the outrage I thought I should feel. 'You can't coerce a person into marrying you.'

'Can't I?' The brush flicked up my labia and circled my clit.

'No! Oh, God –' My breath caught as he increased the pressure by the smallest, most excruciating margin.

246

'Even if you could make me say "yes", what's to keep me from going back on my word later on?'

'But you try very hard to keep your word.' He said this slowly, deliberately, as if the phrase held a secret meaning. 'You try very hard to keep your word.'

At the second repetition, I remembered. I'd made that exact claim to Sean six months ago, when he hadn't believed I meant to stay friends. It had been a private moment, the turning point in our relationship, the day our real friendship began.

'Sean told you that?' I couldn't hide my hurt.

Joe smiled with his eyes alone, gently, and with genuine compassion. 'He told me everything. He knows what I'm here to do. He wants me to be happy. He wants you to be happy.'

'I can't make you choose.' The words were out before I knew it. Abruptly, I knew I was taking this proposal seriously.

'Choose?' His brow furrowed. 'I told you, I'm not in love with Sean – or do you mean choose between men and women?'

'I don't want you to look back twenty years from now and feel you've missed out, that you denied half your sexuality.'

With one finger, he teased a damp curl from my cheek. 'Everyone who marries chooses between the rest of the world and the person they love. Whatever I give up will be nothing compared to what I gain.' His gaze narrowed, a golden laser to my soul. 'I want all of you, the light Kate and the dark Kate. You gave me your heart before. Now I want the rest. I want it for myself and I want it for keeps. I've had six months to think about this, long enough to be sure I love you more than all those other choices.'

This time he didn't ask if I'd marry Sean. My answer would have been the same – that Sean wouldn't ask me. But my feelings about the answer were different. Sean and I had been in each other's pockets for half a year.

We'd been friends, partners and lovers. We respected each other, relied on each other.

Didn't Sean mind? I wondered. Not just losing Joe, but losing me?

Joe waited, following the conflict in my eyes.

'Everyone has to choose,' he said quietly.

I wondered if he meant me this time. But was it such a close race? My heart wanted Joe. My heart said: this man will be true to you all his days. This man makes you want to surrender in a way no man ever has. If a corner – perhaps a substantial corner – of my heart belonged to Sean, then so be it.

'Yes,' I said, and a bolt of pure gladness flashed through my being.

Joe released the breath he'd been holding. 'You'll marry me?' The old Joe struggled in his face, fighting to believe. 'Really?'

'Really.' I laughed, not believing I was doing this, giddy as a schoolgirl on champagne.

'Yes!' His fist punched the air as if his team had won the cup. 'Oh, but I have to get you out of this.' He reached for the scissors.

'Not so fast.' I stopped him before he could cut me free. 'You have some unfinished business, Mr Capriccio.' I stared meaningfully at the calligrapher's brush.

'Oh.' He looked at the delightful instrument of torture, then at my glistening sex. 'No, I'm sorry, Kate. You look too delicious. The brush will have to finish you another day.'

He reached into the bedside table. This time he brought out what I expected, and something else as well: a small black jeweller's box whose eye-popping contents sparkled with the clarity of spring water. Jesus. That diamond had to be three carats. He slid the ring on to the third finger of my left hand, where the gold immediately began to warm.

My first response was to coo the way any woman would at the sight of such a rock. I wished I could pull my hands free to admire it. But the ring made the engagement too real – too real and too scary. 'Joe, it's beautiful, but I can't accept it.'

'Yes, you can.' He clambered between my outspread legs and bowed to me, his muscular haunches rising, the curve of his spine like a reed bending in the wind.

At once I forgot my protests. It had been a long time since I'd felt those silky locks between my thighs. I moaned as his thumbs slid up the petals of my sex, parting me for his kiss.

'Ah, Kate,' he breathed. 'How could I have forgotten how beautiful you are, like a wet pink seashell?' He ran the tip of his tongue up my clit, lifting it gently, his touch as subtle as the Chinese brush. My hips strained towards his mouth. My wrists tugged the ties that bound them.

'Don't tease me, Joe.'

He repeated the feather-light caress. 'Just a little longer.' He nuzzled closer and sighed. 'You don't know what it does to me to see you squirm. It's been so long.'

'Two whole months.'

'Six,' he corrected, and rose to his knees. His sex stood out from his belly, dramatically thick and proud, every millimetre vibrating with power. He propped his hands on either side of me. 'It's been six months since anyone made me feel whole in bed. I need to take you, Kate.' He shifted and the tip of his cock probed my curls. 'I need to take all of you.'

'Then do,' I said, 'and please hurry.'

He grinned, still hovering on the brink of penetration. He lifted the scissors from the pillow beside my head. 'Shall I cut you free first?'

'Oh, yes. Yes, please.'

I wrapped him close as he sank inside with one long, humming, quivering push. My hands roamed his back, loving the furrow of his spine, the fans of muscle at his sides. His breath came in anguished pants. He coaxed my thighs wider with a gentle caress. My calves squeezed him home the final inch.

He closed his eyes in blind pleasure, then opened them and kissed me softly on the lips.

Still and speechless, we throbbed together – our hearts displaced to that intimate juncture of yin and yang.

'You've got to move,' I said, though I, too, loved the hanging pause. 'I can't bear it.'

'Yes,' he said, drawing back and sinking again. 'Yes.'

There were no more words then, only sighs and moans and bodies slapping together with ever increasing fervour. The bed creaked. Joe gripped desperate fistfuls of the navy coverlet. Oh, the noises he made, as though I were stabbing him with that long, smooth spear. Sweet pain. Sweet union. The miracle of body contained in body. Could we ever get close enough? We lunged in sync to double our separate strength. We groaned together. We sobbed for air.

'Now,' I said, soaring through the ache and wanting him with me. 'Now, now.'

But he wouldn't let go. His face twisted as my spasms gripped him. He drove through the juicy internal convulsions, blinking sweat from his eyes.

'Again,' he said, and he changed angles, pumping the sweet spot behind my pubis. 'Let me feel you come again.

I guess he wanted proof of how much I loved him, how much my body loved him. Or maybe he needed to show himself master in this, as well – master of himself.

'Joe,' I began, but the plea was lost in a second rippling crescendo. My spine arched off the bed. My nails scored his back. I didn't want to hurt him, but I literally couldn't control myself.

'Good, Kate, good,' he panted. He rose up on his arms, locked his elbows and quickened his thrusts.

I knew he couldn't continue this way. A vein pulsed at his temple. His lips drew back in a snarl.

'Joe, please,' I begged. 'Please, love, come.'

'One more,' he gritted out. 'One more. Ah, God.'

Then he jolted inside me, coming, shaking, moaning

250

so loudly the sound alone drew the one more he craved from the depths of my sex.

We cried out in unison. We clutched each other like sailors swept overboard in a storm, dying the little death, taking our first step into a new life.

My heart took a long time to settle back to normal. As it slowed, I looked inside myself, trying to determine what I felt – light-headed, mostly, or maybe just light, as though I'd set down a burden I'd been carrying a long time, a solitary burden.

I touched the huge, marquis-cut diamond with my thumb. Could I really marry him? Could I believe in happy endings the way I had as a child? Did I even know Joe any more?

He stirred beside me, turned his body towards mine. 'I want another favour from you, and I want this one without coercion.'

Well, what was one more? 'Name it,' I said.

'I want you to promise you'll never make me do that again.'

I looked him full in the face. He was serious. 'You can't tell me you didn't enjoy yourself. You came like a freight train.'

Annoyance thinned his sensitive mouth. 'You know I liked what we did today. What I didn't like was hurting you.'

'Then why did you?' I went up on my elbow. 'Because you did hurt me, you and Sean both.'

His eyes filled. 'I know I walked a fine line, Kate, and I'm sorrier than you can imagine. But you had to know I could master you. You were afraid to give your body and heart to the same man. So you let Sean master one and me the other. You kept yourself safe that way. But safe isn't good enough any more.' He traced the tiny lashes beneath my eyes. 'I had to prove my nature is as powerful as yours – or Sean's. I simply choose to exercise my power differently. We are equals, Kate. We're just different.'

I stared him down for a minute but he didn't look

away. He believed what he was saying and, after today, I guessed I believed it, too.

Suddenly, I saw the humour in it. He'd mastered me only to beg me not to make him do it again. 'Does this mean you refuse to top me once we're married?'

He realised what I'd said before I did. Not 'if' we're married, but 'once we're married'. Ducking his head to hide his grin, he wiggled my sparkling diamond back and forth. 'I might agree to crack the whip now and then,' he conceded, 'if you ask me real nice.'

Chapter Fifteen
Happily Ever After

I waited for Sean to say something like, 'I'm sorry I
didn't let you know what Joe was up to,' or, 'I'll miss
our Wednesday night workouts.'

Beyond offering the requisite congratulations, however, our decision seemed not to affect him. All through
the wedding planning insanity, he maintained a cheerful
front. He was helpful and sensible, an unshakable voice
of reason.

For instance, I'd married my ex at City Hall. I didn't
see why we couldn't do that again and throw a big party
afterwards. Sean knew better. With boundless patience,
he explained why Joe's family – and Joe himself – would
consider only a church wedding meaningful.

'Don't worry, though. Joe's mother's cousin is an aide
to some archbishop. You shouldn't have any trouble
with the annulment.'

I raked my hair back. 'That's like saying my first
marriage never happened, which is a lie.'

Sean spread his hands. 'God works in mysterious
ways, babe. Who are you to complain if He smooths
your path?'

Not having been taught by Jesuits, I didn't know how
to argue with that.

'Grin and bear it,' he advised, 'for Joe's sake. If he sees

you're unhappy, you know he'll let you elope, and he'll be sorry for it later.'

No doubt this was true, but Sean's attitude unnerved me.

At one point, when it looked like my father wouldn't tear himself away from a long-standing golf date, Sean even volunteered to give me away.

Tears blurred my vision. I confessed that, in a way, I was his to give; part of me would always belong to him.

'Which part?' he asked with a cartoonish leer. But he also gave me an odd sideways glance, as though calculating how much truth my words held – and what advantage that truth might give him.

I told myself I was being paranoid, or thinking wishful. I knew I'd miss him. Even if I didn't love him the way I loved Joe, with Sean I could let my hair down.

One night, tired of playing United Nations negotiator to the future in-laws – and one or two beers beyond my limit – I told Sean I wished we could forget the wedding, just go back to the way things were in the beginning.

We were sharing a corner table at the Irish Pub on Walnut, on a weeknight, so it wasn't too jammed. We had to watch where we went these days. Joe had a knack for throwing on a pair of horn-rimmed spectacles and passing himself off as nobody, but sometimes even Clark Kent blew his cover. Luckily, he didn't get mobbed. His fans could, however, occasionally make pests of themselves. Tonight he was stuck in a potential investor's meeting for the recording studio. Since he was now an hour late, Sean won the bend-your-ear sweepstake for my horrible day. Lucky Sean.

'Don't kid yourself, Kate,' he said, giving his mug a thoughtful twist. 'You're a nester and so is Joe. You need to commit. You need to belong to someone.'

'But I'll miss you,' I grumbled.

Sean smiled into his beer. 'I'm glad to hear you say that.'

Joe walked in then with a flurry of apologies and kisses – so I never did ask why Sean was glad.

* * *

254

The three of us went out the night before the wedding – no drinking, just dinner and dessert at the Osteria Romana, a lovely, old-fashioned restaurant near the Italian market. Its stucco walls and sparkling white tile floors were a far cry from the dives we used to frequent, but the *veal saltimbocca* was worth every penny. Happily, none of us had to count pennies these days.

Joe and I finished with decaf and *biscotti*. Sean ordered a scoop of raspberry *gelato*.

I wondered if he remembered the first conversation we had over the icy treat – when he revealed how he and Joe met, and let me know he wasn't averse to a three-way adventure.

If he did remember, he didn't mention it. We shared other stories: the Robert Cray CD Joe wore out trying to lure me into his room; Keith's pitiful crush on Cheryl; Marianne's new career; the look on my face when I found Sean's uncle's sweaty crew tramping through my house with the makings of our gym.

Our gym. The phrase made me drop my chin to my hand. It had been Sean's and my gym for the last six months. He hadn't removed his equipment yet. Would he come to work out after tomorrow? Would Joe mind? Was he secure enough to assume Sean and I would behave? I certainly intended to. If anything, my experience with my ex had increased the value I placed on marital fidelity. I would never hurt Joe that way. I hoped he trusted me. Still, I didn't dare ask my questions aloud.

Sean burst out laughing, distracting me. 'Remember Captain Blood?'

'And his lucky eye-patch?' I added, revelling in Joe's blush.

'I still have it,' he confessed. His eyes twinkled. 'I remember how it got lucky, too.'

Sharing those stories felt like the last day of summer camp, full of good memories, but wistful. Though I looked forward to going home, so to speak, I'd miss my playmates.

When the three of us started yawning over our plates, Sean and Joe walked me back to Society Hill.

Sean stopped Joe short of the front steps by flattening his palm across his chest. Joe's brows shot towards his hairline. The unspoken challenge did not move Sean at all.

'Sorry, buddy. You can't go in, not even for a good night kiss. She's got the dress laid out in the living room. It'd be bad luck for you to see it.'

'Oh.' Joe took a hesitant step back and looked at me.

I shrugged. I didn't know what Sean was up to, either.

Reading our expressions like a book, Sean staggered in mock dismay. 'I swear I'm not sneaking in for one last slap and tickle. I want to give Kate my wedding gift. You know, the one we talked about.'

The stiffness left Joe's stance. 'Oh. Sure. Sorry, I shouldn't have –'

'Forget it.' Sean waved his apology away. 'I kind of like being considered unscrupulous.'

Despite Sean's promise to behave, my nerves tightened as he dug his gift from the deluge that had recently overwhelmed my dining room.

He emerged with a shop-wrapped white and silver box. Lilies of the valley sprayed out from the bow. Shifting from foot to foot, he ruffled the silk flowers with his thumb.

'I was considering a bun warmer, but I thought you'd like this better.' He thrust the box in my direction. 'Happy wedding, or whatever people say.'

I set the box on the one clear corner of the table and prised off the lid. Inside was a dog-eared stack of letters bound in blue satin ribbon. I touched one loop of the crooked bow. Sean must have tied this one. I skied my finger down to its central knot. The envelopes, all neatly slitted, held letters. Sean's Rittenhouse Square address was printed on the front – in Joe's handwriting.

Curious but wary, I lifted them from the box. 'What are these?'

'Love letters.' Sean stepped closer. 'Though we didn't

256

touch, his body heat warmed my back. 'They're addressed to me, but most of what's in them has to do with you. I hope you don't mind that I cut out the parts that were private.'

I shook my head in confusion. 'Joe was writing to you about me?'

'Yup. About once a week. He asked how you were, who were you dating, what did I think of this dream he had about you, and could I please send some of your favourite lavender soap because he couldn't find it anywhere in New York.' Chuckling, he reached around me and tapped the letters. 'He told me all the things he was too proud to share with you – his setbacks, his triumphs, the fantasies he invented to get off by when he couldn't stand the thought of coaxing another stranger into bed. Not that there were so many.'

I sensed Sean's grin without seeing it.

'All the fantasies starred you, of course. They're pretty hot, so don't read them when he's out of town.'

'But why didn't he write me?' I asked, letting out my last scrap of unsoothed hurt.

'Aw, Kate.' Sean's hand settled to my shoulder. 'You don't know how many times I wanted to tell you he still loved you. But the idiot swore me to secrecy. I'm not sure he was wrong, either. Do you really think you'd have ended up here if he hadn't backed off for a while?'

I thought about that. Maybe Joe did have to leave before I could see him clearly. I'd locked him so firmly into his niche: Sean's bottom, my lovesick puppy. The truth was he'd had power over us both all along. The scales were never as unequal as I'd assumed. I just couldn't admit it back then. Like Joe said, I was afraid to let one man have all of me.

'No,' I said. 'I don't suppose we would have ended up here.'

'That's a girl.' Sean slapped my back. He turned towards the door.

'You're going?' The words were out before I could think better of them.

He rapped a playful drum roll on the frame. 'You bet, Madame Bride-to-be. I need my beauty rest or no one's going to believe I really am the best man.'

He was whistling as he pulled the door shut behind him, and I wondered what he had to be so happy about.

For all my hand-wringing, the wedding went swimmingly. We were married in the little church where Joe was baptised. Happily, the priest did not keel over when he saw my sequinned sapphire gown – the same backless gown Joe had demanded I wear to Halloran's. The short veil was dyed to match and I carried a bouquet of blue violets. Personally, I loved the way I looked, despite the whispers it inspired. My father, who did forego his golf date, said he wouldn't have bothered if he'd known it was going to be a costume ball.

On the brighter side, Sean's sister, the security expert, scored a coup by sending the paparazzi on a wild goose chase to the Cathedral of Saints Peter and Paul. The only pictures the media were able to print were the few Joe's publicist released.

Our pint-sized receptionist, Cheryl, sang a song Joe composed especially for the ceremony. I was biased, of course, but I thought it was beautiful. My mascara was down around my neck by the time the last note trailed away. That pleased Joe. Every time I sniffled, he had to hide his grin.

I caught my mother sniffling, too. When she hugged me afterwards, she conceded that this young fellow and I seemed to suit and maybe Tom and I simply weren't meant to be.

That alone was worth the price of admission.

Joe and I stood side by side at the head of the receiving queue. Every so often, we'd turn to each other and exchange loopy grins. I noticed Cheryl and Keith had sat together, not come together but sat together. This sign of romantic progress pleased me. Everyone should do this, I thought as I thanked the people filing out from the pews. Their well wishes might have been the profoundest poetry, so strongly did they move me. I hadn't known I'd feel so happy, hadn't dared hope.

This is going to work, I thought, brimming with joy. We will live happily ever after.

Then Sean reached the front of the queue.

I opened my arms without a word.

Hands lighting on my waist, he pressed the traditional bridal kiss to my lips – or so it must have seemed. Only I felt the nip of teeth on my lower lip, only I tasted the lightning-quick flicker of his tongue, and only I knew that the subtle clasp and release of his hands on my hips mimicked the age-old rhythm of coitus.

His boldness made me want to laugh. Long live the bad boy.

When he released me, his eyes gleamed with mischief. I couldn't help smiling back. As one, we threw ourselves into a bone-cracking embrace.

'I'll miss you,' I said against his ear.

He chuckled. 'Don't count on it, babe.' His hand slid down to my bottom and squeezed me through the slick, cool sequins.

Then he pushed me back and held me at arm's length.

'Remember I'll never hurt you,' he said.

A strange thing to say . . . until I saw the kiss he gave the groom.

Rising slightly on his toes, he slanted his full, sensual mouth over Joe's startled one. It was a tongueless kiss, but devastating – light as air, subtle as silk. My own lips tingled at the sight. I knew how soft those lips could be, and how hard the hands that slid down Joe's tail-coated back. Sean urged their bodies close enough to touch from lip to ankle. He'd been half-hard when he hugged me, and now his cock stood out flagpole stiff. Shorter than Joe, the tip caught him just below the crotch. The moment the extra pressure registered, Joe's knuckles whitened on Sean's arms. I could almost read his thoughts. Should he push him away and risk hurting his feelings? Or trust him to stop before he caused a scene?

His indecision cost him. In a few short seconds, his

best man's kiss took a predictable toll. Joe's cock jerked upward, lifting the smooth black cloth of his trousers. Not one to miss an advantage, Sean sidled their legs together. Their erections brushed. Joe flinched. His hips swayed forward, then back, as he fought the seductive pull.

When the people queued up behind Sean began to murmur, Joe gathered his strength and broke free.

The entire exchange lasted less than half a minute.

As shameless as ever, Sean winked at Joe and tipped an invisible hat at me.

'See you after the honeymoon,' he said.

Joe shook a scolding finger. Despite his grin, I knew Sean had shaken him – not so much by kissing him, as by making him react so forcefully. Colour stained his cheeks and a vein pulsed double-time above his crisp white collar points.

I stared sharply at Sean, without effect. Still smirking like the cat that stole the cream, he stuck his hands in his pockets and shrugged.

'What goes around comes around,' he said.

Then I understood.

Once upon a time, Sean had used me to hang on to Joe. Now he would use Joe to hang on to me. Joe would not, could not tolerate my seduction. But perhaps he would tolerate his own. If he saw that his love for Sean sparked no fear in my heart. If he saw that I, too, missed our precarious balance of three. And I knew Joe missed it. That rocket in his pocket wouldn't lie, not on our wedding day.

When Sean finally turned to go, the bounce in his step did not surprise me.

'Hm.' Joe slung his arm around my shoulder and leant conspiratorially close. 'Why do I feel as if we should invite him on the honeymoon?'

His words delighted me. 'Don't be so sure he won't pop up,' I teased.

Joe squinted at me, shocked-father-style. 'You two make a very naughty pair.'

'Yes, we do.' I reached under his tail coat to pat his cheek. 'Impossibly naughty.'

Joe licked the curl of my ear. 'I suppose I'll have to show you and Sean who's boss.'

The prospect sent a carnal shiver through my sex. I couldn't imagine how Joe would master both of us. 'Well.' I gave my veil a saucy flip. 'You have my permission to try.'

BLACK LACE BOOKLIST

Information is correct at time of printing. To avoid disappointment check availability before ordering. Go to www.blacklace-books.co.uk

All books are priced £5.99 unless another price is given.

Black Lace books with a contemporary setting

THE TOP OF HER GAME	Emma Holly ISBN 0 352 33337 5	☐
IN THE FLESH	Emma Holly ISBN 0 352 33498 3	☐
SHAMELESS	Stella Black ISBN 0 352 33485 1	☐
TONGUE IN CHEEK	Tabitha Flyte ISBN 0 352 33484 3	☐
SAUCE FOR THE GOOSE	Mary Rose Maxwell ISBN 0 352 33492 4	☐
INTENSE BLUE	Lyn Wood ISBN 0 352 33496 7	☐
THE NAKED TRUTH	Natasha Rostova ISBN 0 352 33497 5	☐
A SPORTING CHANCE	Susie Raymond ISBN 0 352 33501 7	☐
TAKING LIBERTIES	Susie Raymond ISBN 0 352 33357 X	☐
A SCANDALOUS AFFAIR	Holly Graham ISBN 0 352 33523 8	☐
THE NAKED FLAME	Crystalle Valentino ISBN 0 352 33528 9	☐
CRASH COURSE	Juliet Hastings ISBN 0 352 33018 X	☐
ON THE EDGE	Laura Hamilton ISBN 0 352 33534 3	☐
LURED BY LUST	Tania Picarda ISBN 0 352 33533 5	☐
LEARNING TO LOVE IT	Alison Tyler ISBN 0 352 33535 1	☐

Black Lace books with an historical setting

Black Lace anthologies

Black Lace non-fiction

------- ✂ --------------------

Please send me the books I have ticked above.

Name ....

Address ....

....

....

.... Post Code ....

Send to: Cash Sales, Black Lace Books, Thames Wharf Studios, Rainville Road, London W6 9HA.

US customers: for prices and details of how to order books for delivery by mail, call 1-800-805-1083.

Please enclose a cheque or postal order, made payable to **Virgin Publishing Ltd**, to the value of the books you have ordered plus postage and packing costs as follows:
  UK and BFPO – £1.00 for the first book, 50p for each subsequent book.
  Overseas (including Republic of Ireland) – £2.00 for the first book, £1.00 for each subsequent book.

If you would prefer to pay by VISA, ACCESS/MASTER-CARD, DINERS CLUB, AMEX or SWITCH, please write your card number and expiry date here:

....

Please allow up to 28 days for delivery.

Signature ....

------- ✂ --------------------